RED ICE

RED ICE

R. L. CROSSLAND

Originally published by Charter/Diamond Book.

Copyright © 1990 by R. L. Crossland

ISBN: 978-1-5040-3071-7

Distributed in 2016 by Open Road Distribution
180 Maiden Lane
New York, NY 10038
www.openroadmedia.com

RED ICE

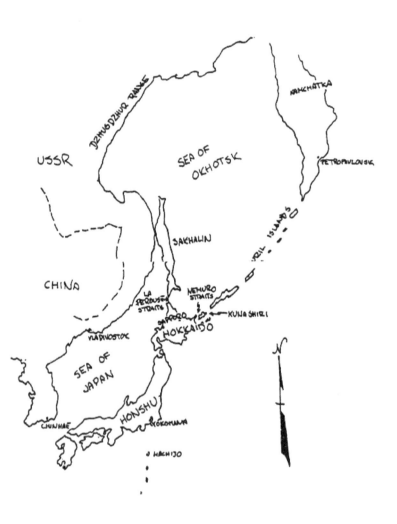

USSR

DZHUGDZHUR RANGE

KAMCHATKA

PETROPAVLOVSK

SEA OF OKHOTSK

KURIL ISLANDS

SAKHALIN

CHINA

LA PEROUSE STRAITS

MEMURO STRAITS

KUNASHIRI

SAPPORO

HOKKAIDO

VLADIVOSTOK

SEA OF JAPAN

HONSHU

CHINHAE

YOKOHAMA

HACHIJO

N

PROLOGUE

Special Prisoner 734 limped to the fallen tree. It lay barely ten meters away, but he was out of breath by the time he reached it. Others trimmed away the branches and slowly began to saw it into sections. Carefully he uncoiled the chain that he had figure-eighted around his shoulders. Though it weighed less than seven kilos, he could not stand upright until it dropped off.

Another man, Special Prisoner 605, made a faint effort to help him fasten the chain to the fallen tree. They kept bits of rag between their hands and the ice-cold metal. The touch of metal in this bitter-cold climate could leave fingers useless for the rest of the day. The guards did not appreciate useless fingers. Neither talked. They had both withdrawn into the zombielike state that pretended to forget the cold.

He noticed that 605's face was chalky and mottled with greenish brown bruises. Emaciated by the exhausting work of timbering and by lack of food, neither prisoner could survive much longer, but clearly 605 was nearer to death. He had collapsed twice already today and the VOKhk guards had beaten him with the butts of their SKS rifles until he had crawled in the direction of the timber cut.

Special Prisoner 734 wondered about the guards. He wondered where in the socialist republic they found such men. It was not a job many would want.

Before the guards could back the armored half-track into position to tow the log, 605 cried out and fell face first into the snow. Two guards hurried over and began to kick him. Not wake-up kicks, but the kind of kick that would send a soccer ball seventy-five meters. They went on like this for ten minutes—the guards did not tire as easily as the prisoners. Besides it kept them warm.

"Comrade guards, it appears he is dead," the gang boss said. The boss of the project was a prisoner, too; someone must lead the timbering. His position permitted him to risk addressing the guards.

The boss, two other prisoners, and 734 dragged 605 to one side of the narrow cut in the taiga. Everyone returned to their assigned tasks. The tasks would have taken a healthy man an hour to complete, but took them each a full day.

"Less than six months here," the boss said, shaking his head. "Why do they send us these Moscow city men?"

The gang boss was like that. Always joking.

PART I

CHAPTER 1

It's not every tenant that gets to enjoy a bath with his landlady. Nor one so attractive as the long-legged porcelain doll opposite me.

But then again the taking of a bath here in Japan has been elevated to a social and spiritual occasion. Furthermore, Keiko, whose well-sculpted form had raised the height of my bathwater, was not your typical landlady.

"You're not too bad looking for *dame hakkojin*," she said, as if studying me for the first time. *Dame hakkojin* meant literally "useless man the color of luminous white paint." Keiko was a bit of a Japanese redneck. "You sure you're not tee-tee bit Japanese?"

I should start at the beginning. Like hundreds of other veterans, I heard the siren call of the Orient and vowed someday to go insanely Asiatic. It was an easy vow to take. A culture as rich and intriguing as Japan's makes the mere act of living, for an Occidental, an adventure. But above all, Japan still reveres adventure and the chivalrous warrior. My association with Japan has been a happy one.

"Look gray-eyed devil, don't start horizon-focus routine on me." She punctuated her comment with a splash. "*Ara ma*, much better to be bathing with the toothless old man picks up cigarette butts at Tokyo station."

Her tone softened. "You will not become serious at a time like this, I forbid it. *Iya da wa!* I don't like it. You make me sad when you become serious. With you seriousness and sadness are one."

In any event, the court martial made the decision to follow my vow all the easier. Perhaps if I had solicited publicity at the trial—receiving attention on the magnitude of the trial of Colonel Rheault of the Green Berets—I could have avoided the final injustice of a trial before the long green table. Regrettably that sort of publicity could only compromise other SEAL operations, and I was a man of codes and values and standards, none of which permitted the jeopardizing of men in the field for personal benefit. In the long run it made little difference, for my effectiveness as a military officer would be equally doomed by the taint of publicity or court martial. So I opted for the long green table, an ironic promotion, and an administrative discharge.

Later I met Keiko while salvage-diving off Honshu, in those first lonely months after discharge. As a remedy, she was over-cure for the Service Dress Blues. Raised among the Ama, women abalone divers on Izu Peninsula, she had, I was sure, cornered half the world's strategic reserve on curves. This in addition to inheriting their incredible endurance and phenomenal resistance to cold.

Like many Japanese women, she giggled into her hands and had a voice that made you think of wind chimes. But there was a pervasive impishness that was uniquely hers. She knew when to bubble with enthusiasm, and still rarer, when to be quiet. Sensitive and intuitive, she could read my moods like a newspaper. She was proud of her heritage and could be damned patronizing in her answers to my foreigner's questions. Aroused, she was the original Far Eastern spitfire.

Keiko was well known throughout Yokohama as the proprietress of the best restaurant and sushi bar on the waterfront. It was an enterprise she administered with the cool efficiency of a head accountant and the firm hand of a boss stevedore. Somewhere, someone long ago had started the rumor that Japanese women were submissive and fainthearted. Perhaps that was true, but I knew that in her case beneath that elfin manner and soft-spoken exterior lay a spine of 440-carbon steel. Stories about her evictions of unruly customers abounded. What she saw in me I never quite knew, possibly a similar inflexibility in matters of duty.

My delightful bathtub rested in an apartment above that restaurant, in a weathered-wood, quaintly Japanese building she owned. The apartment provided a refuge from the rigors of salvage diving—and the increasing number of free-lance military operations I was being called upon to engineer on a cash basis.

So here we both basked in the big boxlike tub, or *ofuro*. It had been a long day diving the ice-water salons of the Kamakura Mara, and every fiber of my neck and shoulders ached. A cool plum wine, an accommodating landlady, and a hot bath were surely the sinful answer to a broken-down frogman's dreams.

Keiko slid lower into the tub until only her beautiful long-lashed almond eyes were above the steaming water. Then, stealthily she kipped from sitting to prone as her eyes glided closer to mine. With an abrupt splash she bussed me and laid her cheek against my shoulder.

"*Koibito*, you have been captured by famed Japanese sneak attack," she giggled. "You must think of suitable ransom. There will be no rescue. MacArthur-sama is not around to rally the forces of right. Old Imperial Navel is gone."

"Have pity, you slippery Ama wench, on an impoverished sailor stranded on these beaches with no hope of ransom. Let's start with a proposition well-grounded in history. Will unconditional surrender do?" Holding my plum wine unsteadily, I gauged the appropriateness of counterattack.

"What hope do I have? I bow to your superior number. Keiko, you are perfidious, semi-inscrutable, and a peril-like credit to Nippon and . . ."

"*So na no?* Is that so? Inscru-table? What means this word 'inscrutable'? I have not heard this word before."

". . . the gal with whom I most enjoy discussing global strategy, unconventional tactics, and matters of state with. Inscrutable? Oh, mysterious . . . er . . . hard to fathom, hard to really know."

"Ah, I understan'. Yes, I am mysterious sometimes, *ne*? But it is you who is inscrutable, true?"

She reached over and gently dabbed her wet fingertips along the zipperlike scar on my right shoulder. "Sometimes I wish I could unzip one of these and get inside to see the true Quillon Frazer. Sometimes

I see you thinkin' so hard but you never let me know what you're thinkin'. . . ."

One of the girls from the restaurant called through the door to Keiko. A messenger had left a note for me downstairs.

Keiko looked at me with an appealing tilt to her head, her round breasts bobbing faintly with the motion of the water. Unconditional surrender. Yes, there is something to be said for unconditional surrender—to a magnanimous victor, accepted ever so gracefully.

The next November morning was crisp and clear. As I shaved, I studied the man beyond the mirror.

Inscrutable might have been an overplayed word because his appearance itself told too much. In his late thirties, the man was trim, hardy, with a relaxed but distinctly military bearing, and weary eyes. His high, broad cheekbones, those of a boxer or wrestler, were impassive, though his jet black hair hinted at Celtic turbulence. The broken nose told of a certain self-destructiveness. Only a faint glimmer deep behind the eyes revealed a wry and sanity-saving sense of humor. Frozen in a snapshot, he might have been an athletic stockbroker, a lobsterman, or a tennis pro. In the motion of real life, an erectness and slight rigidity of carriage betrayed a more adversarial calling.

No, little more than a quick look made it all too clear; here was a stiff-necked, hard-nosed, old-school officer who'd taken that duty-and-honor bilge seriously, and it'd nearly destroyed him. It was an easy guess that off watch he would be unremarkable in general—inclination to be cosmopolitan, perhaps; surely culturally adventurous, as that type generally were; occasionally roisterous, under the right circumstances. Study him stressed under the responsibility of command and all those drearily conventional attributes of the classic military officer oozed through the casing, like sweating plastic explosive. Incorruptible, steadfast, selfless, courageous—all that hokum people had once pretended mattered. Here he is, ladies and gents, a bygone archetype, the warrior monk, in modern dress. Sees command as a moral charge, he does, he does. Ready to share the burden of sacrifice with his men at any moment. Step this way, our next exhibit . . .

In one aspect, however, the display of emotion, he *was* inscrutable; that element remained locked behind a case hardened will. Sometimes, not often, emotion flickered, accompanied by a subtle tightening of the jaw muscles. This single mannerism betrayed a building anger that might someday flare into white hot fury.

Soon I was bounding down for breakfast at Keiko's. Its heavy timbers and sophisticated Japanese joinery lent stability to the early morning. She handed me my usual breakfast of fried eggs and misoshiro soup, along with a business card and a smile. It was a lawyer's card with a note on the back. The lawyer was asking me to visit his office that afternoon to discuss a confidential matter. The address given was an impressive one in the Ginza section of Tokyo, a short train ride away.

As I had just finished the Kamakura Maru job and my next project wasn't for a week, I dug out a tweed jacket to make my turtleneck sweater more respectable. Then I set course for the Ginza.

CHAPTER 2

Ginza in Japanese means market. The Ginza in Tokyo had evolved into the Far Eastern version of Fifth Avenue. Without the shoppers and signs to give it away, a visitor would be hard pressed to distinguish it from midtown Manhattan or the Market Street section of San Francisco.

Here, however, the constant throng of shoppers is quietly different. The crowds are thick yet without jar or aggression, a reflection on the ingrained courtesy of the Japanese. For some unknown reason you must pack the inhabitants of Tokyo more tightly before they reach critical mass than you can their Occidental cousins.

The law office was nestled in a modern tower of innovative design. There the receptionist greeted me with the proper mixture of cordiality and distance befitting a firm of significance. While I stated my business, I noticed her eyes drifted to the perceptible lack of crease in my trousers. She then announced my name into the intercom and remained unerringly polite and courteous as I cooled my heels in that outer office. Looking around the office, I concluded that this lawyer's client could afford the best. In salvage, I was neither the biggest nor the best, and under the circumstances this was the type of work I expected.

"Frazer-san, Sato-san will now see you. Please excuse his delay, he is most interested in seeing you," the receptionist murmured in flawless, inflectionless English, gesturing to the door on the left.

As I entered an office about the size of a small gymnasium, a forceful-looking gray-haired man rose and offered me his hand in firm American style. Sato, the lawyer, had clearly seen something of the world and was used to commanding respect. I sensed the calculating mind of a chessplayer, always three moves in the future, and that this trait fused well with his bearing, which would-have done honor to a Roman senator. Everything about his manner radiated tenacious intelligence.

Another older man—undoubtedly Western—lean, stooped, his beard streaked with white and gray—said something to me in an eastern European language and gave me a Continental dead-fish handshake. On an empty chair next to him lay a pile of outer clothing and a pair of sunglasses. Neither were suitable for November Japan. No, this wasn't going to be a marine salvage job, after all.

I'd never met either one of them before, but there was something hauntingly familiar about the stooped man and those mournful hound-dog eyes of his.

"Mr. Frazer, I am Kiyoshi Sato. I sent you the business card. Please be seated. This meeting must be kept in the strictest confidence. . . ."

I nodded.

". . . for reasons which my client assures me will soon be obvious. The gentleman here on my left, as I am sure you have already recognized, is my client, Sergei Kurganov."

I must have paled. No wonder he had looked familiar; Kurganov was the Iron Curtain exile whose novels had rocked the West to its long-ignored or forgotten foundations. Perhaps no man in this century had endured the fathomless pain or had seen the unquantifiable suffering he had—and still maintained the resilience to skewer the most powerful and oppressive political system in the world with his pen. He dwarfed the other great men of the decade. I could not help feeling humble.

Sato, sensing my unabashed awe, started in, "Mr. Kurganov, as you probably know, does not speak English. I do not know the reasons why he has arranged for this meeting. He has asked me to translate for him and, as a lawyer, keep these communications in the strictest confidence."

Sato began, at first haltingly, to interpret Kurganov's famous sardonic style:

"The creative thinking of the Soviet penal system established a rehabilitative marvel, the Corrective Labor Camp, to attend to its class enemies. Class enemies leave such camps vertically or feet-first. There is, of course, always some doubt about those who leave the camps vertically. It is, therefore, a credit to the camps that the majority of the inmates leave feet-first and unquestionably rehabilitated to the requirements of Soviet society."

Kurganov swayed slightly as he stood up, holding his hands tightly behind him as if still manacled.

"A statistically predeterminable percentage die in the railroad cars and on the trek to the camps. This cannot be helped. Those weak in ideology will be weak in body. In the frozen cemeteries that pass as Corrective Labor Camps, these class enemies—a good many of which haven't the remotest idea what they have done, and whose persecutors often have little better idea—may expect a degrading end in utter despair. Slow death by interminable beatings, exposure, or starvation are the prevalent options; the stronger, however, can add scurvy and pellagra to their choices.

"Families are divided among the camps. Daughters and wives are used by the camp officers, guards, trustees. . . ."

And this stooped, frail man had withstood it all. He had endured fifteen years in an icy hell that, by sheer number of deaths, made Hitler's a five-and-dime operation. It was beyond imagining how anyone could survive the sixty-below-zero winters of Siberia in what we would consider spring street clothing.

But where and how did I enter into all this?

". . . in calling the world's attention to this continuing atrocity, I incurred the wrath of the Soviet Republic (which had been so good as to return to me the freedom with which I had been born). I expected and was prepared to accept whatever treachery lay in store for me personally. By this time my wife was dead, my daughter, as if by a gift, insane.

But the benevolent and all-knowing republic has found a way to bring revenge upon me, though it knows nothing short of death will stop my writing."

Yes, I thought, there was little that could or should stop his writing, yet what cost must a man pay—and keep paying? would he ever have any peace, whether he continued or not?

"As a university student before the war, I studied to be a physicist. At the university an older student from my hometown, Yuri Vyshinsky, took me under his tutelage. We were very close. It was he who introduced me to my wife. Those were happy times, vibrant with laughter in the student drinking halls. I was blissfully ignorant of politics and strove to remain that way.

"Yuri often asked me, in a veiled way, what good was harnessing the universe when at the same time men's souls were being tethered. 'Couldn't I think of any higher calling than physics?' I couldn't understand him. Wasn't he a physics student himself? I sensed he questioned my particular vocational choice. Despite these mystifying exchanges, we remained firm and loyal friends.

"Not until several years later, after capture with my artillery unit and my subsequent escape from a German POW camp, did I begin to understand Yuri. To our Soviet masters, the story of my escape and naïve return to the Red Army had to be the flimsy cover story of a spy. (In retrospect, I now fully appreciate how incredible such an act must have appeared to one who understood the Soviet system—which I did not, then.)

"The first weeks, those weeks before you're sent to a camp, are the hardest. I was thrown into an ancient prison east of Moscow. Despair is simply a word until you have survived long periods of torture and lack of sleep.

"Your thinking changes when the single driving purpose of life is the avoidance of pain. You begin to doubt everything and abandon all you once valued. You decide that you were a fool. Your whole spectrum was off center. If this is the depths of man's depravity toward man then you must shift your moral spectrum a good deal lower. You were aiming too high when you sought the center. You expected too much. Obviously if men permit such a system, this is the system they deserve. I had hit, I believe the American expression is, 'rock bottom.'

"Then, during one particularly savage beating, Yuri's words came to me. Yes, there was a higher calling than physics—not the caduceus, nor the scales, nor the sword, but—the pen. A reason for living now separated me from the doomed. Eventually I was to see thousands die who had no cause but personal survival. My cause was survival, but more, to destroy the system that established and maintained the camps.

"Yuri cared for my wife and daughter until they, too, were imprisoned. He smuggled us all food and notes of encouragement. Yuri's words kept me alive and gave me a mission. I endured knowing someday I would fight back. All this I owe Yuri and can never pay back.

"I have never mentioned Yuri by name, but he appears as a character in many of my books. The KGB wasn't able to establish his identity until recently. They seized him on as flimsy a pretext as they ever need and have transported him to a camp somewhere near the Sea of Okhotsk. Yuri was never a strong man physically. As a special prisoner—a status his association with me will rate him—he can't last six months."

Kurganov brought his trembling, gnarled hands before him and stared straight at me through those mournful hound-dog eyes.

"That is why I need your help. You must rescue Yuri from that corrective labor camp in eastern Siberia."

CHAPTER 3

I whistled two long notes. Q. Frazer Enterprises; the extremely difficult we accomplish immediately, the impossible takes a little longer.

"Lieutenant Commander Frazer, I have never done anything by part measures. You are a top man in your field. I am confident if anyone can effect this rescue, it must be a man of your experience. You must tell me you will do it for me. Yes, you must tell me that."

His confidence was flattering but was it well founded? Admittedly I had done several prisoner rescues and agent exfiltrations while on active duty. Recently, I'd smuggled families out of East Germany and Iran. This was well beyond all that—by contrast those operations were wading-pool exercises. This was a Channel swim.

I rubbed my right shoulder.

But where else could Kurganov go? The Central Intelligence Agency wouldn't touch a bombshell like this in its present emasculated form. Moreover, there was nothing in it for the Company. Bluntly, Yuri had only sentimental value.

Had anyone else asked, I would have politely declined. Access to Siberia was too limited, the number of risks from man and weather too high, the probability of success too low. But this giant had six decades of Russian suffering etched on his face and it was a heavier burden than any man deserved.

"Mr. Kurganov, I'll look into it. There are many reasons why such an operation may not be feasible. I must know all you know about camp life, where Yuri is held, as well as what intelligence I can gather on the region before I can give you a conclusive answer. If it can be done, I will find and train the men to do it. I assure you. One other thing, this is going to call for considerable resources."

Sato translated and Kurganov smiled. It seemed such a shock to see a face like that distorted into a smile. I had the urge to hug him, it must have been the Russian influence.

"Lieutenant Commander, I am a rich man . . . a best-selling author with much, too much money. You will receive . . ." he named a sensible number ". . . plus expenses. I will cover the invoices for *anything* that needs to be done."

He clearly was not overpaying me personally. I liked his emphasis on the job rather than the rewards. Professionalism in this business did not equate with big dollars. Kurganov had done his homework; he knew Frazer.

I don't know who had convinced him he was employing a genuine professional and not some useless driftwood. What would I do with the money? Hell, I'd only spend it. For Kurganov, I'd have agreed to try it for a good bottle of vodka. Well, nearly.

But perhaps he was right and I was the genuine professional he thought my record indicated. Already I was weighing different plans. A thousand questions were caroming about within the inner armor of my brain. Most were about the rescue . . . some were about Kurganov.

CHAPTER 4

Through Sato I explained, "The project contains three basic problem areas. They are, one, determining Vyshinsky's location; two, arranging transportation to and from a point within striking distance of that location; and three, recruiting and training a raiding party."

"*Da, da* . . ." Kurganov agreed before Sato could finish his sentence.

"The first, and likely the most difficult task will be to pin down Yuri's whereabouts precisely."

"Yes, this will be very difficult. Mr. Kurganov believes his contacts in the CCCP should prove very useful. However, the corrective-labor-camp system often moves prisoners among several camps. It is not unusual for a prisoner to be moved through many camps before his . . ." Sato's voice trailed off, leaving the end result unsaid.

A vivid image of human scarecrows in black, numbered uniforms stumbling through knee-deep snow made a sharp contrast with the thick carpet and plush upholstery of Sato's office. It was a discomforting image.

"A further problem, I'll venture, will be that the communications through Kurganov's pipeline will be slow and, out of necessity, often cryptic. It would be the ultimate nightmare to penetrate a camp and find Vyshinsky had been moved. You must make this clear to Mr. Kurganov."

I paused.

"Secondly, it will be no easy task getting delivered within raiding distance of Yuri's camp and still be able to execute an orderly withdrawal. Does Kurganov have any idea of which portion of eastern Siberia?"

"The Kamchatka Peninsula, Magadan, or possibly the Kurils. In one of the timber-cutting or mining camps, or in the Kurils, a construction camp."

I shook my head understandingly. So this was why he had come to an ex-SEAL officer; all possibilities were coastal and good prospects for seaborne raiding.

"Good, that broadens our prospects. I can think of several options. If the particular coastline lies close to a shipping lane, our party can launch from a slow-moving merchant ship in either rubber boats or kayaks. Or under ideal conditions, we would go in along the coast using a low-flying seaplane, still using smallcraft to get to shore. Our best alternative would be to go in by submarine, lockout, or wet-deck launch, and respectively swim or paddle to the first substantial coastal ice."

Fatigue was starting to show in Sato's face. He had to strain for the Russian equivalents of all these unlawyerlike terms. Wearily, he raked his fingers through his hair, yet I felt he could go on for days like this.

"Third and easiest, but by no means without its problems, will be recruiting and training a squad for covert, cold-weather, commando raiding. Through personal contact, I can bring in two or three more SEALs. The rest will have to be picked mercenaries.

"Siberia will be a problem. It would have been easy to recruit for a raid on one of the world's steamy regions. The bars of Marseilles swarm with men 'of experience and resource' who can survive for weeks with a rifle, canteen, and ten sticky fingers. Cold-weather warfare is a different variety of misery, requiring advance planning and discipline. Both of these elements have been rare in the soldier-of-fortune operations of the past several decades. Experienced mercenaries, aware of this failing, will be reluctant to sign on for a trip through the Russian winter wonderland. The mere mention of an objective as dismally grim as ours will deter most. To top all, a six-month outside limit means we will be braving the worst of the Siberian winter."

After reviewing these points and many minor ones, it was late afternoon. I suggested that Kurganov advance me $100,000 for expenses to see if the rescue could be put together. Gesturing acceptance, he gave me a typically middle European dead-fish handshake and I left. Part of Kurganov's burden left with me.

I flexed my right shoulder. Some wounds had memories.

The train from Yokohama cast long autumn shadows on the fields.

Why was I drawn to these projects? I had served my time, eight years as a regular naval officer. I had already earned my red badge of courage; no one could fault me for saying "enough." The system had kicked me out. Nothing could be simpler. The answer "enough" could be explained with a dozen justifications and some very telling legal proscriptions.

But I was a military officer, nothing more. I could not see myself any other way.

I leaned back in the train seat.

Why?

Was it factors beyond my control? Heredity? Genes? Had my family something to do with it? Some family tradition?

My father had grown up in a fishing village in western Scotland and was attending school in Glasgow when World War II broke out. He was graduated with a certificate in mechanical engineering near the end of the unexploded bomb scare in London. In desperation, they gave him a quick course in bomb disposal and a commission in the Royal Navy Volunteer Reserve.

"Ach, by the time I was ready the trouble had subsided, an' I talked ma way onto a wee Fairmile boat. More style, thought I, than diggin' up bombs in cellars," he'd said more than once. "And a different type a grit required. On a dark night, with the wind just right, you felt like Drake."

His boat was assigned to the Coastal Forces and saw only a moderate amount of action. He met my mother, a U.S. Army nurse assigned to patch up Rangers who were attending the Achnacarry

Commando Course in Inverness. "Butcher and Bolt School" he'd called it. His Fairmile had ferried Rangers across the Channel on D-Day.

Time softened his recollections. It must have been rough on him in many ways. The Regular Royal Navy did not look upon engineering officers with high regard . . . or officers with RNVR commissions . . . or officers without university degrees . . . or bookish officers with broken fingernails and noses . . . who ran bloody piddling little boats. I could tell he had been proud of that commission. He had been a naval officer. And that meant something.

My mother, a Dolliver, one of the Salem Dollivers, came from a family of steady distinction and little cash. My mother had never said much about the courtship with the raven-haired Scot, but the family album of World War II pictures was treated like a rare book. I often wondered how my father had managed to win her affections in the running competition with the cocky Rangers and Commandos.

After the war he took a job in the States, in the industrial New England town of Pequonnock, where my brothers and I were born. He had worked his way up to plant manager by the time I graduated from Berkeley.

There was the unspoken assumption that my brothers and I would serve someday. I knew the periodic skeet-shooting sessions were not purely recreational. Nor were the camping trips and long hikes. Doing your duty required a little hardening in the formative years.

"There's a grand lot of bullies can't abide a Frazer. Remember that," he'd say on those stiff-legged hikes. "We're no' big but we can terrier the hell oot a them. And mind you, no' all bullies are big or found in a schoolyard."

Later, when I went into the Navy, he added, "Bear in mind, too, that no' all villains wear a different uniform than you do. I can remember a grand lot of toffy-nosed, ring-cuffed blokes in the Andrew whose actions really helped the other side. There are Chinamen who play three-sided chess. 'Tis a more realistic game. It'll be a rare war when you're fighting only one enemy or where all your enemies are out in front of you."

My second year in the Navy, he died in a plant explosion. They say he was seen rushing to close several key valves when the second blast came.

My mother died of cancer two years later.

A passenger train whizzing by in the opposite direction made the train wobble. Two children in school uniforms played with a toy robot or spaceman the size of my thumb.

Why?

Was it factors beyond my control? Environment? Had there been something in my food? Water? Air?

The town of Pequonnock was a brick-and-cobblestone collage of rubber factories, shoe and sweater mills, and heaps of bivalve shells. It was jammed with a little bit of everything. You could go a mile down the coast from the coal barges and see some of the most impressive sailing yachts in New England. Not many of the townspeople had anything you could call a yacht, though more than a few had boats.

The style was smokestack exotic. Some joked that our phone book had the greatest concentration of consonants in the state. We had pastry shops in four languages. It took a month and a half for the divergent groups to stop celebrating their different Christmases.

My memories were of boyish games played in and about the railroad sidings, the piers, and the barges near where my father worked. And of flashlight tag, led by an Estonian scoutmaster, around upstate ponds. It was a game at which I excelled. You could will yourself into invisibility. Conform to the low-lying scrub, and don't move. Don't flutter an eyelash.

In later years I remember roaming the dunes and tidal marshes that formed an L at one end of town. These coastal badlands were the site of endless imaginary adventures. The occasional old tire, the abandoned refrigerator, and the three-wheeled shopping carts became props for my solitary fantasies. But Pequonnock had a way of jarring you back.

The Hungarian revolution left its mark on the town. The work force, already heavily central European, swelled with Hungarian refugees within the year. A year later a tufted-browed teacher arrived at our school. His fastidious manner, Gabor-sister accent, and firm sense of discipline did not sit well with his students. On my way out of the school building one day, I spotted two schoolmates with DA haircuts loosening the lug nuts on Mr. Horvath's tires.

"Get away from that car."

"Aw, get stuffed, rah-rah."

"You heard me, get away from that car."

I waivered.

"It's old man Horvath's, an' he gets what he gets. Man, you ever hear 'im talk? Sounds like a fairy kraut or weirdo Russki or somethin'."

"You'd be the funny-sounding one where he comes from," I said lamely.

"Well, send him back. Hey, smartstuff, just get out of here. Or maybe you wanna stop us?" one said, working himself up.

I tried. Things were always scuffling and inconclusive at that age. Then, too, they had the tire iron. In the end it cost me twelve stitches, a lump on the head, a jammed thumb, and two weeks of detentions levied by Horvath. He had, however, offered to drive me home after we retightened the lug nuts.

"I am a civilized man," he said with his eyes firmly on the road. "Am" sounded like "ham." "It is my recently learned experience," the weary teacher said thoughtfully, "that it is not very good to be too civilized."

The train passed through a tunnel that reminded me of a collapsed parachute and a training raid in Korea. The SEAL parachutist had broken his back.

Why?

Maybe it was just me.

A series of aptitudes and inclinations marked the course I held. These aptitudes and inclinations stood out like channel buoys among the flotsam and jetsam that defined Quillon Frazer.

Clausewitz had said that war was the province of physical exertion and suffering.

I was good at sports, but particularly drawn to mettle-testing "ordeal" sports: distance running, distance swimming, cross-country skiing, and the like. Then again "punishing" sports like boxing, wrestling, and the martial arts carried great weight in a blue-collar town. If nothing else, they kept the schoolyard predators away from a management kid who read too much. Unconsciously, I had prepared and continued to prepare myself for wars of movement where man alone provided the only reliable momentum, and for battles fought at close quarters where the ability to absorb pain and a strong arm might make the difference.

Clausewitz had stated that war was the province of friction.

You could talk about the world the way it ought to be. Others could do that. The world the way it ought to be seemed a long way off to a veteran with my combat experience. Yet the hot spots of the world were where it was changing, for the better if I could help it. These hot spots were the points of friction for careening political philosophies, religions, cultures, and economies on collision courses.

Some men could change the coefficient of friction at these points. Worldwide, at any given time, there were perhaps five hundred men who had participated in special operations under fire and were ready to participate in them again. I was one.

War was a rough study in abrading contrasts, but it was an important study. There would always be war in the same way there would always be disease. If you acknowledged that and realized that you brought a degree of skill and industry to your side, then you appreciated the parallel between you and the surgeon who, through the destructive cut of his knife, saved good tissue and prolonged life.

And Clausewitz had said war demands resolution, firmness, and staunchness.

A friend of mine had gone to work for the CIA. He had said that through their written testing they could tell if you had a sense of destiny. It was an important point. Anyone who volunteered to put himself in harm's way had to feel that someday, in some way, he would be needed to fit into some important event.

Unconventional warfare was my fate. I was a fast learner in a field where no two operations were alike. I could absorb complex theory and give it concrete and immediate application. Evident, too, was my knack for carving order out of chaos, for organizing and directing. Finally there was something about me, some personality quirk that made me the type of officer the right kind of men wanted to follow. Resolution? Firmness? Staunchness? I could never be sure.

In any event I knew what I did best. It was the *only* thing I could do with more than half a heart. It was, for better or worse, what I was destined to be.

And a naval officer, a specialist in unconventional warfare, was what I knew I could never, ever be again . . . in any sanctioned manner.

My shoulder ached more than ever.

I spent the trip back to Yokohama, gazing out the window, hefting and sorting plans like an old woman buying fruit. My concentration was so total I nearly missed my stop.

An attack on the Russian mainland would be tough enough. The unforgiving Siberian winter narrowed the margin for error until it was the size of the peephole in an interrogation-room door.

Keiko sensed my preoccupation and quietly went about cooking supper. She studied her cooking intently, singing some soft Japanese song as I drafted a barrage of telegrams to Coronado, Little Creek, Manchester, Marseilles, Harare, Ramsund, and Chinhae.

When she was about to go down to work, she kissed me lightly on the forehead, and then as I rose, kneed me full force in the groin. While I staggered back trying to catch my breath, she bowed politely and left.

Ama women require attention and are never, never to be taken lightly.

CHAPTER 5

As the small KAL airliner lifted from the runway at Tokyo's Narita Airport, I unloaded my worn briefcase and reread the telegrams I had received and deciphered prior to takeoff. They had been transmitted using a variation of the book code—not a terribly original crypto method, but for our purposes, effective. Each message left Yokohama in number groupings disguised as the price column on an invoice telegram. The addressee would, on receipt of the telegram, purchase three preselected monthly magazines—magazines without regional editions, and different ones for each addressee—to be used as decoding keys. The first price code group indicated which magazine and which page applied to the subsequent twenty-one characters. Every three characters gave the line and ordinal position of a letter in the underlying message. Then the process was repeated using another group, and this time twenty-four characters, progressing in added groups of three until the message was completed. No printed letter on a magazine page was ever used twice, and this was the marvel of the system. It could not be broken by a statistical frequency of letter-use analysis. In any given English paragraph of a minimum size, the letter *e* will appear most often, then *s*, then *t*, etc., and that's how you broke elementary codes.

Furthermore, our messages were too short for a computerized hit-or-miss analysis. But the code was only as secure as its users.

FRAZER
YOKOHAMA
WICKERSHAM
LITTLE CREEK VIRGINIA

YES STOP BETWEEN ENLISTMENTS COMMA HAVE UP
TO 180 DAYS STOP YOU SUPPLY DATES
    GORDAN

FRAZER
YOKOHAMA
PUCKINS
CORONADO CALIFORNIA

REQUIRED WESTERN PACIFIC DEPLOYMENT IN MAY
STOP TENTATIVE YES COMMA NEED TIME FRAME
STOP WIFE EXPECTING PUCKINS NINTH TWO WEEKS
    BARRY

Petty Officer First Class Gordan Wickersham and Chief Barry Puckins had been members of my platoon in the western Pacific. They presented an odd combination of personalities and would comprise part of the nucleus of the rescue organization.

Wickersham's eternally over-revving mind was held captive in a body as powerfully muscled as a Wisconsin brewery horse. When he wasn't brawling or womanizing, it was his singular mission in life to bring the military into the free enterprise system. On at least three occasions, I'd had to stop him from setting up a corporation to sell shares in captured booty. Yet there was no finer M-60 machine gunner in Vietnam. This Clydesdale of a man lumbered to the sound of the guns.

I could see Wickersham standing before me, grinning not quite angelically, showing a one-inch gap of missing teeth in his upper jaw and thoughtfully stroking his cauliflower ear. He was explaining how he had only *borrowed* the commodore's jeep . . . that the fact that the shore patrol had found it sans tires, battery, upholstery, and canvas top was due to unfortunate vandalism by persons unknown . . . which he would rectify by "fixing their wagons," but first he had to make a visit to the Salvation Army mission in Manila . . . to visit an elderly, ailing lady . . . whom he knew through one of the stewards. As an experienced interpreter, I guessed all this to mean he'd intended to sell the whole jeep but got stiffed; and by elderly, he meant over eighteen; and by ailing, he meant she had a fever that needed quenching.

With his bridgework in, he had the battered good looks that some women found exciting; generally the slinky, long-legged types you found draped off hulking prizefighters. His slabs of muscle weren't only for show. In basic training, several instructors had wagered he couldn't climb a thirty-foot rope with twin steel-90 diving tanks on his back. They lost.

Gordan Wickersham was one of five sandy-haired, heavy-shouldered sons born to a long-suffering beer salesman. How Milwaukee ever survived the intersibling competition among these five brawling, hockey-playing, ever-competing, and always-enterprising young public enemies is a monument to its civil defense organization. The competition was cutthroat, and their dares and challenges bordered on the suicidal. The end product was an odd blend of loyalty, swagger, hostility, and intelligence. As a result of his immersion in this strenuously masculine environment, a good fight, a touch of heavy-handed buffooning, a ready wench, and an easy dollar meant home. And all he needed from life.

The moderating influence on Wickersham was the silent Texan, Puckins. No officer could possibly devote the time required to effectively monitor Wickersham's activities. Fortunately, through some strange symbiotic chemistry, he was given to relinquishing ascendancy to Puckins long before Puckins had ever made chief. It was the Clydesdale and the cowboy. They formed an inseparable team, a vibrant lamination of the physical and the spiritual.

Born and raised in west Texas, Barry Puckins carried the classic lean and bowlegged cowboy build, but he could swim like a Waikiki beachboy. His redheaded Huckleberry Finn looks fit well with his disposition toward silent mirth. He could draw more laughs with a few wordless movements than a good comic working a half-hour routine.

Humor formed only one component of a complex man, a man who was essentially a fundamentalist of the Old Testament mold. He'd graduated from a Texas Bible college—it was surprising how many SEALs had attended some seminary or other. His grandfather had stormed into Texas as a six-gun-carrying, circuit-riding preacher, and I remember Puckins showing me a picture of his parents that bore a dry resemblance to *American Gothic*. It would, however, have been a mistake to label Puckins cloistered or otherworldly. "Easy to see He made the world chock-full of different adventures and places. Cinders of hell, it'd be a sin and darned unnatural not to grab the opportunities laid before us," he'd confided to me in one of his rare wordy moments. "I hold there's gotta be a reason for it. Sure as they'll be no thermostat control for you an' me in the next life. There's somethin' to it." In this vein he had bounced around before joining the Navy. He'd tried everything from miming in Ghirardelli Square to bartending in a Houston skivvyhouse.

Reconciliation of religion with his eventual profession wasn't difficult. Certain Moslem sects viewed the killing of each infidel as bringing oneself another step closer to Paradise. Puckins's attitude toward dispatching communists was analogous, but not quite so simple. In its essence, communists were anti-God, therefore Puckins was anti-communist.

Furthermore, or perhaps as a logical progression from his religious convictions, Puckins was a bedrock family man devoted to his wife and squad of kids. He showed a strong feeling for children in general, and they for him. There's an old saw that men in sapper or demolition units are either mad, married, or Methodist. Since madness is relative and I was a member of the same unit, I would have no way of judging that point, but as to the latter two categories, Puckins was very much married and very nearly Methodist.

The Korean stewardesses alternately hovered and darted about the aisles with gracious laughter and the tinkle of glass.

FRAZER
YOKOHAMA
FITZROY
HARARE ZIMBABWE

REGRETS STOP ON TO DEAL OF CENTURY POSSIBLE
ACQUISITION PRECIOUS STONES STOP MAY NEED AS-
SISTANCE SOON STOP STAY AVAILABLE STAY HEALTHY
JACK

I had known Fitzroy in Vietnam, too. He had been an outstand-
ing trooper with the crack Australian Special Air Service. His tracking
ability was legendary—from a heel print he could give you race, religion, and blood type. I had hoped to use his skills in reverse in Siberia
perhaps to elude or confuse trackers.

FRAZER
YOKOHAMA
DRAVIT
MANCHESTER ENGLAND

AFFIRMATIVE COLD CLIMES RAIDING STOP QUERY
DESPOILING ANTARCTIC WEATHER STATION COMMA
TIBETAN STRONGHOLD OR BIRDSEYE FOOD FACTORY
HENRY

Captain Dravit, formerly of the Royal Marines would be my
second-in-command and likely the oldest member of the raiding party.
His steadfast competence was often downright unnerving, but hardly
surprising from a gardener's son who'd worked his way up through the
ranks. Barely five foot four inches tall in jump boots, he sported a first-
rate handlebar, which had become something of a trademark.

Bantams like Henry Dravit were worth a herd of football linemen
in a tight spot, and his record bore the fact out. His baptism of fire
had been in the frosty over-the-beach raids of the Korean War. On
one occasion, his entire party wiped out and his dry suit shredded by

shrapnel, he inadvertently crawled into a North Korean automatic-weapons position, His dubious luck further brought him into one of the first brainwashing experiments. This he found mildly amusing—until things went sour and they threatened to pull out his mustache with pliers. After which they promised to work on other portions of his anatomy.

"Nasty bit of work. After a while a mustache sort of grows on you, seems to me," he once told me with a laugh. A well-developed sense of irony spiced his conversation.

The next day two North Korean guards were found, their heads twisted northbound and their bodies oriented southbound. Dravit, his mustache, and all his moving parts were gathering momentum southbound. Dravit, then Corporal Dravit, had begun his epic end run from Wonsan to the Funchilin Pass through the entire North Korean army and part of the Chinese. Keeping below ridgelines and moving only at night, he was to skulk three hundred miles in fifteen days, gain two pounds, and retain his mustache.

"Sodding U.S. leathernecks nearly foreshortened my memoirs by several chapters as I entered their perimeter. The retreat from the Chosin Reservoir must have been rather dicey."

In addition to his Korean experience, he brought along the strength of innumerable winter Royal Marine exercises in Norway. He and Pieter Heyer of the Norwegian Marine-jaegerlag would compose the training cadre. Together they were as capable of preparing us to survive Siberia as anyone who'd never set foot there could.

Originally military service had been intended as a brief diversion before Dravit would become a gardener in earnest alongside his father. There was nothing extraordinary in his signing on; the elder Dravit viewed military service as a chance for Henry to get the sand out of his shoes, and Henry had envied the Royal Marine Reservists he had noticed tramping about the countryside. They seemed an appealing sort: trim, outdoorsy, and wet to the knees. No one was more shocked than he was to find he was good at it, far better than at gardening. When it came to fighting, Dravit, as it developed, was a hang-the-automatic-weapons-we-can-set-those-blokes-running-by-positioning-the-mortar-right-there natural.

Only impatience with civilians, abstractions, and grand strategies had kept him from advancing beyond captain. Since the British hadn't succumbed to the "up or out" cancer, so loved by the Americans, he continued until retirement, satisfied in his career.

Dravit would be a strong, energetic assistant. I never knew a man who could think so quickly on his feet. For instance, there was that weekend liberty when he'd quelled a potential riot in Nicosia. He had cleared a crowd from a town square using a broom handle in a rather forceful demonstration of bayonet techniques. The Greek and Turkish factions simply stepped aside. They couldn't believe their eyes. Physically he remained in top condition, and without the gray at his temples could have passed for twenty-nine, though forty-six was closer to the mark. I knew I had been right in guessing he was thoroughly bored with his job as an automatic-weapons salesman. I anticipated he would attend to discipline and day-to-day details in surges of too-long-restrained vigor. A lesser man might not have been able to reconcile such a swashbuckling style with maintenance of high standards and iron discipline.

Dravit contributed one other skill to the project—he had received Russian language training.

A half dozen other telegrams echoed Fitzroy's Micawberesque response. A greater return for less risk lay just beyond the next wave. In thumbing through the telegrams I noticed that I had still not heard from Pieter Heyer in Ramsund. I relied on Heyer to add depth to the training. Dravit had been trained for cold weather; Heyer was born in it.

Perhaps five men as a core group. Training would have to begin without my knowing how many men I'd need for the actual mission. But first I needed the raw material. I hoped that starting with an additional group of about twenty-five, I could distill the group down to five or ten reliable, field-wise raiders. With these men to augment my original five, we just might be able to finesse a clandestine rescue where a larger group would fail.

The last telegram in the stack was a decoded copy of the one sent to a café owner/soldier-of-fortune recruiter in Marseilles. Though the café owner knew my method of operation, it was advisable to remind him of my specifications in case he was tempted to clear the café of deadwood.

CAFE CAMERONE
MARSEILLES FRANCE
FRAZER
YOKOHAMA JAPAN

REQUIRE 25 DOCUMENTED VETERANS FOR COLD WEATHER HIGH RISK OPERATION STOP LIGHT IN-FANTRY BACKGROUND STRONG SWIMMERS STOP REPORTING HOKKAIDO JAPAN 7 FEB NO EXTRADIT-ABLE OFFENSES CONTEMPLATED SEND NO BILLION DOLLAR BALLPLAYERS COMMA MOVIE TOUGH GUYS COMMA PRETTY BOYS JUNKIES ALKIES COMSYMPS
    FRAZER

There was an unfortunately broad spectrum of quality among paladins.

The plane was packed with businessmen virtually spilling over into the aisles. The lure of economically booming Korea had filled every seat. Half of the passengers stared into open briefcases while the other half exchanged information on the price in "real money" of everything from brassware to sweaters. The passenger next to me, a paunchy man in an overtailored Italian suit, droned on about the merits of his Mercedes diesel and seemed to know the smart price for everything.

I restrained my urge to offer advice. It would be futile. My fellow passenger would undoubtedly blunder through his Korean visit re-gardless—patronizing, using first names, and backslapping. In look-ing over the other Western passengers, I wondered what it was that I had been drawn to protect and why.

Yet theirs would be merely human blundering—random, small scale, and self-adjusting. What Kurganov and I fought in our own ways was institutional blundering on a mammoth scale. Its inevitable outgrowth was unending purges, liquidations, relocations, deceptions, and dragooning orchestrated by shortsighted *apparatchiks* whose blueprints were drafted in applied fear. One of the few luxuries of my present existence was that the foe, totalitarianism, was irredeemably corrupt and as black as Lenin's shadow. The cause, however, was tinged with gray. Men of my fellow passenger's stripe left me uneasy. Unlike my comrades in the established militaries, I, as a free lance, righted immediate wrongs and was not plagued with implicitly endorsing the programs that invariably followed. In his present existence Frazer had lost much, but gained purity of action.

A second reason held me back. As a veteran and expatriate I was sadly familiar with the cultural heavy-handedness of the first wave of troops to reach the beachhead. It didn't matter whether the troops were commandos . . . or purchasing agents. The ability to identify with the locals was a gift and as common as broken noses among missionaries. It was even rare among such "go native" elite units as SEALs and Special Forces, where identification was a cultivated attribute. The toughness of mind required to reach your objective was the same toughness that locked out external values and influences. Too often those locked-out influences were some foreigner's seemingly untested values. Within elite units worldwide, perhaps one man in ten stood truly capable of integrating into a combat organization of mixed origin. Yes, Frazer, you were a rare and adaptable fool.

As we began our descent, a stewardess pulled down the blinds on each of the windows. After nearly thirty years, the Republic of Korea must still function on a wartime basis. The blinds were pulled to prevent observation of the port defenses of Chinhae, Korea's principal naval center.

At the small Chinhae air terminal, I was met by a middle-aged naval officer built low and solid like a cinder block. Commander Pak directed the maritime unconventional warfare section of the Korean 25th Squadron and consequently smiled only with his eyes. The rest of the smile had been eroded by too many covert amphibious reconnaissances into North Korea with too many good men lost and too many imprisoned—never to be freed.

The stocky, hard-bitten old frogman had logged over two decades in the simmering war between north and south. North Korea, jealous of the south's ever-growing prosperity and self-conscious of the north's own fall from ascendancy, devoted incredible energy and resources to harassing the south. South Korea had no choice but to counterpunch if it was to hold the harassment in check. Consequently, both sides infiltrated, reconnoitered, and sabotaged. Since Korea was a peninsula, infiltration by sea assumed preeminence as the method of choice. Infiltration by sea necessarily meant heavy use of frogmen. Through the years Pak had risen to the position of head maritime counterpuncher. Year after year, Pak, as an officer in the Naval Reconnaissance Unit, had braved the cold, swift currents of the north, had crawled the shingle beaches by night, and had awaited that final searing burst of fire that had yet to come. His expressionless face was as obdurate, unchanging, and unforgiving as his country's coastline.

Like me, the old campaigner belonged to a thin, uncompromising strain of defenders—defenders, who, in all but the worst of times, the public viewed as embarrassments.

We had met when I was officer in charge of a SEAL Mobile Training Team in Korea. An immediate friendship developed—firmer than most of far greater years. We shared a difficulty in reconciling a sense of duty with the demands of ambitious seniors. The grade of commander was as far as he was ever going to get, and he took contrary pride in that fact.

"Quillon, I would like to think you are here as a tourist,"—fluency in English was mandatory for Korean officers—"to again enjoy our Mongolian beef, drink rice wine, and visit our Kisaeng houses. I'm disturbed, though, by your cryptic message and the fact that you're carrying a briefcase.

"Come to grips with the fact that they chucked you out, and you let them? Can't blame them, you were too hard to control. Inflexible men, I think, give them a pain."

His English was constantly improving. I couldn't say I enjoyed the way it left me more open to his insights.

"They'll know they were wrong someday. Anyway, someone will know.

"My people have threatened to throw me out every other year for the last ten. They never do. They'll put up with me as long as my unit keeps taking the missions."

No grin, just a slight eye sparkle.

"Your shoulder still bother you?"

The Frazer stoicism amused him. It was a useless pretension to attempt to outstoic a Korean.

I held my palm up, grabbed my bags, and tossed them into his jeep. We drove through the narrow streets bracketed by simple one-story buildings with tiled roofs, past the statue of Admiral Yi, Korea's fourteenth-century Lord Nelson. When we arrived at his home on the eastern side of town, his wife made the obligatory welcomes in Korean and disappeared.

"Commander, I need to get in touch with someone in your central intelligence agency with enough clout to get me the use of a ship."

Pak showed no surprise. "Gunboat or submarine?"

"Either. Preferably a submarine."

A submarine would be a godsend provided he could get one. Korean gunboats were really destroyers euphemistically designated "gunboats" for treaty purposes. Destroyers weren't well suited for what I had in mind.

He stepped into the next room and I could hear him using a telephone, his voice growing louder. Moments later he returned with tea.

"A Mr. Kim will be here shortly . . . and reluctantly. I hope you have something to trade, for he will be a hard man to convince to part with anything. He has little patience for non-Koreans of official standing, and within that group even less time for Americans these days. And of course you are an American of no standing whatsoever . . . from a protocol standpoint, anyway."

We didn't have to wait long for Kim.

Tunnel-rat pale, Kim blinked as if the sight of you hurt his eyes. Coldness and oiliness were all mixed up in the man. His feral crew cut splintered in a dozen different directions, like fur on a cat's arched back.

"Now, Lieutenant Commander Frazer—I hope you don't mind me calling you that, your rank at discharge, that is—let me see if

I've got all this straight. You're without a navy, your current ties with the U.S. are somewhat strained, and you've been subsisting on a shoestring for the past decade. It's a pity a man with your talents just can't seem to fit in anywhere. Too bad, too bad. No organization, no government . . . sad, is it not? Granted, you have collected a small nest egg through some of your recent diversions. That Iranian escape was amusing, but unfortunately 'small change,' I believe the expression is. Now, at the expense of appearing rude, what makes you think I'm going to give you a submarine? The Korean navy doesn't have a sub according to *Jane's Fighting Ships*. But even if we did have one, why fritter it away on one of your little projects? You're wasting my time."

I ignored the statement that denied any record of a submarine; we both knew the reason for the denial. "I don't want a submarine permanently, just the use of it for about three weeks . . ."

He blinked at me impassively.

". . . and I will be willing to charter it on an arm's-length, businesslike basis. I will pay all running expenses, manning expenses, repairs and upkeep, plus a weekly charter fee of . . ." I named a very generous fee. "In addition, I will post security in the amount of one-half the value of the sub, with some additional for pensions for crew members' families."

"Out of the question," Kim droned. "One of our submarines, that is if we had one, would have a value beyond price. Really, Lieutenant Commander Frazer, I never considered for a moment that you wanted one permanently. . . ."

"Furthermore," I continued, "we would be presenting your country with a means of underscoring the fact that some of the more distasteful methods of communism haven't changed much in the past thirty years. I would think this fact properly conveyed might be embarrassing to those factions in the U.S. who would have the world believe that Ivan's methods have changed. Especially when it comes time to renew U.S.-Korean defense agreements."

He blinked again. I thought his eyelids had moved perceptibly more slowly.

"How?"

I told him about Kurganov, Vyshinsky, and the camp. I was vague about details at this juncture. He could understand why. But he still appeared dubious.

"Yes, we could get some mileage out of Vyshinsky's escape and subsequent press conferences. His statements would support the allegations Kurganov has been making all along about the hoodwinking of the West. Sort of act as an update. But to risk a submarine . . ."

Well, at least Kim was finally acknowledging they had one.

"We might get the same mileage out of drawing more attention to the Moscow dissidents, without putting any of our security forces in jeopardy," he said, thinking aloud.

I had one last move and I hoped that I had primed Kim properly. We needed that submarine.

"Such a camp is likely to serve a secondary purpose for Ivan. If my guess is correct, it is not far from a railroad line that services the Chinese frontier and does occasional duty as a communications station for the border forces."

Kim had stopped blinking and was leaning unconsciously toward me. The bargaining center of gravity had shifted in seconds from him to me. Not bad for a stiff-necked old frogman. He could hardly keep from rubbing his hands together with anticipation.

A communications station meant crypto gear, encrypting devices possibly common to North Korea's code devices. In any event, these devices would be barterable to some other intelligence agency for North Korean code machines. The prospect of surreptitious capture of crypto gear was enough to make an intelligence czar sell his own mother, though I doubted Kim had one unsold this late in his career.

"We could be persuaded to carry back a few key assemblies," I said as he silently mouthed the words after me.

Kim's smile was positively chilling. He cleared his throat officially. "You will, of course, need weapons, ammunition, and explosives. We will obtain them for you. The Japanese government has a very unenlightened attitude regarding such matters."

I proceeded to tell him my plan in detail, granting some allowances for the lack of specific information on the camp and its location.

He offered a few suggestions and suddenly I was the proud charterer of a diesel-powered submarine of unspecified origin and vague description. I hoped the camp was indeed used for a communications station. In any event, I would soon find out.

Commander Pak, beside me, smiled—but only with his eyes.

CHAPTER 6

The next evening I returned to Yokohama and found a telegram waiting for me from Ramsund, Norway. Petty Officer Heyer of the Marinejaegerlag had accepted my offer, but could only get leave for three weeks in late February. After climbing the wooden steps, I slid the door to one side, kicked off my shoes, and sat cross-legged on the tatami mats.

Pieter Heyer was a painfully quiet naval commando from Norway. His angular features, his pale blond hair, and pinkish-white complexion all seemed hewn from the ice and snow of his North Sea homeland. Equally at home in fins or on skis, he seldom moved or spoke unless he absolutely had to, but once he did, his actions were resolute and invariably faultless. As a group member, Heyer assumed the role of a valuable individual rather than a leader. He felt more comfortable working with the constants of objects than with the variables of people. A rifle you could rely on; people were a sometime thing. He was the man to assign to equipment and rations. He, too, spoke fluent Russian—more fluently, though less often, than Dravit.

The components were clicking crisply into place. I was ecstatic, a submarine and a technical man with a strong background in two days.

With this kind of luck we might pull the thing off, after all. My exhilaration turned to a sudden uneasiness at my rush of good fortune.

I rose from the mats. As I crossed the room I heard my name called from the landing at the bottom of the stairs and turned.

The caller struggled up the stairs with a slightly out-of-sync gait that, with the marbling of scars across his too closely shorn scalp, made recognition immediate. He was a former SEAL point man—one of the best in his day—now patched and mended, but not quite complete.

"Mr. Frazer, how ya doing? Have you seen . . ."

He named a former SEAL, one we both had known, who was currently in Yokohama on a merchant ship. There was sake on my visitor's breath.

"Sir, you think you could spare me a little, you know, to tide me over, just this once?"

I couldn't, nor could I the other times, either. His disability check never lasted him very long. I wasn't sure whether it was the liquor or the high cost of living out here that made the money vaporize so quickly. The steel plate in his skull seemed to cause money to evaporate faster than hope. His color was poor.

"Step in."

He took off his shoes and shuffled around the room inquisitively. When his back was turned, I popped a small wad of bills from their hiding place behind a beam. "Trust them . . . but only with your life," I'd heard a chief say.

"Thanks, sir, now don't forget I gotcha covered." God, he looked vulnerable. It was hard to believe he was the same man I'd seen that night in the U Minh Forest. He'd been badly wounded and, when put on a dustoff chopper, had swatted aside aircrewmen in a raving frenzy. In delirium, he'd hunkered down apelike, and the Army medics didn't go near him until he'd passed out from loss of blood.

"No sweat. Things have been looking up," I said, and winked.

He grinned.

"Get it back to me when you can."

There was no thought of recruiting him. He'd given all he had.

With much bonhomie, he trudged unevenly down the stairs.

Where and when had I become angel to him and so many others? Strange bonds. Trust them . . . but only with your life.

For a beached frogman who took little notice of money, I seemed ever sensitive to the manner in which it fell between my fingers.

Not too much later, I ambled down to Keiko's restaurant. Seconds after I had entered, I felt her squeeze my hand as she glided by into the teppanyaki room. Tall by Japanese standards, she bore herself like a princess of the Ama among the restaurant's well-heeled clientele. Her vibrancy and striking, athletically trim good looks stole your attention. Everyone else in the room seemed bland, part of the background. A Chinese-style yellow sheath dress, a *cheongsam*—one of my favorites—made her particularly desirable in the soft lights.

A faint piston-like fidget of her hips indicated she had more than one thing on her mind. Ever restive, she could still move through a room with a presence that made rough seas placid.

Keiko Shirahama was the hamlet girl who had grown to want more.

Japan, more than most countries, looks to the sea for sustenance. The Ama, as divers for shellfish and edible seaweed, shared breadwinner status with their fisherman husbands. Their fathers and brothers served as boatmen and tenders while these women divers, equipped with the natural feminine superiority provided by an insulating layer of subcutaneous fat, plunged to the sea bottom day after day.

The term *Ama* in Japanese was a homonym for the Japanese word for "nun." There were other similarities; their white scarflike headgear, for instance, bore an eerie resemblance to a nun's headdress. Ama, however, unlike nuns, had a reputation for being, as one Japanese friend put it, "women with sharp tongue." Even spicier in personality than most of her fellow divers and quick to translate her moods physically, young Keiko had publicly boxed the ears and berated the fishing cooperative's headman after a family dispute with the cooperative.

She was prudently hustled off to board with land-bound cousins in Yokohama who treated their novel Ama like a black sheep. Her unmerited status was an affront to her pride, but it offered certain unexpected benefits.

Forced to take a job as a restaurant bookkeeper and hostess in an establishment that catered to—horror of horrors—foreign devils, *gaijin*, she found it surprisingly to her liking. By Japanese standards, foreigners had rough edges, and so did Ama. She bought the restaurant a year or two later. Only after realizing the world she had been born to and loved had grown too small.

The attraction to life in a larger arena was in constant tension with the values and traits inculcated by time and heredity. Undeniably, she had been forged by hard work and tempered in cold water. The Yokohama waterfront presented as pluralistic a community as Japan could offer. Physical courage and hardship endured were the watchwords of the Izu Peninsula fisher folk, and in her adopted world she gravitated to those who traded in those qualities.

She returned quickly to tow me into one of the more private dining compartments. The compartment had a leg well around the table, a concession to Westerners, which she knew I preferred because of a bad knee. She slid the wood-and-paper door shut. Moments later a waiter appeared with *ocha*, green tea, and the, ingredients for *shabu-shabu*, a sort of do-it-yourself beef stew. Another favorite; she wasn't overlooking a thing.

The meal went by uneventfully as I described some of the less sensitive portions of my trip. We alternated tending the small burner on the table. I finally sat back, sated and mellowed by the onslaught of earthly delights. The uneven graph of my stubborn existence, which had too often plunged me into gritty, bloody, hang-by-your-fingernails valleys, demanded I savor these fleeting soft-rich moments. Sometimes they could be eternities apart.

"Quillon, did you enjoy your trip to Korea?" Keiko said gently, breaking a reverie.

I nodded, swirling the tea in the bottom of my teacup. The Japanese found meaning even in teacups. A good teacup in Japan must be faintly cracked. A minor defect gives character and warmth. Weren't the best frogmen always slightly flawed?

"More than on those other trips you take?"

"No, about the same."

"Why didn't you take me with you?"

No doubt about it. Fattened for the slaughter. Beware, frogman, of sirens bearing gifts.

"Because it was just a short business trip and I didn't think you were interested in going."

She thought for a second. "*Honto?* Next time you take me. Okay?"

Whittled to helplessness in seconds. Keiko looked up at me with a slight tilt to her head. Those big, dark, liquid eyes could have asked for virtually anything. It is the eternal male conceit that we are the masters of our own destinies.

Of course, I knew what lay behind all this. Keiko had—justifiably— little cause to concern herself that I might let my eye wander during my trips to the Middle East, Europe, or Africa. But between Japan and Korea there is an ancient rivalry. No right-thinking Japanese woman would allow her man to go to Korea unguarded against the well-known evils of Korean women. Korean women were without shame.

"All right," I said, knowing when it was tactically necessary to give ground, "but bear in mind that I'm going to be pretty busy this next time. I may not be much fun to be with."

She smiled and put her arms around me, her palms drawing me toward her. I could feel the warmth of her body through the sheath dress, her firm breasts burrowing below my rib cage.

"If the restaurant can run itself, perhaps we should continue this discussion topside."

She looked at me slyly and slid the door to one side. "Yes, I think so. It is a small restaurant, not worthy of too much attention. As for you, you are not worthy of too much attention, either, but I make sure you have very little energy except for business when you go back to Korea."

As we turned the corner and passed through the bar, I saw something that put an abrupt chill on the evening.

Keiko was quick to sense it. "*Koibito*, is something wrong? Did . . . ?"

"No, Kei-chan, nothing's wrong. You run ahead. I'll be with you in a second."

There in the bar, in his full-bodied perverse glory was Thomas Alderson Ackert III. All. of him. He revolved ninety degrees on his stool and beamed that tidewater blue-blood smile that said, "Screw you, sucker, me and my career are going to make it to the top standing on the heads of patsies like you."

He raised his glass and waved me over in grand style.

"Hey, Fraze-buddy, how you doin'? Join me for a drink?"

"Some other time, Ackert."

"Now, now, Fraze. Ol' Ackert came here special to see you. Nice place your Nip honey's got herself. Right nice." He gave the room a generous sweep with his arm.

"Look, Ackert, you're a long way from Yokosuka or wherever you're based, so shove off. They're kind of fussy about the caliber of people they serve here."

We were two kinds of naval officer, and they didn't mix well.

"Well, then, you better just come on over here and listen careful." The smile was gone. No use wearing it out.

"I'm out here doin' a nice tour with the Defense Intelligence Agency. You remember them, they feed intelligence to the Company, analyst stuff. Well, the Company asked that I get in touch with you—seeing that we're old war buddies and all. Seems they're a tad upset about some cold-weather advertising you've been doin'. Get the picture?"

The picture unfolded like a recurring bad dream. A bad dream whose uncontrollable momentum brought unescapable horror.

My stomach felt as if it were falling from some great height. *If he knew this early, who else might know? And how much?*

"Don't know what you and they are talking about. Better check to see they're not overpaying their source."

"You don't?" Ackert said nonchalantly. "Well, if it's a third-world operation, who cares? But if it's a Warsaw Pact country, we say cool it." He tugged a shirt cuff into proper alignment—appearances meant everything to Ackert.

"I can play hard or I can play easy. Now I always did say you were a smart boy, just prone to get hung up on things that'll get you nowhere fast. But maybe you already know that. Hangups and all, your problem is you just don't get with the program."

The smile had returned.

"I can maybe fix it so you can't go swimming or skiing for a couple months. Or better yet we . . ."

We again. How much did *we* know? Who else knew?

". . . could get the government of Japan to throw you out of the country permanently. Now, that sure would be a shame. Keep you away from the slinky buddha-head dolly of yours. Course, I'd look after her for you, nice spirited piece of stuff like that. She might not take to me at first, but she'd come around. Hell, they always do. Just got to know how to show 'em who's boss. Maybe dust some of that spirit off 'em." He winked broadly.

My ears warmed and great ripples of anger distorted my vision. Sometimes reaching out and smashing something low and ugly is the best thing to do. Slam it, smash it, grind it under your foot. The trouble was, the habit of command had cursed me with a subdued, rational approach to confrontation. Restraint, I hoped, would protect the mission.

It didn't. That was my second mistake.

My first had occurred many years ago in Vietnam . . .

CHAPTER 7

The procession of eight sampans snaked silently through the choked and twisted mangrove swamp, tracing the barely discernible bed of the core river. The air tasted of steam and smelled of wet, rotting vegetation. We were on a fool's sojourn into a damp green labyrinth.

Each crew could just make out the sampan ahead of it, for little of the quarter moon penetrated the gloom of the triple-canopy foliage. Swathed in mosquito netting like unworldly beekeepers, it was hard to resist the tooth-gritting urge to swat the insects that choked the air around us.

I gave the signal for the lead sampan to put more distance between it and the main body. Smooth, orderly movement to the objective was imperative if we were to succeed.

Soon we would have to eliminate the series of sentries on the next quarter mile of riverbank between here and where the two American POWs were held.

The lead sampan surged ahead, nearly capsizing. Two of the boat's Vietnamese scouts paddled steadying strokes, the third lay low in the waist section.

"*Lai day.*"

The lead boat was being challenged from somewhere up ahead. The procession, now bristling with flat-black steel, halted, and only the lead boat continued.

"*Lai day, lai day.*"

The command was casual, and though I could not see the sentry, I knew he was waving the sampan over to the bank. "Come over here," the Viet Cong soldier had demanded.

Fortunately, the soldier did not expect any resistance, for his experience did not include the discipline of more conventional sentry duty. Like most VC sentries, he planned to assess a "tax" on anything of value in the sampan.

"Ratchet-chet, ratchet-chet, ratchet-chet."

The muffled chatter from the nine-millimeter submachine gun carried faintly over the noises of the swamp. A short groan followed.

Offhandedly, the scout in the waist of the lead boat had fired a burst from a silenced Model 76 into the careless sentry as the sampan had touched the bank. The rounds, well grouped, penetrated cleanly, fatally.

The procession began anew, and as each boat drifted by him, the sentry bobbed and nodded in the tepid water. His gold-toothed smile whispered the forfeiture of failure.

On we paddled, with tensed, weary backs, gripping our paddles too tightly. Disturbed by the lead boat, a great white swamp bird fluttered, then screeched off into the darkness.

That previous afternoon, the jeep's wheels slid well to the right in the axle-deep mud as I had turned to clear the MACV compound gate. As I slowed for a second, Ackert vaulted uninvited into the shotgun seat. I was on my way to the tactical operations center to clear an area of operation with the local Army people. We were Navy but they had overall supervisory authority for this AO.

"Whoo-eee, I think you've really gone off the deep end this time, Fraze."

The air was heavy with humidity and my camouflage shirt stuck uncomfortably to the seat back.

"Glad I'm not part of this one. If the VC don't ventilate your bod', the regional general will fry it. Maybe leave it out in the hot sun 'til it gets nice and crispy-like," he said, nudging me in the ribs with more force than necessary.

Thomas Alderson Ackert III, a big blond-headed charmer and natural athlete, had graduated from the Academy, a first-class ticket puncher and had ever since been collecting career-enhancing billets. With Ackert's tight, winning, and even-toothed smile it was inevitable people were more impressed than they ought to have been. As a one-time starting lineman for the Academy, he found the rigors of basic training for the Navy's elite Sea/Air/Land (SEAL) Teams trying and occasionally an inconvenience. But the prestige that accompanied the role of frogman-commando would surely ease along his career. Shrewd and capable, he got his ticket punched at all the right stops. What he did at each stop didn't matter as long as he didn't make waves.

Someone had once described him as that thoroughly treacherous golden bastard who knew all the rules of the game, had mastered them with great fanfare, but hadn't the remotest idea why the game was played in the first place. He was fond of all the current buzz words like "systems supportive" and "middle-tier management," which he sprinkled generously into a honeyed "good ol' boy" pap. First to "get on board" questionable programs of high origin, he sported an array of staff awards, which he had cleverly harvested as a "bombproof" in rear areas. Each of these attributes viewed individually might seem fairly harmless, but examined in concert they were the unmistakable symptoms of a deep and dangerous pathology. And he himself was a symptom of a still greater pathology.

It began to rain in warm, heavy sheets. Ackert smiled to himself with the satisfaction drawn from the prospect of someone else's risk taking and probable doom. I kept my eyes straight ahead.

Maximum glory and minimum inconvenience were the goals that guided his every action. It was evident in the way he led a platoon. It had been evident to some from the very beginning of training.

The high-water mark of our basic training had been Hell Week. The week was an endless marathon of exhausting physical competition under stress between boat crews for twenty-one hours each day.

Between fifty and seventy percent of a training class melted away during that one week. Sleep became an obsessively precious commodity and during slack periods a few men always managed to crawl away to hide and sneak a mind-preserving nap. Everyone did it at some point, though naps were risky. Some fell into deep sleep and could not be awakened until their bodies had restored themselves. By that time they had been dropped from training.

In Ackert's boat crew there had been a petty officer who had become known as "the Rock." Unshakable, he virtually carried his crew through every event. His endurance was phenomenal. The force of his character pulled weaker men along in his slipstream, and only in the last days did he begin to fade. His self-sacrifice had strained even his strength to its limits. A benign Sisyphus, he only rolled his boulder faster.

During one interval he, too, crawled behind a sand dune—after he had been sure to tell Ackert where to find him. Not long afterward, an instructor called for an immediate muster. Ackert could have saved the Rock, but only by drawing additional harassment upon himself. He didn't. There was only room for one star in Ackert's boat crew.

Things seemed to happen to people around Ackert, and oddly the outcome always seemed to make Ackert look better. The men called him "the Golden One," and it was not meant as a compliment. More than once his rushes to "get on board" had placed them in jeopardy.

"You haven't cleared this with the regional general, have you? You're not bein' smart, Fraze-buddy. Fella's gotta look out for himself. Hell, you'd never catch Ol' Ackert trying a fool stunt like that."

"Sure, I haven't cleared it. You know why? The red tape has been made thick; too thick and stretched to protect too many people. Takes too damn long. That's why no one's been able to pull a successful POW op yet. Those guys would rot before we could save them." The hard edge of frustration slipped into my voice.

Clearing a POW rescue operation through the IV Corps military region's commanding general took days. Intelligence on the location of POWs in the Mekong Delta was only good for hours. The Viet Cong kept POWs in ones and twos moving from camp to camp. In the delta there was no central POW stronghold like the Hanoi Hilton much farther north. And the triple-canopy jungle hid all.

I swerved to avoid a Viet family on its way to the river market in the downpour. It wasn't their fault Ackert was in my jeep.

"Ackert, why don't you fly to Saigon and kiss up to someone career enhancing? Seems a nice fellow like you ought to be sipping highballs with some NAVFORV armchair raiders at the Continental."

He drummed his fingers contentedly on the dash.

"Yeah. Sure, sport, maybe I ought to. Leave the olive-drab-and-camouflage crusades to you. Wouldn't want to hazard this beautifully bronzed body on any of the famous Quillon Frazer missions. You've done too well for too long. Anyway, too many ladies would never forgive me. You know how it is."

He paused.

"So you're going to just trip over those POWs accidental like? Cute, real cute," he added.

Under the circumstances, Saigon would indeed be a safe, comfortable place to be. A blown rescue operation would be bad press, and the whiz-kid managerial types who gave the regional general his orders didn't want any bad press. Bad press tarnished their shiny, newly minted images.

On the other hand, a Viet Cong POW camp was an unsafe, uncomfortable place to be. A camp dictated death by millimeters, from disease or malnutrition. A month after capture, a prisoner became a mosquito bite-blotched skeleton in Viet Cong boxer shorts with barely the strength to swallow.

From out of nowhere a Honda 50 carrying a man and three children passed the right side of the jeep.

Ackert scratched his golden head and yawned. "So you're going to gamble everything on the story of some greasy, bucktoothed gook defector. I always did figure you for a gook lover. Too bad, thought you knew better than to trust those apes."

This was meant to rankle. It was well known in the detachment that the word *gook* was forbidden in my platoon. How could you attempt to conduct a counter-guerrilla war in a country and at the same time degrade the most essential element to your success with the term *gooks*?

"They don't speak English, drink much beer, or play football, so what good are they? Well . . . I'd trust him farther than any tidewater ticket puncher with big ambitions. And less integrity than our platoon's pet boa constrictor."

"Now talk nice to ol' Ackert, hear?" He whispered venomously. "Kind of touchy, aren't we? Wait 'til old IV Corps hands you your head once he's found out you led a deliberate rescue mission without letting him give the whiz kids a chance to take first bows."

"And who's going to tell him?"

"I don't know . . . ," he said with his best year-book smile. "Maybe me."

The jeep stopped with a jerk.

It would be a good fight: in this corner, the rawboned Quillon Frazer in the celebrated and foredoomed tradition of his Highland ancestors . . . and in the opposite corner, Thomas Alderson Ackert III, golden-haired tidewater Goliath, destined to insinuate himself to the mastheads of naval power.

But I had more important matters to concern me. In particular, two captive Americans dying slow deaths in forgotten places.

Ackert would have to wait.

The sampans glided forward beneath the interlocking talons of the unending mangroves. As if anticipating our intrusion, the jungle growth became more lush and more concealing.

With increased confidence the crew of the lead sampan took out the next sentry as quietly as it had the first.

My radioman, Puckins, looking like Huck Finn gone to war, turned in the bow of our sampan and gave me the three-ring okay signal for no particular reason. Puckins was just the SEAL you'd want in the bow on a cold-sweat jaunt like this one. Some men transmit waves of calm and well-being, like brandy on a cold night. It was like him to diffuse the aching tension with some insane pantomime.

He pointed to the sampan behind ours and made gestures indicating a "thick neck" until a strand of red hair fell out from under his hat. I knew he could only mean burly Wickersham. Then, with three quick gestures of a skilled mime, he conveyed that Wickersham's Cholon girlfriend was generous with her favors. Heck of a statement for a circuit rider's grandson to make—in the manner he made it.

I looked behind to Wickersham and then realized he couldn't see any of this. I thanked the god of darkness for this one small favor. We didn't need anyone riling up Wickersham. Fortunately, he was probably preoccupied with computing the fair market value of eight used, slightly bullet-ridden sampans. Yesterday I'd caught him trying to sell a bale of phony VC flags to a couple of PBR crews.

Along the banks the trees grew in ever more frantic postures as if trying to escape the parasite plants choking them.

We now approached the satellite camp and the final sentry. The river was not very deep here—often I'd feel my paddle brush bottom mud. Yet the water was still black and opaque like the blood of a night wound.

From our defector, or *hoi chanh*, we had learned that the satellite camp was one of several small outpost camps that surrounded the center encampment of a battalion or greater of Viet Cong. Nestled in triple-canopy swamp, the satellite camp was secure from air strikes and acted as part of the buffer against major U.S. or ARVN troop movements.

It was composed of eight huts in two parallel rows of four perpendicular to the river, which at that point was fifteen feet across. A drainage ditch ran between the two rows and intersected the river at a right angle. On either side of the ditch were wooden plank-ways connecting the huts.

The *hoi chanh* had indicated that the two American captives would be in one of three places: in the two huts farthest from the river, in the tiger cages outside the huts, or shackled to nearby trees outside those huts—if they were still alive.

It was all very simple, except for the three or four Viet Cong that occupied each of the eight huts, the two hundred or so more Viet Cong and NVA nearby at the main encampment, and the last sentry stationed just yards downstream from the satellite camp.

A small shelter loomed out of the darkness abreast of the sampan just ahead of us. This was the post of the last sentry. Its small roof had offered relief from the monsoon rains. We turned our boat into the riverbank and stepped gingerly into the mud. All the sampans were unloading now. Everyone was wobbling around on tension-weakened legs.

The elimination of the last sentry had been the smoothest, and the reason was clear. His body sprawled in relaxed lines on a plastic ground sheet; he had been asleep on watch. Now his dreams would no longer be rudely interrupted.

My hand signal brought the men silently to their positions. I counted eighteen sweat-glistening, green-painted faces. An M-60 machine gunner stood on either outboard side of the camp. Then the two grenadiers mounted the two inboard plank ways carrying haversacks stuffed with concussion grenades. Two men stayed with our sampans, watching for signs of the main force upstream and uneasily counting the beached sampans that weren't ours. The rest of the platoon split into two files, one for each plank way. Puckins and I stood in the ditch between the plank ways.

Before I could give any commands, an excited Vietnamese voice, one of theirs, broke the silence. The subsequent burst of AK-47 fire made any prompting of the grenadiers to begin their long sprint down the plank ways entirely unnecessary. They tossed two concussion grenades into each hut, slowing only as they approached the last pair of shelters.

"They're here, here outside the end hooches. Corpsman! Mister Frazer!" one grenadier with a beard bellowed as they both attacked the last two huts, which had begun to return fire.

We were moving swiftly but cautiously behind the grenadiers. There was no telling what might be in a hut and it was no use everyone getting killed if one hut turned out to be a mortar factory. The files moved forward to spray down their assigned huts, but it was clear a number of the survivors of the grenade attack had left their huts by cutting back exits through the woven walls. These VC were returning fire from all around the camp. Puckins, with his bowlegged gait, and I, trying to run sideways, began to slog down the ditch to the POWs like a pair of Aqueduct mudders on glue-factory day.

From out of nowhere, a moon-faced Viet bowled into me and, before I could take a swipe at him with my rifle butt, he was gone. He lingered in my mind's eye—rifle without magazine, wearing a blue-checked scarf the VC and Khmer Rouge sometimes wore to transform civilian clothes into a uniform, and padding through the mud like a charging rogue elephant. One other thing stuck in my mind—his haunting gold-flecked grin. It could only have been a grimace, but it struck me that way nevertheless. I turned and proceeded down the ditch.

One POW was shackled to a tree out in the open, and the other was in a tiger cage wrapped in mosquito netting. The shackled one was moving unevenly. His eyes were wild and large with excitement. They were in sharp contrast to his slack, emaciated body. Insect-bite welts covered his blue-green skin like a rash.

"Sergeant Henson . . . United States . . . Army . . . ," he croaked weakly. "Zero four three. . . ."

The initial digits of his serial number made me catch my breath; they matched mine. Henson and I were from the same New England state. Would I look like that someday? Just looking at him made my stomach churn. He looked less than human and I could tell he was fading fast. We had to get him out of here fast.

AK fire flickered the leaves to the left of my head as if to under-score my thoughts.

"The major . . . in the cage. . . . Help him." He gulped, it seemed to help. "He was shackled out here like I was just now . . . without net-ting . . . for a week. Got to help him. . . ."

Henson began to repeat himself and tilt his head at odd angles. Puckins cut the lock off the tiger cage with bolt cutters, but the major hadn't moved in all this time.

"Corpsman! Corpsman!"

The corpsman, a young Hawaiian, rushed to us, then the cage. Running his hands along the major's body, he'd stop at different points. Finally the corpsman sighed, tugged off the major's dog tags, and handed them to me. Instantly he was off to where he was more needed.

"Pull out! Let's get the hell out of here. Let's go!" I yelled, taking a quick count of the platoon. "Wickersham, Serrano is going to need cover fire on rear security."

Puckins took Henson and lifted him like a tired child over his shoulder.

Henson began to sob. "No, no, I couldn't stop them."

The glisten of tears streaked up Henson's inverted face. He was a good NCO and accepted responsibility out of habit—any responsibility, all responsibility. A hard habit to break.

The withdrawal was no more confused than most. We slipped back to the sampans, keeping a watchful eye upstream. The firefight was increasing in intensity. Muzzle flashes resembled popping flashbulbs. The intermixture of red and green tracer fire lent the camp a festive air. One hut was burning.

Our chief petty officer, a black grenadier with a shaved head and an ebony earring, signaled over the din that we hadn't lost a man, though there were some wounded. We then began to work the sampans downstream as planned.

Ackert . . . and regional generals . . . and whiz kids . . . be damned. Warm satisfaction was radiating from this op like heat from a wood stove. Henson was going home and we were going to start him on his way.

The reaction force from the main camp could be heard coming downstream after us. They were firing alarm shots and I could hear their sampans bumping into each other in the eagerness of pursuit.

From the rearmost sampan, Puckins and I stretched booby-trap wire across the river just below the water's surface, the wire was arranged to trigger several claymore mines from the virtually impassable brush on each bank. While we worked, Sergeant Henson lay in the waist of the boat dozing fitfully. Another sampan stayed abreast of us as a lookout. The claymores would provide a little breathing room.

The crack of an AK-47 and a thud in the riverbank next to Puckins announced the arrival of the VC vanguard. We returned fire with a magazine's worth of 5.56, a couple 40mm, and headed downstream. I wondered if we were capable of leaving a rooster tail. Puckins was uncharacteristically intense in his paddling. The roar of the detonation just behind us nearly capsized the sampan. A gust of stinking smoke and a peppering of spent shrapnel emphasized the closeness of the vanguard.

Once more we stretched out prepared booby-trap assemblies. And again a shuddering explosion followed only seconds later.

Sweat was rippling down my back with all the energy this godforsaken river lacked. With my mosquito netting flipped back over my head it seemed every insect in the swamp was seeking refuge in my ears.

As we prepared to rig a final booby trap, Sergeant Henson abruptly sat bolt upright in the sampan. At the same time I heard a rustling to my right. A small party was flanking us along the bank. Puckins sprayed a burst at the sound and there was a return volley. My right leg and shoulder shivered immediately with unexpected pain. I caught a glimpse of several blue-checked scarves, and a glint of gold fleck, I thought.

The world took on a dreamlike quality and I lay back in the sampan to enjoy it. My left hand trailed in the water. Sergeant Henson floated indifferently between the two pinwheeling rear sampans. The aurora borealis ripples of light flashed across the inner lids of my eyes. I seemed to have some question about celestial navigation. But there was no one around to ask.

"Ah, good. Good, Mister Frazer, you're awake. Home is the hero and all that. Hero business ain't what it used to be, is it? Well, you're safe in drydock for now," she said with annoying energy.

There is little more exasperating than a plain Navy nurse with unbridled enthusiasm. Buoyant and cheery, they insist they can heal all by pure example.

This one was absolutely effervescent. They left men no dignity.

Bandages and casts swathed my entire right side. I felt weak, vulnerable, and hung over. My face felt as if it had been sprayed with a Wesson oil atomizer. From the look of the place, I was in the hospital at Binh Thuy. Questions zipped across my mind like tracers.

"There's a commander outside to see you."

That brought back the answers to some of my questions. I remembered seeing Sergeant Henson drift by, clearly dead, in the midst of the running fire fight. Henson dead. The major dead. Two POWs reported dead. It would surely draw some bad press on the IV Corps general and his superiors. Better they had died emaciated, mosquito-bitten, forgotten and lonely, than to impede some ticket puncher's career.

A tall, lean, sad-eyed commander walked in with measured strides. His jungle boots were spit-shined and his uniform crisply starched. This was to be a formal visit.

"Lieutenant Frazer, I have been assigned as the investigative officer by NAVFORV for the investigation into the SEAL operation, twelfth of August"—he drummed his fingers uncomfortably against his briefcase. By raising my head I could make out an Academy ring—"nineteen fifty-something. Anything you say may be used against you, should this eventually result in a UCMJ proceeding. I—"

Then the peace of the room was shattered by hard, fast footfalls in the passageway as two men in civilian clothes burst into the room carrying AK-47 assault rifles. Behind the weapons, Puckins and Wickersham, as inseparable and menacing as Scylla and Charybdis, hesitated just inside the doorway. The presence of the commander had thrown them off a beat.

I could guess what they had in mind: stash Mister Frazer someplace safe until this whole flap blew over. Someplace like Saigon's Cholon district, where all the deserters lay doggo. Sorry, sir, we're not sure just where Mister Frazer is right now. He said something about checking his agent net. Maybe if you came back next week . . .

This maneuver had met some success for others before, but neither Puckins nor Wickersham realized the heat our little operation had generated among the Saigon whiz kids. Someone had to burn—to appease the gods.

I noticed Wickersham glare at the commander and then study his AK thoughtfully. The commander was an unexpected complication. Wickersham's eyes reflected the wavering balance now between hostility and indecision, and soon righteous anger would tip him out of equilibrium. In another impetuous minute he'd commit himself, waving the muzzle of the captured weapon in the commander's face. There'd be words to the effect of, "Commander, sir, damn shame some doped-up, half-crazed VC terrorist violated the sanctity of this place of healing, making your wife a widow. Another ticket puncher lost to the world, a damn shame, a damn mud-sucking shame." As yet the words were unsaid because unconsciously Wickersham knew their futility.

And still the tension in the room continued to build, crackling like a shortening time fuse.

The commander looked sick. But by now I realized that he had looked sick from the moment he had entered the room. He sensed the injustice of his assignment and it didn't suit him. He didn't like it, didn't like it at all.

"RM1 Puckins, GMG2 Wickersham, I think you two had better disengage," I said, praying my voice wouldn't crack with emotion, "and get back to the compound before you get into some real trouble, sporting those unauthorized weapons. I appreciate what you want to do, but I called the shots, I'll take the fall. Thanks, fellas. Now disengage, and that's final."

I felt sorry for the commander. He had drawn a dirty job and only a larger sense of duty made him accept it. He wasn't a ticket puncher; they have a talent for avoiding the unpleasant and inglorious. They'd never draw a dirty job like this one. They never do.

CHAPTER 8

People jammed Keiko's bar. Laughter jarred my senses from two or three parts of the room, bringing me back to the present. Waitresses bustled quickly between the kitchen and their tables.

I was determined that sleazy excuse for an officer would not rile me into a slip. "Ackert, here's a little advice. Watch your drinking, you're starting to annoy people. Drink your drink, then get out. You fellows on the way up have to be careful about things like that. That—and you ought to be careful where you're seen drinking and with whom. Why, I'll bet you've already done your future irreparable harm. Here, let me see you to the door before any damage is done, and you might get out with your reputation intact."

Wearily, I plodded up the stairs. If this mission were compromised, I and everyone who put his faith in me—who went with me—would spend the remainder of our lives chopping frozen wood or digging icy ore in Ivan's desolate cold storage. That is, if we survived to be taken prisoner.

Rage and frustration broke in alternating waves over me. The Ackerts of the world drew spiteful pleasure from a ruthless and unilateral game of king-of-the-mountain with unsuspecting strangers. Any stranger could be a competing ticket puncher no matter what his professed goals, and never give a sucker an even break. The Ackerts were the new gamesman breed of officer. The gamesman, the military manager, the organization man, the careerist, call him what you may; he was a rapid mover in the brass-heavy bureaucracy and a free trader on the moral marketplace.

A woodcut print dropped to eye level; I had reached the top landing. I slipped off my shoes.

Keiko sensed my anguish. She tugged at my hand and led me into the bedroom. Then, quietly and tenderly, we made bittersweet love.

Non-gamesmen could play at Ackert's game. I would start a variant of the game with my own rules, call it . . . king-of-the-abyss.

PART II

CHAPTER 9

Two weeks later, a wintry December rainstorm blew Kiyoshi Sato through the doorway and created a lake the size of Siberia's Baikal on the inner landing.

"It's the Dzhugdzhur Range on the western shore of the Sea of Okhotsk," he said breathlessly. "Haven't got the coordinates or the camp description yet. They're going to be hard to come by, most of the prisoners aren't sure themselves where they are. Other than Siberia, that is." He shivered. "We're losing precious time. At best, Vyshinsky can't last past April."

I motioned him upstairs and sent for some green tea.

His news foretold worse than I had guessed. The Sea of Okhotsk. Grim, gray waves sprinkled with massive chunks of ice. Moreover, its waters would test every dimension of our Korean-supplied submarine skipper's skill. He must deposit and later snatch our commandos from between the cocked jaws of a bear trap. Two major Soviet naval centers lay ready on either side of its entrance, Vladivostok and Petropavlovsk. As if to improve the probability of disaster, strung across the throat of the Okhotsk like a noose of pearls, sparkled the tiny Kuril Islands, Ivan's electronic eavesdropping posts on the Pacific. As much of the credit for the success or failure of the rescue would rest in the submarine skipper's hands as mine.

Sato, looking less soggy and regaining his usual dignity, estimated the information was over two weeks old. A reliable source, an old prison comrade of Kurganov's, had obtained it, and the series of human relays that had brought it had a long history of trustworthiness. It composed part of the *zek* pipeline. *Zek* in labor-camp slang meant inmate.

"I still need a precise location for the camp, and the composition of its garrison. Do you think the *zek* pipeline can come up with that sort of information?"

Sato shrugged. "Who knows? Might as well ask for the camp's spring menu, in case you like Siberia and decide to stay."

Charts and nautical publications dealing with the western rim of the Okhotsk proved sketchy or out of date. I needed a reference library.

Swearing Keiko to secrecy and yet betraying very little of my plan, I asked her to find me someone who knew the Sea of Okhotsk. This was not as tall an order as it appeared, since her family had many contacts in the Japanese fishing community.

Several days later she gave me a name and address, that of Hiizu Matsuma, on the northernmost island of Hokkaido.

"He is skillful old fisherman, *ne*? His mother was Ainu," she added. "He does not like Americans very much; they hurt the whaling industry and his sons work on a whale factory ship. *Roshiajins*," she said, using the Japanese word, "he hates. It is almost a sickness with him. An understandable sickness."

She went on to relate that prior to World War II, Hiizu Matsuma had been a fisherman living on one of the center Kuril Islands. At that time the Kurils belonged to Japan. Occasionally storms swept him onto the Soviet coast—sometimes at Kamchatka, other times north of Vladivostok. The local Evenki, Siberian relatives of the North American Eskimo, gave him food and shelter until he could make the necessary repairs and return to sea. Of course, the official Soviet thinking would have frowned on that, but the Evenki at that time lived a life unaffected by political upheaval in general and the dictates of the

Kremlin in particular. Siberia remained as untouched by European civilization as it had under the tsars, until after World War II. There were only some minor infections. Corrective Labor Camps, marred its chilly purity.

When World War II finally reached its fiery bloom, he took a contract to provide fish for a local Japanese army garrison. At thirteen he was too young to serve, and as the war progressed, too important to the garrison's commandant's palate to allow to enlist. Often, as Matsuma went out to fish, he saw Russian cargo ships bringing supplies to trade on the Japanese main islands. Despite Russia's war with Germany it did not declare war with Japan. In fact, Russia carried on an extremely active trade with Japan, high-handedly ignoring the fact that Japan was inflicting heavy losses on Russia's Atlantic allies, Britain, the Netherlands, and the United States, in the Pacific. Russia finally mustered the nerve to make war on Japan a few days after the atomic bomb fell on Hiroshima. Russia courageously seized the Kuril Islands and threw virtually everyone with any military connection into a Corrective Labor Camp.

Matsuma was imprisoned with the famed Colonel Kondo, one of the few guests of the Soviet penal system to give nearly as good as he got. Though Russia had never exchanged more than a teapot full of lead with Japan in the war, it seemed to have harbored some bitter personal grudge against the individual Japanese soldier. It did its worst—it treated them as it did its own citizens and gave them infinite sentences for no reason at all. Few were ever repatriated.

Matsuma bided his time and gradually learned Russian. Few Europeans successfully escaped the camps. But Europeans' physical characteristics contrasted sharply with those of the majority of the thinly scattered local peoples.

One very cold winter day—cold even by Siberian standards—Matsuma, as part of a woodcutting party, saw his opportunity. The guards and their dogs had become preoccupied with their small fire and little else as a frigid wind blew snow uncharacteristically from the west. Ducking into the storm, he kept the wind at his back and stumbled eastward for three days.

"Cold, much cold," Keiko said, hugging herself. "Makes Hokkaido in January like Okinawa in August."

Matsuma's tongue was raw and swollen from eating snow when the Evenki found him. Frostbite had cost him toes on each foot, and the scar tissue on his face is still sensitive to cold, Keiko added, now over forty years later.

Though the Evenki were nomadic and land oriented, Matsuma managed to pick their brains of every bit of information concerning local tides, currents, and weather. Their reindeer drives showed him much of the Okhotsk's western rim. At each encampment he gained experience sailing a homemade punt.

He stayed with the Evenki until midsummer, by which time he had perfected his skill with the sailing punt. Twice he was turned back— once by the sight of a patrol boat, the second time by a storm. The third time he set off with a wild look in his eye and didn't stop until he staggered ashore at Hokkaido.

Several days later I flew up to Hokkaido to interview Hiizu in Japanese. His pole-frame house, with its corrugated-steel roof symbolized the mismatch of industrial Japan and the traditional Ainu. Confirming my expectations, he wore the look of a hardened old fisherman. His features were Japanese—high cheekbones, round face—but his heavy beard and longer earlobes indicated Ainu ancestry. His short, though long-trunked, frame, together with an uneasy alertness and fluidity of movement, made you think of a sea otter.

I introduced myself as an American anthropologist interested in the environmental factors affecting the Siberian Evenki—a thin, short-term cover.

He responded in rough, harsh Japanese. Was I, he asked, one of those useless Caucasian scientists making it impossible for his sons to hunt whales? No, I responded, pointing to ancestors who had hunted whales over the entire Pacific. After all, it was true. That seemed to satisfy him.

"We spent an hour or more talking about the sea and marine life. Finally I asked him if he'd be interested in talking to a few of my associates in Korea about the western rim of the Sea of Okhotsk. Mentioning a fee that must have been too much, I sensed a resurgence of suspicion.

"It has been many years since I cut the waters of the Okhotsk. I would think that now the *Roshiajins* are on such affectionate terms with the western countries that there would be better sources of the information you ask . . . at less expense. But fishing is poor, ignorant work, and I know little of such things. Perhaps in scientific matters one should not put trust in what they say."

His impassive oak brown face could have belonged to the Indian of a nickel, an Aleutian eskimo, an Amazon head-hunter, or a Mongolian border guard—it told nothing. I held the vague suspicion he was laughing at me behind the tight-skinned mask, but could not be sure. In any event he was a man to respect and I needed his help. I wondered if he, too, knew, or was I just getting jumpy about this project?

PART III

CHAPTER 10

The mid-February snow lay like a crisp, pale comforter across the volcanic mountains of Japan's Hokkaido. The thin evergreen tree cover approximated Siberia's, and the terrain reflected other similarities. The lonely wind wove in and out of the volcanic peaks and then struck out with its icy fangs at an isolated ski resort nestled among the comforter's folds.

Known for its volcanic hot springs, the resort evidenced an architecture teetering unsurely between the design demands of a Swiss chalet, an Ainu village, and a Victorian hotel. Bear totems mixed with soft-drink machines in its main lobby, but its aged, unpainted wood exterior seemed at peace with its surroundings.

I had waited as long as I could for firm intelligence. Training must start now. A review of my muster list revealed a cadre of four: Dravit, Heyer, Puckins, and Wickersham. Puckins couldn't join us until the last week of training and Heyer would only be around for training. Depending on the size of the prison camp's garrison, an additional three to ten men might be required. Estimating a two-thirds dropout rate, I had requested my Marseilles café owner send out thirty men. He had sent twenty-five. On his own initiative, Dravit had recruited a Gurkha rifleman.

We had booked nearly every room in the small resort describing ourselves as a foundation-funded ex-con readjustment clinic. The manager's reluctance had been dispelled by generous flurries of cash. The cover story, I hoped, would account for some of our recruits' disreputable appearances and keep away fainthearted meddlers.

At five A.M. Dravit jammed everyone into one suite and held muster. Most of them looked athletic and carried the usual assortment of scars and broken noses. On the slopes and cross-country trails they would appear to be just a few more Caucasian ski bums, some perhaps who had not found their way back from Sapporo 1972. Dravit laid down the rules in English.

"Since we're training in a civilian resort, the usual military courtesies will be dispensed with. From here on out you are ex-cons communing with nature for the good of your souls on some screwball American grant. This does not, however, mean that orders are not to be obeyed, it only means that orders won't sound as much like orders as they might, ay?"

He punctuated his points with neat jabs, using his left hand. Dealing with weapons and men, the tangibles came so easily to Dravit. He fell into the right rhythm naturally. I envied his easy ability to control the day-to-day problems always fought at close quarters.

The men, sitting on the floor or on the beds, gave him their complete attention. Few showed any expression.

"Lieutenant Commander Frazer will be in command. He will be paying the accounts and calling the tune. Should any of you get out of tune, it will be me you'll be seeing, then. Not a lad amongst you wants to see me, do you, lads?

"If anyone wishes to drop out at any time prior to deployment, all he has to do is check out of his room and use the open-return airline ticket—the one in the top drawer of the bureau in your room."

A battler, the ravages of physical pain and hard use were etched across the nose pounded bridgeless and the high, broad cheekbones. His mustache was the only part of him that didn't look repaired. Changes in mood rippled across his ruddy face like a series of flag hoists, and kept his audience deftly off balance.

"Once we leave Japan things will get more difficult. Our destination will become a bit more obvious; therefore, no one leaves the project—alive, that is. We're a trifle touchy about security, the truth be known. A flamin' rear-echelon type with a big mouth could do us a world of harm. I'll send a beggar to his reward before I'll let him send me to mine. Right?"

The trim little Englishman tilted his battered head back and forth as he talked, bobbing and weaving, unconsciously flicking combinations into empty air. The heavy scarring around his eyes gave the lids a droopy cast, but the overall impression was one of vigor and determination. You could knock Dravit down forever and he'd still keep getting up. Pick a fight with Dravit at your peril; to keep him down you had to give serious consideration to killing him.

"Like a little toy tank," an aristocratic-looking German whispered irreverently to the man next to him.

They each nodded as he caught their gaze. The terms and conditions of employment were fairly standard in this work.

He was drawing them in masterfully.

So intuitive and self-disciplined. You'd never believe his home life was so much burning wreckage. Two divorces. Three children in their mother's custody.

Military marriages had been rough on Dravit. The odds had played against him. In the service, your time with your family was short and intense. The relationship tended to run to one of two extremes: either you played the benign, good-natured patsy home from the seas or you attempted to make up for lost time and brought your job's iron discipline and hard attitudes home with you. Dravit had played both extremes, and lost both times. No matter, I liked him and relied on him. Unlike his families, we had his exclusive attention for the full duration of the job. In any event, he would be the closest thing I would have to a friend on this project. That is, if there were such a thing as a commanding officer having friends.

"Mr. Frazer here will fill you in on the general nature of our sojourn into the frosty climes"—he grinned villainously—"where it's always double drill and a frozen canteen."

I rose slowly. I knew I didn't have Dravit's casual, cultivated menace acquired from years below decks. Ghosts of the room's earlier conversations hung in the air.

So this was that naval officer they'd been talking about . . . A SEAL, huh? . . . Well, he looks like he's in shape, got the bearing of a bloody brigadier . . . Sure, sure, very impressive, but can he fight? . . . What the hell's the Navy know about free-lance war making anyway? A likely bunch of paladins those white-linen boys would make. . . . Tight-lipped bastard, ain't he, I'll bet he can be a thoroughgoing son of a bitch when he wants to. . . . Man, are they gonna lay heavy words on us without a drink?

First impressions counted, and I had to convince twenty-five adventurous men—to follow me to some unknown place—in order to do some unknown martial deed—against some unknown adversary. My right shoulder ached again and I tried unsuccessfully to avoid clearing my throat.

"I'm Frazer . . . ex-U.S. Navy . . . SEALs. I've led a raid or two in the past fifteen years—nothing that ever showed up in the newspapers—and lived to tell about them. Wickersham, Dravit, and Heyer will vouch for me. Most of you are wondering what this is all about, and if you're getting paid too much or too little. From the look of most of you, too much. In looking around, you've probably figured out that after the required dose of SEAL-type training, we won't have enough men to depose a small government, or even knock over its treasury. You're right."

Heads were leaning toward me attentively. I scanned their faces; they were from everywhere: a Norwegian, a Frenchman, a Gurkha, a Cuban, a German, a South African. . . .

"We're going to execute a long-range amphibious raid requiring extensive cross-country skiing, some small craft work, and perhaps some swimming or scuba diving. We will be bringing back a willing passenger, code-named Eurydice for now. We can expect that Eurydice's hosts will take a dim view of our intrusion, not to mention Eurydice's abrupt departure . . ."

Wickersham had climbed up on a bed and was bouncing up and down, executing imaginary stem Christies like a slalom racer. His bridge was out again and he was grinning maniacally. Dravit moved to coldcock him but I waved him off.

". . . which may occasion the use of arms, the demolition of some buildings, the detonation of a booby trap or two . . ."

There were shouts.

". . . and, if my SEAL inclinations can be satisfied, the sinking of a few ships."

Three or four had sprung to their feet. A chair tipped over backward. There was a rush of secondary conversations. The excitement of it was in the air.

"Listen up," Dravit barked.

Yes, we had recruited the right men. Tired of scrambling for dollars through seedy con games, flyblown hijackings, smuggling small things for hawk-faced dowagers, gigoloing fading heiresses, futile searches for galleons and Aztec gold—they craved the simple, incisive action of combat seasoned with the smell of powder and the exhilarating sense of life where death stalked closest.

"But before we deploy I must, I will, be sure that we are ready, that every man going is in crack physical condition, his reflexes sharp, his knowledge of his responsibilities to the group thorough, and his ability to survive in the cold total. Your skills will be as good as they have ever been or could ever be.

"Before then you will be tired, frustrated, and hate the sight of Dravit and me. For we are going to torment you along through our own graduate-level course on war prowling; teach you the rudiments of a strange language, bring you to the edge of freezing so you'll know that cold is death, not just negative-degree readings; exhaust you until you know what second wind is, third wind . . . hundredth wind; all so we will survive and succeed where a conventional military unit would not dare to begin."

Wickersham stood shaking his ham-sized fist like some comic-opera generalissimo, then hosing down waves of invisible ski troops. His buffooning offered a good sign. Capture their imaginations and they would follow you into the cocked jaws of hell.

CHAPTER 11

Two days before the recruits had arrived, Sato visited me late in the evening there at the ski resort. He had scribbled a message on a notepad and handed it to me. It read: "EURYDICE Vic. 56° 05' 37"N 135° 40' 16"E LUMBER."

Without saying a word he tore up the two pages below the message so no impression remained.

"How reliable is all this?" I had a right to ask.

"Very, I think."

"How about giving me a little background so I can judge? I will be wagering lives on this information. You don't have to give me your whole network, just some indication of how it works."

"Even so, I will probably be jeopardizing the entire network," he said, sighing. "It's easy to follow threads back and forth. Well, anyway, I suppose you do have a right to know. Let's step outside for a walk. They have eavesdropping devices for outdoors, too, you know. Parabolic reflectors, I think they call them, but their application is difficult."

I put on an old convoy coat and stepped out into the lightly falling snow. For once the flakes were dropping straight down.

"An underground pipeline smuggled Kurganov's first works page by page out of his camp and Russia. After his exile, he managed to get in touch with the man who was the western termination point of the pipeline and on occasion transmit to Russia's forgotten men as he had once transmitted when he, too, was a forgotten man.

"One point on the pipeline, in the middle of Moscow, is run by someone who goes by the code name Myshka. He had developed a certain flair for eliciting information from the local ministries, not a usual pipeline requirement. His information is invariably accurate, but until now of little real value to us.

"For a long time, Myshka had an ineffectual neighbor who walked a pitifully mangy dog of indefinite breed. Everyone in their cooperative apartment building avoided the pair on their daily sorties. Fortunately Myshka endeavored to befriend the miserable pair, not without benefit. The man worked in the Ministry of State Security. The dog was without redeeming social value." This is the tale that Sato told:

Aleksandr Gorshnov, a lower-level bureaucrat, often complained to Myshka about his lack of future in the ministry. Wiping his glasses, Gorshnov would bemoan his meager salary and puzzle over the prosperous life-style of another civil servant of the same grade in his office.

"Watch him closely," Myshka suggested sagely. "Maybe he augments his income; we all know there are limits to thrift."

It turned out that the fellow civil servant held a post in the Camp Administration Section, Prisoner Transport. He knew where each prisoner was going, but only by place-name and mailing address. Gorshnov's associate sold that information to relatives who were often afraid to inquire or correspond with the imprisoned relative. Each movement meant the relative still lived. No movement for years could only mean death, if you knew the system. Access to such information brought personal prosperity.

Gorshnov learned his associate's habits more energetically than he had ever done anything in his life. Within a few weeks he had become adept at rifling through his associate's desk and soon knew the details of prisoner transport. Pain, anguish, and death turned a nice profit. And he was grateful, telling Myshka the source of his newfound success.

Shortly Myshka developed a relative named Vyshinsky and had to plead with Gorshnov—though not too long—to accept money for disclosure of the camp's place-name. He himself worked in the Moscow Forestry Institute. He compared the camp's place-name with maps and lists of lumber-product sources in eastern Siberia and crosschecked it with large-scale maps showing railroad spurs. In this way he managed to identify the camp industry and pin its location down precisely. In a sparsely settled area where place-names could cover hundreds of square miles, the location had to be exact.

"He then enciphered the coordinates into one rather bad poem, which he smuggled through the pipeline. If intercepted by the KGB, the simply coded message would likely be overlooked by the KGB in its joy of interception. Finding evidence of one crime, they would be too satisfied to search for evidence of another.

"Myshka, in a flash of literary bravado, code-named Vyshinsky Eurydice—an allusion that would be obvious to any literary-minded pipeline receiver."

"Eurydice?" I questioned. The name sounded familiar. "Eurydice . . . now I remember. It's mythology, she was Orpheus's wife. Orpheus tried to retrieve her from the home of the dead, from Hades. Yes, very good, the allusion seems appropriate."

"Not too appropriate, I hope," Sato whispered. "Orpheus failed."

"Vyshinsky. Tell me about Vyshinsky. I need to know him when I see him. We will have gone an awfully long way to pick up the wrong Vyshinsky," I said slowly, trying to work some of the stiffness out of my right shoulder.

"I have a file taped into the dead space of my car door," the Japanese lawyer responded. "It should tell you as much as you need to know."

I sat in his car and read by the glove-compartment light.

The file contained a grainy full-length photo of a small, thin man in coveralls. The photo was poor but it showed the receding hairline, the glasses, and the small schoolmaster-ish goatee. He was alone and his posture was stooped and stiff.

The first thing you noticed was that the eyes held you. They expressed a deep lingering, but contained pain. They were sad, compassionate eyes. *Pallbearer's eyes.* Here was a man who had lived life as a human punching bag, but instead of bouncing back, he had just *absorbed*, and the leather had begun to wear thin.

The second quality about Vyshinsky that caught my attention was the pipe-cleaner unreality of his physique. He seemed awkwardly assembled, like a mannequin. Despite his work clothes, it was clear that this was a cerebral man, to whom his body was a mere accessory.

I scanned the photo once more—a round, sensitive head connected to a pencil-thin neck, mounted on uneven, narrow shoulders, teetered on an unlikely waist that left a good deal of coverall fabric to spare. The overall picture was of a man as frail and brittle as an oyster cracker.

Kurganov knew his man; Vyshinsky wouldn't last six months at forced labor in a gulag.

I flipped through the various entries. Sato's file had been expertly done.

In 1930 Stalin decided to liquidate the kulaks.

The kulaks were moderately successful peasant farmers who had made their appearance after the overthrow of the feudal landlords during the Russian Revolution. For a little over a decade, the peasants were forgotten while the Bolsheviks turned their attentions to the industrialization of the cities. Untouched, the kulaks gravitated toward a market economy and eventually made the error of holding back the sale of their crops until prices reached what they considered to be the proper level.

To safeguard his industrialization program's food supply, Stalin set in motion a program with multiple objectives: to break the kulaks' hold on food distribution, to generally drive the peasants into the cities, and to soften rural Russia for the advent of agrarian collectives.

Setting out with their usual heavy-handedness, Stalin's henchmen rounded up land, crops, and livestock in the name of the state. The kulaks constituted a very small percentage of all Russian peasants, but once the Soviet machine began rolling, it ground up everything in sight. Five million Russians were displaced. Some were executed outright while others were sent to factories, underpopulated regions, or corrective labor camps. The Red Army managed the program and it was pursued in a warlike manner. Unfortunately, no one was exactly sure who qualified as a kulak. In the interest of "Soviet thoroughness" all peasants became fair game, and the program was expanded to the uprooting of whole villages to clear the way for farm collectives.

In 1931 the Vyshinsky family stood face-to-face with Soviet thoroughness. The Vyshinskys had been peasant farmers and occasional blacksmiths for generations. The grandfather was a farmer and blacksmith; the father a farmer and blacksmith; and the sons, Sacha, age ten, Pyotr, age eight, and with the exception of Yuri, age four, were expected to become peasant farmers and blacksmiths, too.

Yuri's birth had been difficult and his mother had died in childbirth. A sickly child, Yuri Vyshinsky was deemed ill suited for farm work because of his delicate constitution and because . . . of his gift. At four, Yuri could complete basic problems in farm math flawlessly. He could play a respectable game of chess on the village's one chessboard (which did not have carved pieces but only symbols stamped on disks). This game he played endlessly on each *pech* or brick oven of the many *izbas*—family huts—in the village.

There were some in the village who said he should be sent somewhere to learn how to read and make himself useful. Others attributed his strange aptitudes to something more sinister, in some way related to his Rumanian grandmother's alleged Gypsy blood, and very likely to result in ill fortune. The second group announced that he would come to no account and end up in the company of fortune-tellers, actors, musicians, and mountebanks. Unknowingly, Yuri possessed a rare talent for harnessing abstractions.

That spring, a party commissar came to the village meeting. He explained the new farm policy with commendable Soviet thoroughness. It became evident that the new order placed industrialization and the well-being of the cities well above peasant sensibilities. The commissar, clearly a city man, countered sanctimoniously every awkward question with generous use of the new term *kulak*. The picture presented to them did not sit well with peasants who were only just getting used to the idea of owning their own land. Now someone had come to take it away. There were angry words. The Vyshinskys' patriarch closed the meeting with an old slavic political custom, a defenestration. The commissar was lucky the meeting had been held in a typical one-story *izba*.

"We are not 'kulaks,'" bellowed the senior Vyshinsky out the window to the retreating commissar. "This is hard, ungiving land. Do you think some air-sniffing Muscovite is going to tell us how to wring a living from it?"

Isolated and illiterate, the villagers were surprised when the armed men of the GPU arrived. They rounded up the families of the village and herded them to a holding camp at a railroad station tens of miles away. They awaited their unnamed Siberian destiny in despair.

"We must write Kalinin, Grandfather," the small, awkward boy suggested one day. "Pyotr heard the train master say that he is the head of the Bolshevik government," Yuri added shyly.

His grandfather smiled at the naïveté of his reedy grandson, but Yuri seemed to function at a level beyond them. Anyway, the assistant train master could write and seemed sympathetic. Who knew when their train would come?

The letter started, "We beg you, Comrade Kalinin, a mistake has been made. We are not 'kulaks' but honest peasants who wield our humble sickles in the fields. . . .'"

The Vyshinskys tried a one-in-a-million shot. In the end, no one dared to tamper with a letter addressed to one so high up. Though Stalin was the real power, Kalinin was president of the Union of Soviet Socialist Republics.

Perhaps the party leaders were having second thoughts about their attack on the Russian breadbasket. Perhaps it was time to demonstrate that Soviet thoroughness could distinguish between peasants and kulaks. Perhaps Kalinin, who had made so much of his peasant background so often, found it expedient to underscore his ties once again. In any event, that fall when the train finally came, the Vyshinsky family alone was spared. Quiet young Yuri was torn between his pride of achievement and the knowledge that his playmates were gone forever.

The family's fortunes reversed abruptly. Yuri's grandfather was a man who corresponded with the president of the Soviet Union. Consequently, Yuri's father was offered the position of assistant to the colonel who supervised the new collective. Yuri's father could not admit he found the job distasteful. The family had come perilously close to oblivion and too recently for him to decline. Yet he would never really adjust to constantly thrusting himself between the system and his people. The new inhabitants of the collective were surprised that Yuri's grandfather, once so vigorous, died not long thereafter. Yuri's father understood and suffered on.

Yuri, his father, and his brothers weathered the foreseeable harvest of the kulak liquidation—three years of famine, the death of millions by starvation, and destruction from which Soviet agriculture never recovered.

The three sons were placed in the party youth organization, the Komsomol, and in a special school for peasants. The special school made good propaganda. Moreover, with the elimination of the feudal landowners, and then the kulaks, someone on the collectives had to know how to read the *pyatiletka,* the first five-year plan. Later, Sacha was inducted into the army and attended the Frunze Higher Military School. Pyotr followed by attending the Leninskiy Higher Naval School. Less robust, Yuri was chosen to study physics at a lesser-known university west of Moscow.

Yuri had little say in the matter, so it was fortunate it was a discipline he enjoyed. Unlike some of the other disciplines—genetics, for instance, under Lysenko—dealing in force, mass, velocity, and acceleration carried no politically charged baggage. Reticent, soft-spoken, but already hardened to the realities, he began to find subtle ways to challenge the new Soviet thought at his university. Though painfully shy, he became adept at counseling indirectly and at serving as a sounding board for his fellow students. Vyshinsky's paternal influence was to change Kurganov's life. They grew inseparable. Vyshinsky's introverted, theoretical disposition complemented Kurganov's vigorous, extroverted style. Among his many classmates—in peasant tradition—Vyshinsky had begun sowing seeds. In keeping with the trend of the new Soviet agriculture, there was little promise of a significant harvest.

Then came the Great Patriotic War. Yuri's father and oldest brother, Sacha, died in defense of *Rodina*, the Motherland, in the first weeks of fighting after the German invasion. Still in school, Yuri Vyshinsky learned of the purges that had wiped away the cream of the Russian officer corps, just a few years before the attack, and which had helped to pave the way for German advances. The German planners had noted the purge carefully. As with the kulaks, the liquidation of the Russian officer corps resulted in the loss of millions of Russian lives.

Not long afterward, he was called up for service with a military intelligence unit that specialized in code-breaking. He demonstrated a remarkable aptitude for the work. Surprisingly, the secret lay not in his well-developed mathematical skills, but rather in his sensitive understanding of human nature and his ability to visualize and handle people—at a distance. It had to be at a distance. Something in him did not trust his ability to act directly. Like the Wizard of Oz, Yuri Vyshinsky was at his best hidden behind a curtain.

Eventually declining party membership, he advanced no further and was released at the war's end.

Not long afterward he completed his degree and took a teaching position. Outside of the classroom, he was sought as a counselor by his students. Once again the shy physicist resumed his pattern of sowing seeds, as he called them, "of doubt and truth."

By the 'Fifties, his brother Pyotr had risen to an important position in the Soviet submarine service. Pyotr's influence brought Yuri an assignment to Lomonosov State University in Moscow, and secondarily won him tenancy in a communal apartment, a coveted privilege.

At Lomonosov, Yuri Vyshinsky's students nicknamed him—with some warmth—*krolik*, the puppet, for his airy, disjointed mannerisms. They hypothesized that a stiff wind would tangle his strings and would send their professor flapping all the way to Gorky Park. The sobriquet held some truth, but would have been more accurate had it been the puppet *maker*, because his "sowing" was taking on more active aspects. Like a puppet maker, he created and inspired; but his was a gentle puppetry that guided, rather than controlled, the steps of his adopted charges. His method of pressing his dissension from behind a curtain was well suited for survival in the Soviet system.

By the mid-sixties, Yuri Vyshinsky had in his invisible way contributed to establishing the *samizdat*, the secret self-publishing network. Years later his brother Pyotr, now a captain, first rank, in the Baltic Fleet, came to him.

"There is no appropriate way I can think of, my brother, to convey the feeling of dying by millimeters. I am dying. Radiation sickness is now the official professional ailment of the Soviet submarine service. Through diligent application and loyal service in boats designed without people in mind, I have become an official casualty."

He sighed with resignation. "When the choice is between the people and the state's objectives, the people always pay for those objectives with their lives. The final joke is, the state's objectives are never met anyway."

Yuri, reticent as ever, spoke slowly. "You must leave the Soviet Union. You must get medical help. After Chernobyl it would appear the only reliable radiation-sickness treatment is to be found in the West."

At once Pyotr understood the staggering impact of Yuri's words. A naval officer, especially a submariner, would not be allowed to leave the Soviet Union—not with radiation sickness. In essence, Yuri was telling Pyotr to take his family and defect. It was an eventuality Pyotr had only contemplated in a mental whisper. Yuri was inviting disaster because he would not be able to go. He did not have the mobility that accompanied his brother's naval officer's internal passport. The relatives that a defector left behind were punished for their unhappy status. Knowing he would be left behind, Yuri was implicitly agreeing to make an extraordinary sacrifice. Yuri was surprised at his own directness.

Using some of Yuri's *samizdat* contacts, Pyotr and his family slipped into Finland. Unfortunately, Pyotr's exposure had been too extensive and he was dead within a month.

Yuri Vyshinsky, professor of theoretical physics at Lomonosov State University, received the usual amenities. A year's "medical attention" in a psychiatric ward left him in broken health and with a certain slowness of speech. His job and apartment were taken away.

But the brain was still intact . . . and the spirit. "Krolik" took a job as a sweeper on the underground economy. He slept on a cot in the boiler room of the university's physics building. His new quarters reminded Yuri of those wintry days as a child in the village when he slept on *apech*. Occasionally he ghost-wrote technical papers for his former students.

The KGB attempted to visit him periodically but he was difficult to find and completely behind the puppet maker's curtain now. Guiding the steps of *samizdat* writers and related dissidents, he was a consultant who specialized in dissidence in the shadows.

There were now no distractions from his struggle with the system. Under a naked light bulb, the boiler room walls echoed, "If they take Shevschenko, get letters to the American Academy of Science . . ." "That Ukrainian nationalist manuscript must be printed in Austria and smuggled back here. . . ." "The Irkutsk Writers Union is completely infiltrated, I wouldn't even bother . . ." "The short Baptist tract can be smuggled in a container like this. . . ." "Have you heard Rimsky got ten years in Magadan for housing the blacklisted Armenians?"

The KGB never caught on to him. But two years after Pyotr's death, he was thrown into Lefortovo Prison for initial interrogation. The KGB had at last discovered someone dear to Kurganov. Kurganov was a great irritation to them. One whom they could not touch directly. But Kurganov could be made to regret his actions indirectly, through the punishment of others. That was one established way of dealing with men who shouldered a strong sense of obligation and responsibility. Their file labeled "Kurganov" now had a second subheading after "retribution": it read "Special Prisoner Vyshinsky."

There was, I knew, a point when after having fought hard and well that a man deserved to be pulled out of the contest. Someone else could pick up the banner. Vyshinsky had earned a rest.

I looked at the picture again and tried to visualize him with a full beard and without glasses. I couldn't.

The body, the posture, but most of all, the eyes, would have to do it. The peasant puppet maker's sad and compassionate eyes. *Those pallbearer's eyes.*

"Were we able to get information of the size of the garrison or the layout of the camp?"

"No," Sato said quietly.

"Keep Myshka on it. I don't want to play a long shot like this by the seat of my pants."

The coordinates placed the camp in a valley just west of the Dzhug-dzhur Range, over eighty miles from the coast. Navigation would be tough. Magnetic compasses would spin aimlessly in that portion of the world. Solar compasses, which gave readings using the angle of the sun's rays at a specific time of day, were no more help, since we hoped to move at night.

The stars and terrain features offered our primary means of night navigation. Confronted with a heavy overcast or a good snowstorm, we might have to drop crumbs to find our way out—a procedure which the pursuing Soviet army might find amusing.

CHAPTER 12

In the predawn darkness, I put the twenty-five men through an hour of heavy calisthenics, then took them on a 10,000-meter run. Four or five of the Marseilles group wheezed in a full half hour behind the rest.

"It's too cold for running. . . . What was all this jock stuff for? . . . The only muscle that needed conditioning was the one connected to the right index finger. . . . We've already been through basic training once, we don't need it again." One, a chain smoker, quit on the spot. He flew home that night.

After breakfast we mustered in one suite, which became a makeshift classroom. Dravit and Heyer drummed Russian phrases and some written words into heads of varied receptiveness. During breaks, rumors swirled about like blizzard snowflakes. We were learning Russian to impersonate Russians . . . we were learning Russian to abduct Russians outside of Russia . . . we were learning Russian to survive in Russia. Dravit, who knew the nature of our mission, smiled enigmatically. I simply pretended not to hear.

In the afternoon Heyer began the cross-country instruction in his quiet competent way. The pale blond Norwegian paired the experienced skiers with the inexperienced and put them through the basics. We carried no packs at first, nor any weapons. Japan put severe restrictions on firearms and in any event, we did not want to attract attention.

As far as anyone knew, we were some burly tourist group. The Japanese are used to tourist groups moving around with martial precision behind a host of flags in matching apparel. We reversed the norm by peppering our wide range of cast-off military clothing with enough civilian items to pass for American casual chic.

The next few days went by without incident. I increased the pace and stress of the physical training and the group sorted itself between the fit and thriving, and the unfit and downward spiraling. Three were keeping up with the cadre of four, a middle-aged ex-French Foreign Legion officer, the Gurkha rifleman, and an ex-German Kampfschwimmer. The legionnaire, d'Epinuriaux, was from Chamonix, where he had at one time tried downhill racing. He was called Chamonix or 'Nix. The stocky Gurkha, Gurung, despite coming from the snowiest region of Nepal had never skied but nevertheless led the novices by sheer force of will. Lutjens, a wedge-shaped German frogman, had been a world-class gymnast.

The ex-Foreign Legion officer, Gaston d'Epinuriaux, had a hawklike face and a long, lean configuration, which combined to remind you of a French halberd. Laconic, precise, he was not the fellow you'd go to first with a new joke. Then again, I was hardly the one to be critical on that point. His cold, unblinking blue eyes were accented by a long-discolored scar that streaked down one side of his face like a bolt of tropic lightning. The steely gray stubble over his ears looked as if it could strike sparks on a hard surface. Everything about him was either hard, cold, or contained.

In the hotel's hot-spring pool, he'd created a stir among the Japanese guests when they'd seen his bare torso—dimpled with more zippers than a motorcycle jacket. Bayonet work, I'd say. At its dirtiest.

He was a gloomy old soldier, the kind they fear in the Legion because of the *cafard*. *Le cafard* was the black beetle that, according to legend, gnawed into men's brains at those lonely, desolate outposts of which the Legion was fond. It accounted for all manner of murder, madness, and suicide. The quiet ones were always the most dangerous, the morose ones who did their work mechanically. The merest trifle might set them off.

That was the easy answer to his manner, I suspected there was more to it.

The second excelling new skier, Amarsing Gurung, was a Gurkha. It seems useless to say more. "Gurkha" says it all. He was one of those stocky, bandy-legged mountain men from Nepal whose weathered brown faces opened into a dazzling white smile when there was mischief afoot or at the prospect of action with heavy doses of cordite and cold steel. He shaved his head in the old way, leaving only a jet black topknot by which the gods could pluck his fallen body from the field of battle.

Gurung had served Great Britain, as his father, his father's father, and his father's father's father had. He knew his duty, and his wife, who waited loyally for him in Nepal, knew hers. It was somewhat irregular for him to hire out individually, but he was with Dravit, and surely wasn't wherever Dravit stood a piece of the British Empire? Gurung had languished too long in the garrison in Hong Kong, and a Gurkha must fight, or he was no Gurkha at all. Finally there was the Kampfschwimmer, Lutjens. Physically he could have been Wickersham's younger brother, but he was a delicately dark Bavarian whereas Wickersham was an oakenly buff Wisconsinite. A top-notch gymnast, he seemed to be always in the air, balanced on his hands, or moving with graceful lunges. Where Wickersham's face had been hammered into shape, Lutjens's was chiseled to leave a thin nose and those narrow creases on either side of the mouth associated with well-bred yacht captains, Grand Prix drivers, and men in ads for good scotch. Something about him exuded evening in black tie, svelte debs, and fine crystal. His heavily accented English was hard to follow but I remember overhearing him say, ". . . a boring death, don't you t'ink? T'ese escapades of mine will drive Aunt Elga *verriickt*, which would be a reward in itself, *ja*?" From the most sophisticated backgrounds sometimes came the simplest motivations of all: Lutjens waged a dangerous rebellion against a gilt-edged family.

*　*　*

At the other end of the scale, two of the Marseilles group, an ex-British para and an ex-U.S. Marine, developed injuries whose authenticity I doubted, but which gave them an honorable way out.

Heyer, following my lead, increased the complexity and difficulty of our ski maneuvers. Local skiers often glided through small groups of men digging snow caves, bivouacking or assuming strange formations prone in the snow. These skiers whisked by, shrugging off the odd behavior of foreigners.

On the fourth afternoon, after a timed fifteen-mile ski trek, I let the men go into Sapporo. The liberty would be good for morale and I knew they'd eventually start sneaking off for local color anyway. Consequently, I opted for Sapporo, which could absorb our group without trauma.

A knock on the door interrupted some map work. "As I remember, you said liberty was for all hands, Skipper."

It was Dravit.

"A good officer must lead by precept *and example*," he said, storming into the room before I could reply. "And it is about time you guided me through the mysteries of Kobe beef and Kirin beer, otherwise I will be thought horribly backward by the local ladies and justifiably branded a big-nosed, hairy barbarian."

"Okay, okay. This map work can wait. Seems about time I renewed my acquaintance with bright lights and civilized living."

Ice demons menaced us in Sapporo—great crystalline, reptilian demons who had slithered out of crevasses somewhere on Hokkaido and crept down to Odori Park to squat among the snow sculpture. The eighty-foot figures defined the perimeters of the *Yuki Matsuri*, the snow festival. Their threatening frozen stares sent the hotel bus scurrying down the thoroughfares until it found safety within the brave lights of the entertainment district.

The bus deposited Dravit and me before a well-known businessmen's nightclub. Dravit's primary interest was pub crawling, and when I told him what the price of a drink and charming conversation in this expense-account-geared club totaled, he became even more convinced we ought to make our donations to the local economy over a broader range of recipients. "Share the wealth and all that. Might ossify staying all night in one place, actually."

In addition to the many businessmen, the district swarmed with Japan's strayed souls. Japan categorized them tribally: the *kaminari-zoku*, motorcyclists of the "thunder tribe;" the *yoromeki-zoku*, the voluptuaries of the "philandering tribe;" the *taiyo-zoku*, the affluent, aimless members of the "sun tribe." The West didn't have a monopoly on rudderless ships.

We had no trouble finding other places to visit. The district teemed with bars, tearooms, cabarets, nightclubs, pachinko parlors, and restaurants: the Miyako, the Fuyago, the Kamakura, the Moulin Rouge, the Jazz Inn, the Nevada. . . . Every street tout offered to guide us to a "number-one nice place." Instead we followed out our own instincts and concentrated on a string of cubbyhole bars.

The Kamakura—the snow hut—proved attractive. Its frosted-glass booths resembled Japanese igloos or snow huts. "*Irasshai-mase*," welcomed a predatory hostess. "Sit down . . . you drink scotch? . . . Joni Waluka Red, I bet . . . best music here, *ne*? she fired off without taking a breath.

Despite an earlier warning to steer clear of scotch, the most coveted liquor in Japan, Dravit ordered it anyway. He inspected the bottle of Royal something or other when the bartender poured. Dravit twisted the label for me to read.

"Says here this scotch is distilled by appointment to the Queen and 'manufactured from the finest Scottish grapes.'"

We threaded through the *yoru no cho*—butterflies of the night—of three more bars, including a *karaoke*, a tavern for very amateur solo vocalists, until we hit the Transistor Dolly Bar. The name had me puzzled until Dravit—sensitive to these things—noted that not one of the hostesses stood over five feet tall.

The bantam Royal Marine's eyes lit merrily and several of the girls buzzed about attentively. Each wore a distinctive electronic symbol that matched a button on a console at our table. Dravit punched two buttons, which lit corresponding symbols on a display board over the bar. We heard a short electronic ditty and all but two girls disappeared.

They sat down and graciously listened to Dravit burn out his circuits in pidgin Japanese.

"Bothers you a bit, doesn't it? That ruddy gentleman's cashiering they gave you. You hide it well, of course."

"Of course," I said, wishing he'd change the subject, but he'd had a few by now. He worried for people doggedly after he'd had a few.

"Try to do some good with no hope of reward and they'll stomp on your fingers every time."

He thought a moment.

"Too bloody dedicated, that's what it is. Ramrods like us are too dedi-bloody-cated for the bleeding system to understand. No frame of reference. They don't want us 'cause they can't figure us from a self-interest point of view. I mean, all right, self-interest is a valid enough spur for most pursuits, but getting shot at is just basically contrary to a beggar's self-interest, bloody clearly it is."

Dravit's micro-component dolly refilled his glass.

"So it figures they can't appreciate a first-rate officer when they see one because they don't understand why ruddy integrity is so important to the military in the first place. Well, bugger them if they can't take a joke, that's what I always say. But it hurts, doesn't it? Down deep, I mean. You won't let much show, but an old jolly can tell. You gave it your heart and they rubbed your face in it. Sod 'em. Here's a chill to the vocationless bastards."

"About time we moved on," I said somberly. "Wasn't someone saying something about spreading the wealth and terminal ossification?"

A few blocks farther on we heard the busy chimes of a pachinko parlor. Pachinko—vertical pinball with marbles instead of steel balls—ranked high among Japanese addictions. We would have gone on had I not seen a familiar bowlegged figure leaning against one of the machines.

Leaning wasn't quite the right word—propped, maybe. Barry Puckins of west Texas had flown in for a few days on his way. back from the Philippines. The chief would return stateside tomorrow and be back for keeps in a week. Now he stood in a frozen stance, his palms up and his forearms parallel across his stomach. Pinned to his anorak jacket was a note in katakana, and next to him a bargirl he'd liberated somewhere laughed uncontrollably.

Soon a dissipated teenage girl in a motorcycle jacket and a few of her friends shuffled over to Puckins to read the note. She reached into her pocket, tucked something into the pouch of Puckins's anorak, and touched one of several buttons sketched on the note. Slowly, Puckins rumbled to life like a coin-operated machine.

The girl, a world-weary urchin, had pressed the button "oil." With uneven movements he removed his scarf, wrapped it around his head like a turban, and began to drill. When he struck an invisible gusher, he grabbed the girl, danced a mechanical polka of joy, then abruptly wound down and resumed his original fixed and lifeless position. The girl and her friends were in stitches. Something made me think they didn't often have much to laugh about.

Someone else inserted a coin and pressed "overdrive." Again he rumbled to life, this time leaning backward as he moved and assuming the appearance of a pilot functioning under high G-forces.

Throughout, his eyes showed neither mirth nor recognition. I figured he'd go on like this until the parlor owner threw him out or he passed out. (The bargirl ran across the street for bottles of beer, which he chugged every time someone pressed "lubrication.")

By the time we'd left, the pouch of his anorak bulged heavily with coins.

Several bars later we reached the Fuyago, the nightless castle. Its ladies came on shrill and competitive.

At a corner stool I noticed Chamonix with a bargirl as hard and time worn as deck plate. She was doing all the talking—in French, perhaps—in any event he wasn't holding up his end. He just sat there glassy eyed and expressionless, pouring them back with a vengeance. I saw no reason to disturb them. Empty stools surrounded them like barbed wire.

He downed drink after drink at a steady, unfeeling, unrelenting pace.

*　*　*

"What say you to heading back to that electro-voltaic, double-switch, single-transformer-gizmo saloon, pardner?" Dravit asked brightly.

"Er . . . danger high voltage?"

As we walked back I thought how there was something drearily automated about this band, that had chosen to march like clockwork pallbearers into the endless cold. At least two mechanical men, one comic and the other grim, had mustered under the command of a weary-eyed, wooden frogman. It must be catching, because now the second-in-command had become partial to ladies whose most intimate workings might be transistorized.

Later that evening, commotion in an alley caught my attention. Dravit had been comparing the economic outlooks of Japan and Korea—at length. I couldn't see anything as we had passed the alley but there was a distant gritty shuffling of feet and heavy uneven breathing.

"Let's take a look," I said, wheeling back into the alley. The alley was deep and intersected another, making a thin T. As we quickened our pace, the clear sounds of a struggle issued from the right arm of the T.

Turning the corner, we were suddenly watching three Japanese men, their backs to an open doorway, holding a resisting fourth man while a fifth flicked a sap at his head. The resisting victim was Wickersham. As I rushed at the man with the sap, he heard my footsteps and whirled into me, flicking the black leather sap at my face. I ducked into *Tai otoshi*, a judo body-drop throw, smashing his head and shoulders into the brick building's wall. In the corner of my eye I saw Dravit, his fist wrapped in a scarf, popping neat combinations at another of Wickersham's assailants. That left two men trying to restrain Wickersham, which was hardly enough. They both let go at once, and one attempted a karate front kick at my groin. I had just time to rotate a hip into the kick and to grab the extended foot with my right hand as I swept away his other leg with my left foot. He dropped hard to the ice-covered pavement. The other, in a brown suit, opened his jacket, reached into the front of his shirt, and under a wool belly wrap. A flash of green-and-red tattooing showed across his bare stomach and I knew what to expect. I brushed Dravit aside and grabbed brown suit's moving wrist with both hands. The razor-sharp *tanto* dagger flashed for a split second before I could turn it back into him. The ten inch blade slipped into his visceral cavity to the hilt. He doubled over, then dropped to the pavement. Three men lay on the pavement, the fourth had disappeared.

"Let's get out of here, they're *yakuza* or hired *katana*."

"Wha . . . ?" Wickersham started.

"Move, this is all we need." I surveyed the alley, no one had seen the fight. "I'll explain later."

Snaking through more alleys, we finally came to a boulevard and flagged down a cab. Out of breath, we tried to appear casual as the three of us jammed into the little Toyota. Once we were back at the ski resort I began to explain.

"You must have crossed some real pros. The fellow with the short sword either is, or was, *yakuza*."

"*Yakuza*?"

"Japanese gangsters, Oriental organized crime. Centuries ago they were strictly gamblers, but now they're thugs with traditions and codes."

"How could you tell? Something special about that knife?" Dravit asked.

"Well, yes. That and the belly wrap and the tattoo. *Yakuza* are fond of tattooing an entire kimono design on themselves and of using one of those daggers instead of a gun. Now I've got a question: What the hell did you do to get them riled?"

"Nothing, honest. What was that other word you used, kata-something?" Wickersham asked.

"*Katana*, sword. Hired sword. Some *yakuza* fall from grace with their clans and hire out, like hired guns. Okay, now tell me what started all this."

"Well, I was over at a place called the Miyako blowing my retainer on . . . Well, anyway, after a while I noticed a Japanese fellow in a mod brown suit in the corner seemed to be paying me a lot of attention, but never really looking at me. Well, I figured he could mind his business and I'd mind mine.

"Pretty soon this bar dolly was letting me buy her drinks, so I don't really think too much about my mod friend in the brown suit."

Wickersham took a deep breath. For the first time I noticed the side of his face was the color of a ripe eggplant.

"Well, this fine bar dolly and I decide to see the rest of town, and it seems everywhere we go I catch a glimpse of Mr. Mod Brown Suit. Later on I don't see him but I see this other fellow with a turtleneck—a Caucasian maybe—and now he's everywhere."

I remembered the man with the turtleneck—Dravit had knocked him out—he might have been Caucasian.

"The night was still young so the bar dolly and I go to this tiny apartment of hers for a nightcap, maybe more, maybe less," he said with bloodshot discretion.

"About oh-two-thirty I decided to head back here . . ."

It was 0500.

". . . and just as I was going out the door Brown Suit and Turtleneck and two guys I never saw before try to put me out with a sap, but Brown Suit missed me on his first solid try, and from then on I wasn't standing still for nobody."

I could imagine their plight. They had missed their chance to coldcock Wickersham, and then were stuck with a 240-pound, five-foot-ten wildcat on their hands. From the look of the side of his face they had managed to tag him a few times.

"I think I broke Turtleneck's wrist, but the sap man kept trying to make a good tag. I went out, I think once, but came back to, before they could get me anywhere."

A mugging? Perhaps. But there were easier victims. This carried the earmarks of an attempted kidnapping. I had the uneasy feeling that this attempted snatch and our project were connected.

"Captain Dravit, from now on everyone uses the buddy system on liberty. No one leaves the resort alone. Everyone carries a blackjack, brass knuckles, or a knife."

Dravit caught my glance. We were under siege and someone wanted one of us to talk with or to. What had been up until now a winter snow festival had taken on a dangerous mood.

Wickersham edged toward the resort's main building.

"And where do you think you're going?"

"Get some rest?" Wickersham piped up enthusiastically.

"Uh-huh. You get poleaxed on your own time, you can rest and recuperate on your own time. Be back here in PT gear in fifteen minutes."

"Yes, sir," was the sheepish reply.

You're a hard man, Quillon Frazer. A hard-nosed, stiff-necked, true-to-type ogre. Heaven help you if they ever found out you were fond of them.

CHAPTER 13

The weary days of training seemed to blur together. Even aches and pains took on an undefined quality until they manifested themselves into one single collective throb.

We found that high-camber mountaineering skis with cable bindings offered the simplest, most serviceable combination for our purposes. We allotted one multi-fuel stove for every two men. The stove was for cooking and for melting snow for water. Water in its different forms constituted the single most influential substance in subfreezing travel. It provided both danger and salvation.

Petty Officer Heyer warned that dehydration was the greatest threat to the ski trooper. Any raiding party was duty bound to stop periodically to melt snow for drinking. Otherwise, the party risked the collapse of its members one by one as assuredly as they would drop on a waterless hike across the Libyan desert. Each skier must examine his urine en route and be sure to drink enough water to keep it nearly clear white. He advised against eating snow directly for it puts a severe strain on the body's heating system and the crystals cut up the inside of a skier's mouth. It was only a last-resort procedure.

As dangerous as it was to dry out on the inside, it was equally dangerous to become wet on the outside. Water is a coolant. Its use for that purpose in a car's engine, he explained, was a good example of that property. Water allowed to turn to ice was an even more effective coolant. It would be a fatal error in Siberia to get wet and stay wet. "Therefore," he said, "the whole object of movement in cold weather is to stay dry. And that doesn't just mean don't go swimming with your clothes on."

The pale Norwegian tapped his ski pole against the inside of each ski and continued. The threatening source of moisture could be the sea, melted snow on clothing, or sweat generated by overexertion. All these sources would cause discomfort and, over time, hypothermia.

Sweat was the most prevalent problem and it called for constant trade-offs. At any given temperature, less clothing was needed by a man moving vigorously than by a man standing still. If, however, that man moved too vigorously, he sweated and his lighter clothing instantly became a liability. Each skier had to know his sweat threshold and at what point to peel away clothing to avoid sweating.

Heyer explained that it was a squad leader's responsibility to maintain an efficient "no sweat" pace for all, allowing periodic stops to adjust clothing. One of the liabilities of cold-weather cross-country movement was that a group of men, each fit enough to run twenty-six miles in four or five hours, might take three days to cover the same distance on skis in rugged, uphill, tree-covered terrain. Siberia's taiga-covered coastal plain and mountainous interior would be slow going on skis, but impossible going without them.

On Heyer's last day with us, Dravit took over the Russian language instruction. He drilled basic Russian into the troops with the tenacity and subtlety of a pile driver. We weren't really expecting fluency, just sufficient understanding for survival. The emphasis was not on textbook phrases such as "Which way to your uncle's pastry shop?", but rather on the ability to read Danger: Mine Field, or say, "Drop your weapon, comrade, unless you're prepared to enter the real worker's paradise." In any event, the program wasn't for everyone, and one ex-U.S. Army Airborne veteran threw up his hands in frustration. He later flew back to where people spoke "simple, decent American."

By that time, we had continued to accelerate the pace until somewhere during the blur, the survivors had become rock-hard, Russian-babbling, marathon-skiing zombies.

That evening I took Heyer to the airport. It was the end of his leave, but I could tell he really didn't want to miss out on an adventure. He kept brushing his blond hair out of his eyes and beginning sentences and not completing them. Finally, before he boarded his plane, he kicked at a lump of snow and said, "They'll do all right. Just remember, the Soviets were badly mauled by Finn ski troops in World War Two. They've never forgotten that beating. Soviet troops teethe on cross-country skis now."

Then, as an afterthought, he added, "It's a good mission. Luck will be with you." Then he stormed off to the boarding ramp.

A few hours later, Puckins flew in from California. I watched him leave his plane. The west Texan hadn't changed much in ten years. He still had those same smooth, freckled Huck Finn looks. I thought of Wickersham, whose face carried the marks of ten years' innumerable battles and had launched a thousand bar fights. Puckins moved down the ramp with a cowboy's economy of energy. Several Japanese children waving a paper menagerie of origami foldings—fellow passengers traveling with their families—trailed along in his wake as Vietnamese children had once done. Children had always enjoyed his pantomimes and wordless magic tricks.

Now, as a chief radioman, he was entitled to the sedate coffee-cup world of chiefs. Yet Puckins had rejected a chief's prerogatives. In his quiet way, he preferred the world of action and causes.

"Myshka's been rolled up."

Sato's news stunned me; Myshka's work was still unfinished.

"We think the KGB has him, though we can't be sure."

I lay back in the hotspring pool, trying to ease the pain in my ski-weary legs and to collect my thoughts. The tiled vault echoed with the chatter of hot-spring pilgrims. A busload of them had arrived earlier that afternoon to sample the alleged medicinal qualities of the spring. Though the acoustics of the spa made it virtually impossible to bug, Sato and I whispered anyway—out of habit. Steam rose about six inches off the water, then disappeared.

"He missed his last mail drop and his apartment is empty."

"You're sure Myshka was one of us?" I asked.

"Us?" He paused. "He's a dissident, if that's what you mean. No doubt about it, he's been reliable for years."

"Still could be a mole." We both knew of double agents who had been left dormant for years and allowed to burrow deeply into a network.

"Possibly . . . but I doubt it. The literary pipeline isn't worth that kind of an investment. Anyway, if he was being used against this operation, they pulled him too soon. We'll be wary now."

"Wary? Not much to be wary about, we simply can't go until I have some sense of the size of the camp's garrison and if Vyshinsky is still there. Was Myshka able to get us any of that information before he disappeared?"

"No . . . but he was getting close."

"How so?"

Sato wiped the steam-created sweat from his brow and looked around confidentially. "He was waiting to intercept the quarterly report from Kunashiri, the eastern Siberian payroll center. We learned that much from his last dead-drop message."

I searched for the meaning of dead drop. It was a safe place to deposit written messages, which kept sender from ever having to meet receiver. Sato's law practice seemed to have brought him a rather singular vocabulary.

Sato went on to describe the administration of the Corrective Labor Colony Section, the agency which ruled the camps in Siberia. The section, a bureau under the Ministry of State Security, had moved its Siberian regional headquarters from Sakhalin to Kunashiri, one of the Kuril Islands, for alleged reasons of efficiency. In 1979, Ivan had moved over 12,000 troops in the Kurils to intimidate Japan. Kunashiri lay just twelve miles off Hokkaido. Perhaps the officials of the section were just lonely and wanted to be where the action was. The actual reason was unimportant. The move could be justified by the extensive use of slave labor right there in the Kurils.

The quarterly report Myshka was after was very routine. It summarized administration difficulties of the past three months and the status of each of the hundred-plus camps. Interestingly, it appended—with bureaucratic efficiency—current rosters of the VOKhk, or militarized police, guards, and the prisoners at each camp. By directive, this report had to be sent by military mail to Moscow every February 20. That was in two days. Myshka had intended to pry the report out of Gorshnov, the wimpy bureaucrat with the dog. But now Myshka had disappeared.

"Too bad we haven't anyone else in Moscow with access to that report. It's really the key to this operation." Sato sighed, leaning back into the steam and closing his eyes.

"Yes, it is too bad, but assuming the dead-drop message was reliable, I have another idea."

CHAPTER 14

On several occasions during training, we had broken out the folding kayaks and our rubber boat for paddle practice on Hokkaido's eastern coast. Usually on these days, we would also do a few long distance swims in dry suits. I had intended to give greater emphasis to swimming and boat work when we shifted to Korea, but now I knew familiarity was going to come with a more realistic exercise.

I pulled Chief Puckins aside. "See if you can come up with seven shotguns—the kind with magazines, not the double-barreled variety."

He looked at me quizzically.

"Our weapons for the ultimate raid are waiting for us in Korea. We haven't time to smuggle military weapons into Japan, and we're going on an excursion tomorrow. Pick up one hundred forty rounds of buckshot, too. Tell Chamonix I want Wickersham to get some six-round magazine extensions flown in. Customs will never catch on to them. They're too innocuous looking."

Puckins sauntered off with his forefingers aligned, shooting imaginary clay pigeons.

"Henry"—I motioned to Dravit as we waited for the troops to show up—"we've got some business to attend to. It's going to churn up your training schedule."

"Quite right. We were getting into a rut anyway. A little skulduggery?" he queried brightly.

"We're going to read Ivan's mail. Break out the Zodiac F470, its motor, and the dry suits. Have Lutjens test the Nikonos camera and load it with fast film. I've got Chief Puckins rounding up some shotguns; they're the only firearm we can come up with in Japan on such short notice. Let's take a half dozen of our best students.

"One other thing. I'm going to call to Yokohama and have Keiko charter Matsuma's fishing boat for a little night fishing. He'll probably appreciate the night off."

Russian gunboats regularly patrolled the Russian half of the foggy Nemuro Straits between Hokkaido and Kunashiri. Sato had ventured that the volcanic topography of Kunashiri limited the possible location of the Corrective Labor Colony Section offices to the main village on the island. Dravit and I knew that once we found the offices, we would have to play it by ear.

By remote good fortune, no moon pierced the tendrils of fog drifting over Matsuma's village as we drove among the shanties. I was walking to where Keiko said the dinghy would be beached when Matsuma stepped out of the shadows.

"Matsuma-san, you needn't be here. We chartered the vessel bare boat."

"It is not my boat. You wanted a boat with radar. My boat doesn't have radar. It is a friend's boat."

"But the arrangement was just for the boat, the boat alone. . . ."

"I arranged for the boat, and I will pilot it. That is the situation, take it or leave it." His voice was cool and mocking. Puckins had worked around to one side of Matsuma. The others were unloading gear.

"Look, there won't be enough room for you. We're going to have quite a few men aboard, and some special equipment . . ."

Puckins struck like a cobra. In seconds he choked Matsuma unconscious with a come-along grip. Puckins gently lowered him to the gray sand, rolled him over, bound his wrists with plastic handcuffs, and taped his mouth.

We had no choice in the matter. We had to see that quarterly report tonight. There wasn't time to find another boat.

Puckins and I put him in the dinghy and signaled the others to assemble the gear on the beach. Puckins rowed out to the boat with Matsuma, and when he returned, we loaded the dinghy and the now-inflated rubber boat, or F470. We managed to load the old fishing boat quickly. I looked into the cabin to see how Matsuma was doing. Who would give me coastal information about the Sea of Okhotsk now that we had alienated Matsuma?

Matsuma was sitting upright. The corners of his mouth beyond the tape were curved in a great smile. Baffled, I tore off the tape to see what the devil he was laughing about.

"*Okiijodan, ne*? Big joke, yes? You think I did not know you were not anthropologist from beginning. You think all old men are fools? Your Keiko, she told good story, but I asked around, and her friends say she has an *Amerikajin* friend who looks like you. That friend is no anthropologist. More like *ronin*, masterless samurai," he guffawed through clenched teeth. "That is, if a foreigner could ever come close to being samurai."

"Now, you try to start boat without Matsuma's help." I tried to start it as the men in the F470 pulled alongside. The key turned, but it wouldn't start.

He smiled superiorly. "I have hidden part, will take maybe all night to find."

I knew when I was licked. "Okay, okay, what's the deal? What do you want?"

"You seem very interested in the Sea of Okhotsk. I think you intend to do harm to the *roshiajin*. I wish to do harm to the *roshiajin*, too. I have a debt, an obligation to my brothers . . ."

He could only mean the Japanese with whom he'd been imprisoned.

". . . to show the *roshiajin* they are a country without honor." His jaw muscles tightened. "They are a country without shame."

"What do you want from me?" I said, fully knowing what was to come.

"Let me go with you. My heart burns to watch *roshiajin* die. They deserve to die the way they made my brothers die."

The Japanese concept of *giri* had a strong hold on some. *Giri* was an all-consuming obligation of honor entered into on behalf of one's comrades. Revenge in its name carried no stigma. Rather, such actions reflected one's commendable personal integrity and strength of character. *Giri* did not stem from some contrived fit of pique, but from a sincere sense of obligation.

I sized him up. He was physically up to it. Fishing was grueling work. Yet he had no military experience.

"We are not going on a vendetta. You will take orders from me, an *Amerikajin*, a foreigner. If you cannot take orders, you will not live to return with us, if we return at all."

He nodded.

"We are going to attack a corrective labor camp. Don't let the others know just yet. Before we're through, you'll see plenty of Russians die, all right. And then again, you may end up right back where you started—in one of those camps again, along with the rest of us."

His eyes flared. "I will die first."

"You may. Very well, we need your help, no doubt of that. You may come along provided you meet the standards everyone else has had to meet. Tonight we're going to make a covert raid on Kunashiri. You'll stay with the fishing boat on this side of the straits. We'll straighten this all out when I get back. Now let's get under way."

After I cut away the handcuffs, he rummaged belowdecks for a few minutes, and then the ancient engine rumbled to life. I took a quick look at the radar. It was an inexpensive bottom-of-the-line model.

By now, everyone was aboard, and the inflatable half-deflated below the gunwales of the boat. The men of the landing party were oiling down their shotguns and wrapping them in plastic bags. They put their camouflage uniforms in watertight canoe bags. The two boat guards, Wickersham and Lutjens, stood lookout with their short-ranged weapons.

"We should have brought some rocks aboard," Wickersham muttered, "Could throw rocks farther than I can shoot this fowling piece."

Using our chart, I showed Matsuma where we intended to launch the F470 and where we wished to be picked up.

At about 2230, we loaded the inflatable and headed for the rocky shores of Kunashiri. Wickersham and Matsuma stayed with the fishing boat. The rest of us—Dravit, Chamonix, Puckins, Gurung, Lutjens, and I—all clad in dry suits, wedged into the small inflatable boat. Our muffled outboard engine pushed us along at about five knots. Seaweed kept jamming the prop, so we stopped periodically, cursed silently, and prayed intently the engine would restart. The seaweed of the Kurils was notorious. I figured a good sprinter could race from island to island in the chain, just resting quick footfalls on the seaweed.

We didn't see land until we nearly ran into it. Visibility in the fog was about one hundred yards. We heard breakers and then a great black cliff loomed ahead of us. I had Lutjens cut the engine and drop anchor.

Without hesitation, Gurung and Chamonix, acting as scouts, slipped over the side. It seemed like hours before they blinked the all-clear signal by light to us from shore. Then the rest of us slid over the slick black thwart tubes with our bags and shotguns. Lutjens stayed aboard as a boat guard. I made a mental note of two distinctive rocks as a navigational range. They'd point the way to the F470 when we returned.

There's nothing like a night dip in dark, frigid waters to make you doubt your sanity. The shock of the cold water against the dry suit makes you inhale sharply and wonder if you'll ever master regular in-and-out breathing again. A night swim has that deceptive peacefulness that foreshadows doom.

Swimming in pairs, we let the waves wash us in to shore and smash us against the rock-strewn beach. A barnacle-encrusted rock scraped at my knee and I felt a cold trickle of seawater flow down my shin. Dravit nearly lost his equipment bag to a heavy breaker and Puckins's shotgun clattered against a rock. Quickly, Gurung and Chamonix led us to concealment below an overhanging cliff.

Like so many volcanic islands, Kunashiri rose from the sea in a series of rocky-sloped surges. This was the most desolate portion of the island. The wisps of fog, the heavy waves on the seaweed-covered beach—it would have made a picturesque setting for some less grim activity. But we didn't have time for reveries, the port and main village were still several miles away. We changed hurriedly into camouflage uniforms, turtlenecks, and watch caps.

Gurung clicked his tongue against the side of his mouth to catch my attention. He pointed up and about ten yards farther down the ledge. A small red spot glowed above the edge of the cliff. As I started, I gradually made out the silhouette of a man with an AKM rifle, a fur hat, and the long gray belted coat of Soviet winter field dress.

"Approaching sentry—not to stalk just now," he whispered thoughtfully. "Too much smoking."

I understood. The worst time to attempt to take out a sentry was when he was smoking. In most militaries, smoking on sentry duty is forbidden, so when sentries do smoke, they are extra wary. They aren't wary of some enemy stupid enough to be out on a miserable night like this, but wary of their own sergeant of the guard—who knows how to make sentries even more miserable.

"I am tempted to turn him in," Gurung said with mock anger.

Several minutes later, the glow dropped to the ledge. With my nod, Gurung pulled out his big *kukri* and tested the knife's edge with his thumb. He turned noiselessly, and then glided along the base of the cliff beyond the sentry. The sentry was very close and we shrank into the overhanging cliff. I could just make out the stocky Gurkha methodically scaling the cliff with the *kukri* in his teeth. Moments later, the sentry crashed down from the cliff in two distinct thumps—head and fur hat, body and rifle.

"Son of a bitch!" Puckins exclaimed as the body rolled toward him, stopping inches from his feet.

"Get the greatcoat before it gets bloody," Dravit ordered. "Never a bad idea to have an enemy uniform."

The ever-gloomy Chamonix, still in his dry suit, jammed the segmented body between two large rocks in the surf zone and piled rocks over it. In a few days, the body would work loose and drift onto the beach. The only man who fit the Russian's uniform was the man who had buried him—Chamonix.

We tucked our dry suits and fins into the haversack we'd brought in the watertight bags. Then we began our ascent, with Chamonix close behind us wearing the uniform of a corporal of naval infantry—his AKM at the ready. Shortly, we reached the shoulder of the cliffs.

"There it is. That dirt road should eventually lead us into the main village. It's on one of the pre-World War Two maps I found."

We patrolled along two parallel ruts, which soon became a pot-holed macadam road. Twice the oncoming, fog-rimmed headlights of military trucks forced us to dive headlong for the cover of drainage ditches.

By 0200, we had reached the main village. A massive seawall defined the rim of the harbor, and below the wall stretched a half dozen yards of pebble beach. We kept in the shadow of the seawall until we were even with the point where the old map indicated the police station would be. The single-story building that abutted the seawall evidently hadn't changed purposes in forty years. It was still a police station. As Dravit and I had guessed, the Ministry of State Security building was not far away—in fact, a sign indicated it was the large old building of pre-World War II vintage on the landward side of the police station. The imposing two-story concrete building towered over the police shack. A foghorn, strange and haunting, sounded in the distance.

I hand-signaled for Gurung, our point man, to reconnoiter the two buildings. A half hour later, he reported that the first building was a joint civil and military police station, with a policeman posted outside on the road that led to the seawall. The second building, the State Security building, was darkened except for an inner hallway. A VOKhk guard sat in the hallway and made rounds of the building at regular intervals.

We wound our way to the street, which ran behind both build-ings and moved single file down the three-foot-deep stone drainage trench that bordered it. This street divided two rows of shops—all closed—but whose owners lived in their back rooms. Farther down, a saloon resounded with the singing and carousing of Russian sol-diers. The State Security building stood right behind the saloon. We vaulted a fence and ducked into the long row of shop backyards. A slow-motion steeplechase through tiny gardens, over plank fences and bamboo trellises, and around large fish baskets ensued. Finally, we arrived at the hazy void between the saloon and the ministry building and scrambled over the fence that separated the two.

The lower windows of the ministry building were protected by steel bars. The upper windows were balustraded and covered with shutters. Gurung pointed to the built-up ridge crest at the peak of the tiled roof and then to the quoins leading like rungs up the corners of the building. I waved Chamonix forward. The straight-backed legionnaire stood an impressive six foot four. He immediately recognized what Gurung had in mind and, dropping his haversack, pulled out a rubber-coated grappling hook and a coil of yellow left-lay mountaineering line. He backed away from the building and began to swing the grappling hook like a pendulum to gauge its weight and feel. In a sudden release of energy, he hurled the hook just short of the ridge crest and watched it bounce noisily down the tiles. We waited several minutes to see if we had attracted any attention. Apparently, the nightly ruckus at the saloon had dulled the neighbors to things that went bump in the night.

The legionnaire's second toss caught the ridge crest solidly. He gave it three strong tugs and then kept steady tension on the line. Meanwhile, Gurung clambered from quoin to quoin until he was at a slightly higher level than the upper set of windows. Next, Chamonix angled the line over to the Gurkha. Gurung transferred his weight to the line and let Chamonix jockey the line to the balustrade of the nearest window. A resounding crack from above indicated that one of the ridge tiles had given way and the grappling hook had come loose. Gurung threw out his arms and started to fall.

CHAPTER 15

The Gurkha lunged for the balustrade, his boots clawing for footholds in the air. With one hand he caught a pillar as the grappling hook plunged past him. For a few moments he just oscillated by one hand. Then he mustered the reserve to thrust his free hand to the railing and kip over the balustrade. He was safe.

Immediately, he set to work on the shutters. They were old and poorly maintained. Gradually, he managed to pry enough space between them to pop the hooks with his knife. Using a pry bar, he raised the window and peered in. Then he disappeared through the window.

Seconds later, he was beckoning for the free end of the mountaineering line. Gurung anchored it to the balustrade while Chamonix tied off the other end to a fence post. The sloping line, now taut, could not be seen from the lower window. Dravit was the first to hoist himself up the line, then Puckins, and then myself. Chamonix, in his Russian uniform, posted himself at the base of the building and attempted to look routine and nonchalant.

From the second story, I could just distinguish the rest of the village through the night mist. A gray carpet of chimneyless roofs stretched uniformly in all directions. The pattern was marred by thirty-five years of deterioration, a few Russian-style chimneys, and an occasional concrete shoe box.

We closed the shutters and entered the passageway. The title and responsibilities of each official were etched with bureaucratic orderliness to the left of his office door. The Corrective Labor Colony Section held the third office on the left. Its door was locked.

Dravit tested the transom. It was locked, too. He reached into one of his cargo pockets and unrolled a cloth tool kit on the floor.

"It's a key-lever tumbler; this may take some time."

He inserted a Z-shaped tension tool into the keyway and applied pressure. Then, with a curved pick, he began locating the individual tumblers, raising each one to the unlocked position. Sweat beaded on his forehead.

Precious minutes passed.

"Open, yon great muckin' door of the bloody Bolshies." He pushed the door open cautiously. "Ah, the old magic's still there. Remind me to tell you about my night in the strong room at Pusan."

Dravit went through the desks and cabinets, skimming every document by flashlight. There were reams of documents. If the camps' prisoners could have eaten the documents they generated, they would have grown fat.

A half hour went by. An hour. An hour and a half. "Got it! Got it! Got it! Just like the bloody Bolshies to wallow in ruddy paper," Dravit exclaimed under his breath. He drew the Nikonos from his other pocket and clicked away.

We nearly didn't hear the footsteps moving down the passageway. The guard had walked past the office earlier. This time he hesitated before the relocked door. Dravit and I ducked behind some desks with Gurung. The bolt shifted in the lock. Puckins slipped behind the door just as it opened. The guard swept his light across the room. As he stepped forward to look behind the desks, Puckins dropped him with a sharp tap, using the butt of his shotgun.

The four of us dragged the unconscious guard to the bottom of the stairway, just out of sight of the front doorway. We positioned him as if he had fallen. As we were about to turn away, Gurung pulled a flask from his jacket and sprinkled some fluid over the VOKhk guard.

"Oh, sergeant of the guard being very much pissed if finding guard in such condition," Gurung signed. "I know surely this guard will not report irregularities of the evening to his sergeant, him now smelling of cheap vodka. I know, having much fear of sergeant of the guard myself for many years."

He returned down the passageway chuckling elfishly.

"We do have our fun," Chamonix mumbled dourly on hearing of Gurung's prank when we rejoined him outside.

Chamonix's words were premature. Our return to Hokkaido was anything but fun. By the time we returned to the seawall, the wave height had increased and the fog had grown thicker. We moved as quickly as was safe down the road to our original landing point. Once there, we noticed a vehicle parked on the dirt road and heard Russian voices. So as a precaution, we entered the water farther down the beach, then located the rock range. Lutjens and the rubber boat were right where we'd left them. The first thing I remember seeing was the yawning muzzle of his shotgun as he challenged us from the bobbing boat. He pulled us aboard and started the engine. Once I had given him the course heading, we all leaned back and relaxed. The sense of relief was as potent as hot sake on an empty stomach. The rolling swell rocked everyone but Lutjens asleep.

"Heave to, rubber boat," a voice called out in Russian. "You Japanese fishermen never learn, do you. Time in one of our corrective labor colonies will cure you of that and many other things."

The voice laughed. It carried over the gurgling rumble of a patrol-craft engine. They couldn't have picked us up on radar. Our courses must have intersected by pure chance.

The dark silhouette of a patrol boat, with its officer of the deck, helmsman, and two lookouts outlined clearly, parted the fog. One of the lookouts trained a .51-caliber machine gun on our frail craft.

We froze. What could we do now? A vision of the camp flashed through my mind. Perhaps we would be seeing Vyshinsky sooner than we had expected. What now? Had to hold this show together.

"Lutjens, steer straight for them," I whispered. "Dravit, you're a captain of naval infantry, hard of hearing and mean."

I held my breath.

Dravit looked at me peculiarly. "Have a go."

"Boat, this is Captain Dravonitch, Naval Infantry. What are you doing in this sector? This area has been cleared exclusively for us by the Kurils Naval Infantry command. We are engaged in a classified operation. What is your authority to be here?"

I could see the officer's face. He was puzzled. Our dry suits could have been Russian and Chamonix did have a Russian greatcoat across his lap. The boat officer's thin lips twisted into an arrogant sneer.

"I know of no such clearance. I am Lieutenant Deltchev, Navy. Let me see your orders."

"Orders! And where would I keep orders in this monkey suit? Lieutenant, who in the name of the Worker's Paradise gave you your commission?"

Deltchev stiffened and focused questioningly on the shotgun resting in Dravit's lap. The lookout at the machine gun pulled his thumbs from the trigger plates and leaned back. A couple of officers bickering, he might as well stand back and enjoy the fun. A second later the lookout was slammed back over the engine box by a shotgun blast, Deltchev and the other lookout slumped to the deck, wounded, as at the same time our rubber boat nearly capsized from the recoil of our discharging shotguns. The helmsman dived into the cabin and in the subsequent silence I could hear the clanking sounds of hatches forward being buttoned up. There had to be a few more crew members aboard. The wounded second lookout lunged for the machine gun and managed to stitch several rounds into our rubber boat before a half dozen shotgun rounds made him disappear in a blood-red mist. Some of our men had been hit, I could not tell how badly.

I vaulted into the patrol boat and put two rounds apiece into the radio antenna, the radar scanner, and the compass. Skeins of smoke swirled into the sea mist. The pungent smell of ozone from the shattered equipment was everywhere.

Let them find port now, let alone bother us again in this fog. I spun the helm over and stepped back down into the F470.

"Bullying fisherman isn't as easy as it used to be," I bellowed in Japanese for the benefit of the surviving crewmen.

Then to our own people, "Cast off!"

The .51-caliber rounds had destroyed our tube on the portside, punctured the floor plating, and silenced the outboard. Chunks of the motor had hit everyone, causing minor bleeding. Chamonix's leg had been gazed by a round and Lutjens had been peppered by pieces of splintered paddle. We jettisoned the outboard and its gas tank. The rubber boat limped back into the fog with some swimming alongside, while others attempted to straddle the starboard thwart and paddle with shotguns. It was 0500.

Fighting the heavy seaweed, we struggled to keep our heading to the rendezvous point. Everyone worked hard, but I knew we were largely at the mercy of the frigid currents of the Nemuro Straits.

At about 1000, a cold rain washed away the fog and we found we were on the safe side of the Nemuro Straits. The fishing boat was southeast of us and we attracted their attention with a small survival mirror.

Wickersham and Matsuma brought the fishing boat alongside. Everyone was numb from exposure and we'd abandoned swimming and paddling hours before. Puckins's teeth chattered like castanets, and, dazed, Lutjens groaned softly.

Wickersham reached down from the boat and hoisted men aboard like wet kittens. Matsuma reached for Gurung, who was babbling in hypothermic stupor.

"Keep away from me, Japanese devil. I am Amarsing Gurung, whose father killed more Japanese soldiers than you have teeth in your head," he said absently. "There being a Russian soldier last night who tasted the kiss of the *kukri* of Rifleman Gurung."

Matsuma smiled gently and dragged the soon-unconscious Gurung up over the gunwale.

CHAPTER 16

The Norwegian wood stove crackled and sizzled in our hotel suite. After thawing out, I had slept for twenty-four hours straight. Each one of us had experienced some of the cold-induced symptoms of hypothermia—the dopey sense of well-being, headaches, lethargy—for which rest and warmth were the best therapy. My side was tender where a bit of outboard motor housing had broken the skin. My thighs and knees ached as they always did after a patrol. Legs seemed to absorb most of the tension.

Dravit and Chamonix sat across from me. Neither looked very happy.

". . . and I didn't bother to ask Chamonix to develop the film until just a few hours ago. It didn't seem necessary."

He tapped his pipe against the stove.

"The film had been overexposed—all of it—not just the six photographs Captain Dravit had taken," added Chamonix.

"There were several beads of water within the housing of the camera. You know how watertight a Nikonos is. I opened it with dry hands. The film is useless to us now. *Merde!* All our efforts for nothing."

The sullen Chamonix was even more laconic than usual. The legionnaire carried some undisclosed bitterness. He rose, stood rigidly erect, then walked to the door and left the room with a sharp salute and a click of heels. The .51-caliber bullet that had grazed his thigh had been a tracer and instantly cauterized the wound. He didn't permit himself the luxury of a limp. Vinegar may have flowed through his veins, but the old trooper was flawlessly competent.

"There's no doubt about it, is there?" Dravit stretched his legs, placing his heels on the stove. "Our tight little band has been penetrated."

"Can you remember any of the information from the quarterly report?"

"I can remember it all," he said with a smirk. "It was too hard to come by to trust exclusively to a camera."

He handed me a scrap of paper. It read: "Garrison of Camp R-3; 43 militarized police—15 with radio or electronics specialties; 207 prisoners; Vyshinsky still carried on the camp roster as special prisoner."

I placed the scrap in my pocket.

"Put all that on the stock of my shotgun with a grease pencil when we were in the administration building. Didn't think of it then, but on the way back the bleedin' camera was on the boat, where anyone could get at it."

Penetrated—it was bad enough to have others working against us. But one of our own?

"Skipper, it's about time for the first cut."

Now that we knew the size of the garrison, we could determine the number of men we would need. "Well, it's a trade-off: the more men we take, the better our chance of success in a firefight, but the greater our chance of detection—and the more cumbersome the logistics. Let's make it the Kunashiri eight and take Alvarez and that South African, Kruger, as alternates. Send the rest home with the bonuses."

The turncoat had to be one of the Kunashiri eight, but they were my most valued men. I couldn't afford to eliminate any one of them.

I jammed a few more logs into the stove, but it didn't help. I didn't seem able to get warm.

* * *

The new men were part of the two dozen who'd been recruited in Marseilles. These were the next most talented after Chamonix, Gurung, and Lutjens, and they showed promise.

Juan Ortega Alvarez was a Miami Cuban who specialized in heavy weapons. His high cheekbones; broad, straight nose; and heavy beard made it possible—depending on the depth of his tan—to pass for any nationality inhabiting the zone between 15° South and 35° North latitude. Nearly as massive as Wickersham, his bulk was less sculpted and more evenly distributed than the Wisconsinite's.

Alvarez found growing up in Miami's Little Havana a painful, stifling experience. There were pressures, always pressures. His uncle and a brother-in-law had died at the Bay of Pigs. Pressure: he must be prepared to do his part when the next revolution came. He was a mediocre student. Pressure: he was a Cuban and must bring credit upon his family and nationality. He had no occupational goal. Pressure: he must enlist in the Army until he arrived at some other trade valuable to his community. The pressure from family and friends was subtle but deadly.

Halfway through his reluctant enlistment, he realized he liked the life and volunteered for Special Forces, where his bilingual background would be an asset. Despite Army regimentation, he felt freer than he'd ever been in Florida, straitjacketed by the rigorous standards set by desperate, disillusioned émigrés. Ironically, with this sense of freedom came a new pressure, the internal pressure of a growing sense of destiny. It was not that unusual. A haunting sense of destiny was something I, too, could understand. After his second hitch, he left the Army to free-lance so that one day he would have the experience, credentials, and contacts to leave a mark on Cuban history. Castro couldn't live forever; when the time came, Alvarez would be ready to contribute.

And there was Kruger. It took only one word to set Johannes Kruger trembling: that word was *women*. He wore a badgered look, a seedy walrus mustache, and no visible muscles. He stammered, too—he had always been that way and it had never mattered—all his troubles emanated from his pursuit by women. Life had been relatively quiet for him as a "recce" corporal with the South African Reconnaissance

Commandos. A bit of tracking, an occasional fire-fight with a handful of Cuban-trained Angolans, it was all downright peaceful compared to what followed. After his discharge, Kruger drifted north to Kenya and eventually took a job as a white hunter. He didn't mind the fact that Kenya had a Kaffir government. After all, it didn't govern much worse than those bandits in Pretoria, and anyway it wasn't Marxist. He just didn't mind. It was the white-hunter job that started it all— this trouble with women. Predatory, continent-hopping socialites who were in the habit of seeking ornamental, absentee husbands stalked white hunters like their male acquaintances stalked wild game. Kruger didn't mind that, either; conversely, he played it to the hilt. He juggled three transcontinental marriages simultaneously. His expeditions into the bush provided required excuses and much-needed rest during those rare instances when all three wives were in Nairobi at once. It couldn't last. It didn't. One night he came home unexpectedly to find wife number two in bed with another man. In a shocking reversal of tradition, and in the heat of the moment, the lover shot the husband. "B-b-bloody fool, if he'd only waited a moment I would have said, 'Excuse me, I seem to have the wrong flat.'" A battery of lawyers, wives, and girlfriends drove the hobbling Kruger out of Kenya and into the more celibate Brotherhood of Arms.

As the day wore on, the crowd in the next room grew more and more rambunctious. Wickersham and Gurung, its inhabitants, were on a good-to-be-alive high and inviting the others in for beer or hot sake. Their room resounded with the bumps and thumps of the spirited horseplay typical of these get-togethers. I could hear Wickersham organizing "Hokkaido's First International All-Services Arm-Wrestling Tournament." Before long, Lutjens, Wickersham, and Alvarez had risen to finalist level. I could hear bets called out and furniture being rearranged.

Dravit was poring over Russian newspapers when someone knocked at our door. "Party's in the next room over!"

Frazer-san?" The words had a heavy Japanese intonation. We let the man in. It was a ferret-faced, round-shouldered Oriental in his mid-thirties. He kneeled on one knee like a crapshooter. "*O-hikae nasutte, o-hikae nasutte . . . ,"* he began, giving the traditional self-introduction of the *yakuza.*

"Thank you for kneeling so quickly," I said, giving the standard response.

He went on to describe his native province, his clan, its chief, and his connections with the other clans of Sapporo in great detail. None of it meant anything to me, but this was the traditional recitation and it would have been impolite to interrupt. Dravit stood by dumbly, not understanding a word.

"Frazer-san, a Korean acquaintance of mine in Sapporo who makes a business of knowing things . . ."

One of Kim's KCIA agents must have sent him.

". . . has requested that I relate what information I have gathered about a man who recently met his demise in an alley in Sapporo. This man wore the tattoos of the gamblers' brotherhood."

His words were punctuated by a loud crash and a roar of approval from the gang next door. The semifinals were over. Put your money on Wickersham.

"The man's name was Aoki. He left his clan several years ago after an argument with his *oyabun,* his clan chief. It was well known that he hired out. The rumor has been that he was recently retained by a foreigner. My Korean friend mentioned an attempted kidnapping. Kidnapping is not a normal *yakuza* undertaking."

I had been surprised by the fact that there had been no further attacks or approaches on members of our group after Wickersham's night in Sapporo. That could have meant one of two things: one, they had given up, or two, they had succeeded in turning one of our men against us. This *yakuza's* information plus the camera incident made the latter alternative more likely. I had taken a greater risk than I had realized by raiding Kunashiri. We could have very easily been maneuvered into an ambush. I hoped whoever it was would be content with small-scale sabotage. His position allowed him to effect far worse damage.

The *yakuza* reached slowly into his waistband. Dravit took a cautious step forward. The *yakuza* drew a tanto dagger, then flicked it into a log by the stove. "This is Aoki's dagger. He brought disgrace to us, and it. Perhaps it will be more use to one who has shown he can use it."

An immense crash from next door shook the room. It was followed by yelling and cheering. I could hear Wickersham bellowing over the din, "I win! There's no match for a Navy SEAL, a rootin'-tootin', parachutin', SCUBA-divin', double-crimpin' . . ."

I thanked the nonplussed *yakuza* with the ferret face.

". . . lead-spittin', pineapple-throwin', rubber-coated, K-Bar knife-totin', star sapphire ring-wearin' gentleman of experience and resource whose punctuality is only limited by the accuracy of his big fat Rolex diving watch. Oh yeah, one other thing—"

"Cut the malarkey and drink up. You realize there are children sober in China?" an unidentified voice scolded.

"I'm the last of the bareknuckle fighters!"

Third crash.

Dravit and I burst out of the door to put a halt to the impending brawl.

When we returned, the *yakuza* was gone.

Several nights later, a barrage of knocks on the suite's outer door startled me from a deep sleep.

"Open up, please. We are police."

Dravit, in the adjoining room of the suite, was already up. He had his boots and trousers on. He shrugged his shoulders. Maybe they were police, maybe they weren't. This could be a setup. He picked up a chair and hurled it through a back window as I grabbed my clothes. Then we both dropped sixteen feet into a thick blanket of white powder. I could hear glass breaking in the other rooms. Gurung and Wickersham plummeted into the snow a few yards away.

We found ourselves in the crossed beams of several floodlights. Gray-uniformed policemen circled us—some holding revolvers on lanyards. Wickersham took a poke at one policeman and found himself flat on his back. The Japanese police take their hand-to-hand training seriously.

"As the inspector said, we are police. Excuse handcuffs please."

They herded the nine of us into a waiting police van. Puckins was missing, he'd probably stepped out of his room for a second. Matsuma looked dismayed.

"Poor showing of Japanese hospitality," Dravit said, looking around the inside of the van for cameras or bugs. "Seems a group of outdoorsmen can't enjoy a back-to-nature, consciousness-raising session in peace."

Some time later the van rolled into the central police station at Sapporo. Puckins was brought in moments later. They put each of us into a separate interrogation room. I rated one in restful pale green. Two men told me to take a seat.

"I'm Chief Inspector Koizumi of the Sapporo police. We have reason to believe you are planning to launch a mercenary operation from Japanese soil."

He had said "mercenary" as if it hurt his mouth. He ran his fingers through his gray hair.

"Not me," I said in partial truth. He didn't look convinced.

"Horikawa-san of the Ministry of Foreign Affairs"—he flicked his head toward the other younger man in a well-tailored blue suit—"and I are authorized to forestall any such military operation—by any means we deem fit."

"Don't know what you're talking about."

The chief inspector raised one eyebrow.

"We can hold you indefinitely if we find you constitute a threat to our national security," said Horikawa, rising from his chair. "And despite your persistence in maintaining this little charade, I am confident we can foil your plans."

He was polished and unflappable.

"I'm sure your contracted services are on some sort of timetable. Most military operations, no matter how ragged, seem to be. We can hold you until your organization and its project have become quite stale."

I was beginning to dislike Horikawa; he understood too much. I wasn't sure about my right to a lawyer, but perhaps I could get one in here anyway.

"Maybe we can straighten this misunderstanding out," I said, hoping "straighten" would not mean explain. "Call Kiyoshi Sato at . . ." I gave them his office number.

Koizumi and Horikawa looked skeptical as they led me to a cell.

Legally we had little to offer in our defense, and I couldn't bring up moral arguments without disclosing the objective of the operation. I didn't see where Sato could be of help, but it'd give me time to think.

Someone had tipped them off convincingly that there was an operation afoot. Japan didn't want to awaken one chilly morning to find that it had been the springboard for a surprise attack against one of its neighbors. Japan had had a bad experience with surprise attacks. Its stance was no different from the United States' squeamishness over Cuban refugee attacks launched from Florida against Cuba. The conventional diplomatic wisdom deplored such vulgar self-help. I felt the foul, self-serving presence of the Ackert hand in all this.

The next morning, Sato showed the talents that had earned him a Ginza letterhead. Immediately, with a flurry of accusations, he put the police on the defensive. Furthermore, it developed that he had considerable political clout with the Ministry of Foreign Affairs. His coup de grâce was suggesting deportation as a solution. That jewel of an alternative could save face for everyone.

"To where? Who would accept them? They're bound to be the focus of an international incident wherever they go," Horikawa stammered.

I waved Sato over for a whispering session. Then he turned to the two officials. "I believe the Republic of Korea would react favorably to a visit from a small anticommunist veterans group."

The chief inspector looked bored, and Horikawa exasperated. Again I was led to my cell.

Twenty-four hours later, Sato—using the contacts I had suggested—secured our informal deportation from Japan. Horikawa told us in very strong terms that we would never again be granted visas in any sequence that would allow us to assemble in Japan as a group. When pressed, he did admit that as many as four of us could enter Japan during a given period without sanction. And of course, Matsuma maintained his Japanese citizenship. They couldn't touch him.

It had been a close call, too close. Our schedule was thrown completely out of kilter. But Korea had been our next stop. What really disturbed me was the uneasy realization that someone—Ackert, perhaps—was determined to stop us and had upped the ante. Each passing day increased our vulnerability.

The walls of the police station seemed suffocatingly close . . . but never as close as the walls of a Soviet prison would be.

CHAPTER 17

The KCIA put us in isolation immediately upon our arrival in Korea. They quartered us in a hermetically sealed farm village on the eastern coast. For everyone but myself, there would be no further communication with the outside world until we returned from Siberia.

The village complex consisted of several tiled-roof, one-story structures surrounded by rice fields that gradually acquired, with distance, the energy to bunch up into a rugged mountain chain. Our new home had none of the resort charm of our Hokkaido quarters; it was clearly an often-used staging area whose buildings were nothing more than glorified barracks. Our common opinion might have been prejudiced by our lack of freedom. Korean soldiers carrying submachine guns waved at us whenever our maneuvers brought us near the fence that surrounded the village fields—but they carried submachine guns just the same. The mature, rational view was that they were protecting us from ourselves, but there was little comfort in it. Even the occasional evening movie—black and white, in Korean, with subtitles—heightened the dismal sense of isolation. At least our turncoat could not make contact with his parent agency.

Keiko delighted in being the only female among the eleven visitors. The troops adopted her wholeheartedly. She was easier on the eyes than any of them were, and she made the whole setup seem more routine.

Keiko was mesmerized by the Koreans. "Korean people eat with chopsticks," she observed with great gravity one day.

"Well, what did you expect? Doesn't everyone in the Orient?"

"I was always told they ate with their hands," she responded confidentially.

The Japanese and the Koreans were Asia's eternal Hat-fields and McCoys. Neither nation gave the other much credit. No Korean women ever entered the complex, and despite her growing respect for the Koreans, she was pleased.

Late the second evening, after a long day's workout with the kayaks, two Mercedes trucks arrived with the equipment Heyer had requisitioned. I ordered everyone out into the crisp night air to unload the ordnance and equipment.

Chief Puckins led the working party, which sorted and stored the gear. "Now here we have," Wickersham started to lecture in grandiose style, "one AK-47, with Chinese markings and a spike bayonet, sometimes called a Type-56 assault rifle. Designed by Kalashnikov, it is gas operated, and carries a thirty-round magazine. . . ."

They broke open another box.

"And here is a Type 67 light machine gun, also Chicom. Well, well . . . gas operated, and belt fed with a range of eight hundred meters. . . . Now here's a delight. A Dragunov SVD sniper rifle with both Chinese and Soviet markings and a convenient little four-power sight, integral range finder, and infrared night-sight accessories.

"My, my, isn't this interesting, boys and girls. White camouflage over-uniforms and fur hats with big red stars on the front. Considered very chic in Shanghai."

The troops' eyes were opening wider and wider. The back of the truck was cloudy from the vapor of their breaths.

"B-b-botha's beard, what's this all about?" stammered Kruger, who could restrain himself no more. "Are we doing a rem-m-make of Mao's Long March?"

"Close, very close," I replied.

Puckins stepped forward. He threw his arms to the heavens in mock despair.

Keiko gradually assumed the role of cruise director. She participated in training swims. She demanded better food from the KCIA support section and finagled mulberry-paper watercolors out of the guards to brighten our quarters. Irrepressible, she unearthed obscure holidays for us to celebrate at the evening meal. There were special "guest" chefs. Chamonix and Alvarez presided with great success. Kruger and Lutjens's contributions were utter disasters. She even cajoled Gurung into cooking up a Nepalese meal.

We normally broke from training an hour or two before the evening meal. The small makeshift galley had the only tables and chairs and the best lighting, so everyone gravitated there.

In back, Alvarez was cooking something with beans. To one side, Dravit was poring over schedules and equipment lists. At two joined tables, Lutjens was loudly losing at cards with Puckins. The German *kampfschwimmer* carried on as if he were at Monte Carlo and the croupier had miscounted his chips. Redoubtable, Chamonix sat in a corner with a book, alone as usual.

"M-m-mama-san, could you stitch up this . . . ?" Kruger started, pulling at his wispy mustache.

"Mama-san? Who you call mama-san?" she responded, her eyes narrowing. She gave a defiant pistonlike flick to her hips. "*Mama-san to wa nan da, kisama!* I don't remember ever wiping your nose for you, you with the Okinawa stone-dog face. But maybe I flatten it for you, if you call me "mama-san" one mo' time. I look old enough to you to be a mama-san?"

"No. No, mum. Actually you 1-1-look like a first-class bird, too young to be a commanding officer's girl . . . ," the Afrikaner backpedaled.

"*Ara ma!* So now you think I look like teenie-bopper, *ne?* Fresh from the cradle, no wisdom, no character." She whipped her French braid from one shoulder to the other.

"Hey, Kruger, you got the chart for . . ." Wickersham bellowed as he stormed through the door and into the line of fire.

"You, Petty Officer Wick'sham. This walrus face call me 'mama-san.'"

"Uh . . . hum . . . er . . . uh-oh. Kruger, you can't address Shirahama-san that way," he offered, shifting his heavy shoulders uncomfortably.

Unfortunately, he couldn't resist the compulsion to be evenhanded. "Then again, Shirahama-san, we're a pretty small group and he can't very well go around addressing you as . . . as . . ."

His words had run ahead of his thoughts. He fished futilely for a way to complete the sentence.

"Miss Kosong Perimeter, *ja*?" Lutjens proposed, gleefully adding fuel to the fire.

"Miss Kosong Perimeter," Wickersham echoed with as pleasing a smile as he could muster with his bridge out. Wickersham could be devastatingly charming. It wasn't going to help him today.

"Beauty queen name! I carry my own weight. Miss Kosong Perimeter. Korean name. Big joke, very funny."

"Now, Kei-chan," I began, trying to smooth things over.

"I carry my own weight around here, don' I?"

"From where we all stand, you carry it quite well, Kei-chan."

"Ha, you'll see. Not just pretty face. Walrus face, Wick'sham, you'll all see. You should know better."

She turned and rushed off.

Kruger and Wickersham looked scared.

There was a tension to being part of the group but not participating in the main event.

After supper I took a walk around the complex. I found Chief Puckins at the perimeter fence looking down into the valley.

"You can see lights down there, Skipper. I reckon it's a real village." The Texan rubbed his freckled nose with the back of his mitten. "Kids down there, too.

"Don't really know how I can tell. . . . I just kind of know. Sometimes I think I can hear them laugh . . . on the wind, sort of. Sure, that's a village down there by the creek. Villages always have children."

"Seems likely," I replied. There weren't that many lights. We were fairly close to the DMZ. It might not be a village.

"Some of the Korean kids look kind of like my half-Viet kids."

His strawlike hair flickered in the cold northerly wind. Children meant a great deal to Puckins. In theory they stood for hope, renewal, a reaffirmation of the larger plan. In practice, they were a very personal touchstone for energy and life.

"Funny, when I'm with my own kids I always know I'm going to have to ship out again, and that doesn't bother me. It's just something that's gotta be done. If I didn't do it someone else would have to. But I'd do it better because I understand. My kids wouldn't be anywhere if I hadn't gone to Vietnam.

"Did I say it didn't tug at me shipping out all the time? I'm glad they've got a strong old lady. They all hold up pretty well. All and all."

He patted his pocket. "I should have worked up a pretty good passel of magic tricks to show them when we get back. It'll take some practice."

We just stood there for a while, until the lights went out.

The next morning spotted Wickersham preparing to go through the house-to-house pop-up range on his own time.

I climbed into the range tower, where Chamonix, unsmiling as usual, was manipulating the target silhouettes.

This was the other Wickersham—quiet, intense, exacting. Extra hours spent to make it look easy. Extra hours spent to be sure.

I focused my binoculars on Wickersham. It was snowing gently and Wickersham was halfway through the course. As he rounded a comer, a single gray silhouette popped up with a puff of snow.

I watched his lips move silently, "Two to the body, one to the head. . . . "

It dropped back.

Another gray silhouette appeared in a window.

The triple tap of bullets occurred once more. "Two to the body, one to the head. . . ."

The second silhouette dropped.

Quiet, intense, exacting—this was the other Wickersham, the second Wickersham who rarely showed himself. The first Wickersham, the more visible Wickersham, clowned as a defense.

Four silhouettes rose: two black, two gray. He peppered the two gray silhouettes, making a little polka step as he shifted his muscular frame to fire from one target to the other. The gray targets were guards. The black targets were prisoners, *zeks*. I read "two to the body, one to the head" on his moving lips again.

To Wickersham, dealing in life and death was as heavy and ponderous as surgery. It had to be lightened somehow. *The warrior should not act too proud or self-important.* A trace of Anglo-Saxon fear tinted his view, fear that success and elation brought punishment by the gods. At the banquet, after the slaying of the Grendel and the Grendel's mother, Beowulf is praised but also warned that conspicuous skill and pride can bring ill luck. The fact that Wickersham had never heard of the Old English tribes or their beliefs did not matter, because a similar manner of living, the same requirements for survival, and a kindred collection of values caused him to arrive at comparable conclusions.

Pride internalized made a good fighter; pride externalized brought bad luck. Since death came so easily on trifles, above all, a man needed luck.

Three gray silhouettes appeared above a courtyard wall. Nine rounds expended and they were down.

"Two to the body, and one to the head/better be sure the rascal's dead."

Wickersham's various business enterprises basically served as a variation to the clowning. The Wisconsinite played bazaar merchant for comic relief. Yet understanding Wickersham wasn't that straightforward. He *did* derive secondary satisfaction from making a profit, winning another kind of contest—and creating laughter—which had a way of smoothing over so many rough spots in his travails. Essentially, however, Wickersham did not rest easy with the high stakes of his vocation.

Two silhouettes popped up in the doors on either side of him. They rested on opposite edges of his peripheral vision. He knocked both down with two short bursts.

An alarm went off on the range and Wickersham's broad shoulders drooped. He sat down in the snow and looked at his AK-47.

"Which one?" I asked Chamonix. The Frenchman flicked the switch on his right with a dour look.

The silhouette on Wickersham's right rose slowly. It was black with a blowup of Vyshinsky's picture pasted on its head. *Pallbearer's eyes.* The pictures was perforated. One to the head.

"One error equals failure," Chamonix stated calmly over the range mike.

"*Tant pis.* Let's run it one more time."

In the seclusion of our new training area, we were able to combine live firing with movement on skis. Each man carried an AK-47, except Wickersham, who carried the Type 67 machine gun, and Chamonix, who carried the Russian-made, but Chinese-modified sniper rifle. With us we towed two *ahkio* sledges. These oblong curved-bottom sledges, when towed by several skiers, could carry a man, or up to two hundred pounds of equipment. We modified both *ahkios* along the lines of a Norwegian *pulk.* They were shortened and fitted with tubular towing braces. Once these changes were made, the *ahkios* could be towed and controlled by just two men. In the *ahkios* we carried food, tents, and ammunition, but most important, a single Chinese 57-millimeter recoilless rifle. Ironically, the 57-millimeter recoilless had been copied from the American version by the Chinese during the Korean War. It had been discounted as a U.S. weapon only recently. Now the pirated weapon was going to change hands again.

Daily, Dravit conducted classes on anti-skier booby traps. Using token amounts of explosive, he showed us how to lay out the charges and trigger mechanisms. Then he showed us how to conceal them. Finally, from a distance, he'd slide a weighted ski over the booby trap to demonstrate its effect. Near the end of the third day, one charge didn't go off. He slid several old skis over it, but it just wouldn't detonate.

"Bloody spring must have ice in it. Have to blow it in place."

The meticulous operation of disarming a booby trap was an unnecessarily risky procedure. The more prudent course of action was to set another charge alongside the dud and in detonating the second charge, sympathetically blow the first "in place."

Dravit skied gingerly to where the booby trap had been set. It was a pressure-, not trip-wire-activated assembly. Near a small tree—about two yards from where it should have been—the charge went off under Dravit's right ski. It flung the ski up violently and twisted his ankle at a bad angle. Surprisingly, Dravit managed to keep his balance. He coasted backward a yard, then fell over to one side, cursing venomously.

We were around him in seconds. Chamonix, our acting corpsman, took off Dravit's ski and mountaineering boot.

"It's broken, isn't it. Ballocks, I know that isn't where I placed it. Only thing to my credit is that I underloaded the charges. Otherwise, I'd have lost a leg and eaten a ski."

Chamonix shook his balding head sourly.

Wickersham turned to me. "I remember him putting it over there, farther from the tree, too. Someone must have moved the charge."

Wickersham was right. Some member of our group had moved it—intentionally. And now my right-hand man wasn't going.

His lunch, a few small cups around a stainless-steel rice box, lay nestled in the eye of a storm of paperwork. Concealed behind a stack of binders was a *changgi*—Korean chess—board with its pieces actively engaged. So he had a passion, *changgi*. Well, that made him human and more likable, but I wasn't about to let him know it. For once he was vulnerable.

"Look, Kim, what the hell have you been doing about security for this operation? I've just had a man booby-trapped right out of action while you're in here diddling with rainy-day games. You'd better set a fire under your people or this project's over, finished, ended."

He blinked and shifted uncomfortably in his chair. The bunker lighting was poor. I pressed on.

"Let's understand each other. I'm not irrevocably committed to this rescue or your wonderful code machine, and unless I see I'm getting more support than your acting as a glorified storekeeper for us, I've had it." The words came through clenched teeth. "We're on *your* turf now . . . and we're *still* being monkeyed with!"

The bunker was part of a warren of tunnels deep in a hillside overlooking the Korean eastern coast. The underground fortifications were a legacy from the occupying Japanese forces in the thirties. They now housed Kim and Associates.

He made mollifying motions with his hand and forced a thin-lipped smile. He'd have to do better than that.

"Commander, please calm yourself. We haven't been totally remiss, you know. But you must look at it from our point of view: it is an incredible undertaking to run security checks on your colleagues, for clearly mere surveillance won't work. Look at your roster. D'Epinuriaux, for example, has had twenty-three address changes within four countries over three and a half years. Most of your people have more nom de guerres than decent suits, and have disappeared off the face of the earth at one time or other. Most couldn't come up with enough credit references to swing a soft drink in Hong Kong. We are watching them all closely, but the key is probably in their past contacts, and that's really slow going. Frankly, you and your comrades have moved outside the sphere of acceptable behavior too long and they're all suspicious. Give me the authority and I'll polygraph them all, but I'm sure they're all going to show some sensitive readings."

"Run it anyway. "There was too much at stake to do otherwise. Lie detectors, I knew, could be beaten on rare occasions by psychopaths and extremely facile examinees.

Kim was hunched defensively behind his desk, his professional pride wounded. He searched the piles of paper for a report.

"Your former colleague, Commander Ackert, has been cultivating some interesting acquaintances."

I'd mentioned my mistrust of Ackert when we'd first arrived in Korea.

"He met with Max Brown at Narita Airport for an hour yesterday."

"Brown? That revolutionary-chic flower bastard? What possibly could those two have in common?"

"More than you think. Max Brown has become quite respectable lately. He's forsaken the behavior that landed him in jail during the Days of Rage in Chicago. Why, he's even written a book and taken to wearing ties. In fact, as administrative aide to Senator Denehy, he is a strong and open supporter of reform through working within the system. Really a heartwarming turnaround, don't you think?"

"Oh yes, very touching. It's a shame some of the former guests at the Hanoi Hilton aren't around to write him character references. No doubt some of them still hold bitter memories of Brown and his actress friend. The North Vietnamese did some extra shoulder dislocating to coerce those POWs into making anti-U.S. statements alongside Brown and her. Somehow the POWs held out," I said irritably, and added, "Sure, Brown's working within the system now. Why, I'll bet he owns a station wagon and belongs to a country club."

Kim just blinked. "We're fairly sure he's an agent of influence, but there's no way to prove it. Anyway, that doesn't matter right now. It's Senator Denehy who's our big worry. Denehy is number two in seniority on the Senate Armed Services Committee, and number three on Foreign Relations."

"And?"

"He wants to make—what's the expression—a big splash. And Ackert, I'm sure, would like a patron on that committee. A friend in the right places can win a star or two for the collar of an enterprising naval officer, I suspect. You understand."

I did, all too well. A deal was in the making: help my political career now and I'll back your naval career in the future. So Ackert's interest in my activities was prompted by more than spite. The story he'd given me about the Central Intelligence Agency's interest had seemed an unlikely half-truth. For Ackert, the military courtier, this was more in keeping with his character.

Kim studied the pieces on the *changgi* board. "Denehy's causes have been growing wilder as his influence within the Senate has increased. His most current cause is to establish virtual control of the U.S. Armed Forces by a new special congressional oversight committee."

"Control?" I questioned. "Paralysis would be more like it. But maybe that's what he has in mind. A neutering of the U.S. defense organization would mesh neatly with his philosophy on how to solve the world's problems. But how do we enter into all this?"

Kim picked up a checkerlike *changgi* piece and pushed it against the edge of his desk. "Denehy's constituency has been getting impatient with him and he's up for reelection this fall. He ranks ninety-eighth in attendance at roll-call votes and hasn't been very responsive to his blue-collar base. He needs an issue for this fall—badly. An exposé of some sort would be best: a Watergate, a Koreagate, an anything-gate. The ideal exposé would underscore his committee seniority and be consistent with his image. He styles himself as an authority on foreign affairs and abuses of military power—by both governmental and private militaries. Oh, how he'd like to link an unsavory paramilitary organization with a big-money U.S. corporation. Kurganov isn't paying you directly, his corporation Samizdat Publishing International is. Samizdat has made millions and spends much of what it makes on Kurganov's projects.

"Despite the fact that there were only a few Americans involved, Denehy wrung incredible mileage out of the mercenary flap in Angola during the mid-seventies. I think he's preparing to put on a similar show. Here's his last release."

Kim handed me a newspaper clipping.

The ruthless machismo of the mercenary creed does not lend itself to ideas of democracy, fair play, anti-colonialism, and world peace. I seek a resolution that it be the sense of the Senate that the U.S. government should seek out and foil any vestige of this brand of soulless enterprise. Its practitioners are men without sense, conscience, or compassion.

"And men like Brown, Ackert, and Denehy *are* men abounding in sense, conscience, and compassion," I commented. "Funny. I wouldn't have characterized Kosciuszko and Pulaski as soulless men, or the Lafayette Escadrille and the Flying Tigers as soulless enterprises."

So Ackert was making his grand play. If he could bring them my head at the right moment and under a dark cloud of failure, it would keep a senator with all the perverse ambition and wrongheadedness of a soap-opera patriarch *in power*, a closet Marxist *in influence*, and a naval careerist *on the inside track*.

From that point on, I pulled out all the stops on training. It did not take the men long to realize they had a traitor among them. If I kept them busy, at least I could keep their minds off that threat. Chamonix stepped into the assistant patrol leader spot. Alvarez, the Cuban who had been an alternate, I added for good measure.

Skiing, running, swimming, kayaking—we accelerated to a grueling tempo. All anyone could think of was sleep. I moved everyone out of the buildings into our low-profiled Norwegian tents. Keiko was not particularly happy about this development. She felt awkward and lonely watching us from the main building. About the only time she saw me at this stage was when, out of boredom, she strolled to the firing range, and I showed her how to fire an AK-47 and the recoilless rifle.

There are limits to what you can demand of men in a training situation, so I knew they were glad to hear about the submarine. A message brought word that it would pick us up at Chinhae in four days.

By way of graduation, Kim arranged for a three-day party for the troops—a three-day knee-walking binge, I suspected. There were a few loose ends I could only tie up in Japan, so I was permitted to break isolation and arrange for a flight to Japan for Keiko and myself. A "last good-bye" trip it could have been called, if I had allowed myself the sentimentality.

Keiko and I flew by chartered plane to Hachijo, a small island south of Honshu. With its stooped, windswept evergreens, mist-hidden ravines, and moss-covered rocks, the island was straight out of a Japanese woodcut. There we settled into the Three Sisters' Inn, a quaint old *ryokan* whose subtly magnificent garden overlooked one of the few stretches of sandy beach on the island. Keiko and I had once judged it the best bodysurfing beach in Japan. Gathering our swim gear into a *furoshiki* bundle, we jogged down to the evenly formed waves and assaulted the breakers.

Winter bodysurfing in Japan is not for the faint of heart or the fastidious of technique. It called for compromises. A wet-suit top was a necessity against the cold, but the top prevented a surfer from achieving maximum speed or enjoying maximum mobility. The perfect ride had to be found on another beach in a different climate.

We gamboled like sea otters in the dark gray waves. I had the raw strength to lunge at a wave, then catch a short reckless ride, before tumbling out of the wave to avoid the rocks some ancient spoilsport had erected. In contrast, Keiko surfed with limber finesse. She let the waves catch her and carry her down their face. With each ride, she'd execute several directional changes before lacing between the rocks unharmed. The effort was more conscious and plodding for me—stroke, kick, bunch shoulders forward in the wave, raise my head, put my hands to my thighs, and let rip. Once in a dozen tries I might remember to tuck a shoulder in order to turn right or left. Twice I succeeded in sliding both down and sideways through the wet, translucent pipe and heard myself whooping with unrestrained joy.

The silky sheen upon Keiko's wetsuit seemed to amplify the swell of her hips and the thrust of her chest. In athletic exhilaration, she never looked lovelier. No cream-puff beauty queen forever fearful of messing up her hair could compete in the same universe with this almond-eyed naiad.

We returned to the *ryokan* by alternately shivering and hopping from mossy rock to mossy rock. The dull ache of lung-seared fatigue rated scant attention as we collapsed onto the tatami mats. In the twilight, the physical theme of the day's activity turned to a sensual preoccupation. We warmed up in the inn's steambath and then scampered to the hot tubs, which we had reserved that morning. Our supper, though sumptuous, was eaten hurriedly as events built in rapid acceleration. Like two leaves whisked down one of the island's streams, we, too, were drawn ever faster toward a foreseeable end.

In the flickering light of a paper lantern she slid aside the door to my room—as if for the first time—proud and erect. She wore an old camouflaged shirt of mine, softened by age, which hung open at the throat, between her generous breasts and down to her firm, flat stomach. She gave a spirited flick to her long ebony hair, and for a second flashed teeth as white as the winter moon. She lifted her arms and crossed them in front of her gravely.

"You, Frazer, come take what is yours and only yours."

She paused.

"If this be the last time, let us make it a time for remembering in the miserable days ahead."

And we did. And it was. I was proud that she did not cry.

PART IV

CHAPTER 18

The trip back to Korea was sobering and lonely. Once there, I learned we had developed a disciplinary problem. Puckins and Wickersham had given the KCIA people the slip during the "rest" period and flown to Japan for the remaining days, returning only hours before me. They refused to explain their unauthorized absence. Questions from Dravit and me only met mischievous grins and hard silence.

The breach of discipline didn't disturb me as much as the breach of security. Clearly we had a spy and saboteur in our midst, and though I had known both Puckins and Wickersham for over a decade, no one was above suspicion.

"Captain Dravit, make sure these two are kept busy until our departure. It seems that when they get bored they get the urge to go globe-trotting. Chiefs and first-class petty officers notwithstanding, I believe a good healthy dose of weapons maintenance and barracks cleaning would be in order."

Puckins and Wickersham's faces fell.

"And maybe they ought to re-pine-tar all our skis. When they finish that, let them shovel a walkway from here to Seoul."

"But, sir . . ." one of the culprits started.

*   *   *

Nine sets of weary faces and bloodshot eyes manhandled personal gear onto an old bus and ordnance onto one of the Mercedes trucks. That three-day party must have been something. Tiny Gurung would start laughing uncontrollably for no reason at all. Kruger wore a pair of pink lace skivvies over his shirt pocket like a decoration for valor. Lutjens and Alvarez walked as if they were made of glass. Even Matsuma, who had fallen into the martial way of things, grinned whimsically when he thought no one was looking. The only one untouched by the graduation festivities was Chamonix, whom I'd never seen smile.

Most of the men slept as the bus raced south through the snow-covered countryside, slowing only as it entered an occasional village. Not until we reached the long tunnel that marked the entrance to Chinhae did everyone become alert and begin to sense the full impact of what lay ahead. As we cleared the gates of the navy yard, the men speculated on where we were going and how and why. The consensus was that we were going to Red China since our equipment was primarily Chinese, and we were going by ship since our destination was Chinhae, Korea's naval center. No one had a clue as to why we were going.

We stopped at the end of one pier at a deserted portion of the base as instructed. The truck pulled in ahead of us and we began to unload it. Between the scuba tanks and the ski gear, the truck looked like a mobile sporting-goods store.

There was no submarine in sight. Several patrol boats lay at anchor in the evening haze. There didn't seem to be anyone around interested in doing anything.

At about 2000, two patrol boats rumbled to life and came alongside the pier. A crewman dogtrotted over to us. "You come," he said. "Now?"

Puckins had the men transfer the gear with painstaking care to the two boats. I noted that the boxed ordnance seemed excessive. The Korean crews looked bored, as if this sort of smuggler's transfer was becoming wearisome. If that's what they thought, they kept it to themselves.

"Did we order all this ordnance?"

"I did," Dravit said, inviting no further discussion. No use questioning the inventory. After all, he was the professional ordnance salesman.

Since their punishment detail, Puckins and Wickersham had become very formal and ill at ease. I couldn't tell if I had been too hard on them or if they were up to something. The transfer was too hectic to watch them carefully.

The patrol boats took in their lines and soon we were cutting through the wintry chop and dodging the tiny islands that freckled the harbor.

"There it is," Dravit called out. I moved to the lee rail of the boat for a better look.

The submarine lay dead in the water, dull black and menacing. Its bold, sleek lines seemed poised for attack. Forward of the conning tower, a single five-inch gun thrust ahead determinedly. Emblazoned on the conning tower was a large red star and identification numerals—in Chinese characters, not the way they would do it, but confusing nonetheless. According to these markings, this was a Chinese "Romeo" class patrol submarine. Yet the hull configuration and superstructure were all wrong for a Chicom boat. Furthermore, few modern subs carried deck guns and seldom so large. There was something faintly familiar about this sub and it disturbed me. A lone silhouette in a bridge coat descended from the cigarette deck to meet us.

"Welcome aboard, Mr. Frazer. You like our artwork?" he said, pointing to the markings. "They were applied especially for your cruise.

"Would you and your men kindly follow me below? A working party will stow your equipment for you. I expect you will want to leave one man to supervise the transfer?" the round-faced Korean officer said in matter-of-fact tones.

"Gurung, keep an eye on the unloading of the gear," Dravit, behind me, ordered.

That sense of familiarity grew stronger and began to haunt me. I checked the frame markings. All markings were in Korean characters.

The odor of kimchee-fermented cabbage pervaded the boat. Many of the fittings weren't U.S. made, but by now I was convinced this was a U.S. submarine.

When we arrived at the control room, the round-faced officer turned and introduced himself as Commander Cho, Korean navy, the sub's skipper. He seemed indifferent to our arrival. I supposed that we were just one of the many small military and paramilitary units he deposited yearly on hostile doorsteps. I had been aware that Korea had a submarine of some sort since my days as an adviser.

"Excuse me, Captain, but what ship is this?"

He looked at me sidelong. "This is the Korean navy submarine *Taegu*. You may remember it—though you seem far too young—as the USS *Wahoo*."

"Damned," Wickersham exclaimed half-consciously. No wonder she had seemed familiar. I had toured her sister ship, the USS *Croaker*, which was a World War II relic. But hadn't the *Wahoo* disappeared years ago?

As if reading my mind, Cho added, "She sank with all hands in forty-three while in the Sea of Japan. The Japanese began salvage work a year later but had to stop at the time of the surrender.

"We took over the project in fifty-five, raising and concealing her in a remote submarine pen not far from here, she's been used for intelligence work against North Korea ever since. Your government knows about her, but has never filed a formal protest."

He was all business.

"My former government."

He turned to look at me, then had his executive officer show us the troop compartment. Dravit and I shared a stateroom.

The boat began to vibrate faintly—we were under way. Hell-bent for Siberia in a flat black museum piece.

Sometimes little things should tip you off. First, I should have sensed when Wickersham and Puckins deposited two seabags with such tender loving care in my stateroom that something was afoot. Second, I should have become suspicious when those two asked Dravit to take a look at some mysterious problem in the armory. I should have sensed skullduggery on their part of unmitigated proportions. But I didn't. Instead, I gave my full attention to charts of the Siberian coastline and English translations of the long-term weather forecasts. Then I went to the head.

When I returned, lying in my rack—nonchalantly reading a book, oblivious to the fact that we were gliding at periscope depth through the Sea of Japan aboard a vulnerable old commerce raider, crewed by eighty hard-nosed Korean seamen and carrying nine desperate naval commandos—reclined Keiko in a faded set of bell-bottoms and a dark blue turtleneck sweater. *Damnation.*

"Dravit!" I bellowed out the stateroom door.

"Yes?"

"Get Chief Puckins and Wickersham in here ASAP."

Keiko looked up at me uncertainly. "Not their fault. They only suggested this stowaway after you left Hachijo. It was my fault for taking them up on it. They said it would be good for 'skipper's morale.'"

She rolled over to face the bulkhead.

Dravit, Puckins, and Wickersham came barging through the door. Dravit was smiling but quickly dropped the smile when he saw the wild look of fury in my eye.

"You two"—my index finger shook uncontrollably—"are hereby appointed head cleaners on this boat until further notice. If in the future you have any plans to buoy the spirits of 'your skipper,' or anyone else, you can take those plans and stick them . . ."

Dravit seized the seconds it took to fish for an appropriate receptacle to hustle the culprits out of the stateroom and added some choice advice of his own.

I went aft to the control room to tell the captain of his stowaway. The captain's reaction, clearly, though not overtly, indicated he was of the opinion he had embarked ten rank amateurs.

The humor of the prank escaped me. My full concentration had to be on my men and the mission. There would be no second chances, no coming back to pick up forgotten items. Keiko would be a distraction—albeit a pleasant one—but a distraction, nonetheless. A malfunctioning radio or a shortage of food, it didn't matter. I was responsible.

* * *

The submarine rushed headlong through the brooding waters of the Sea of Japan. After the prank, Dravit had limped out of the stateroom and berthed in the troop compartment. He had said, with ponderous sarcasm, that he could not abide officers who encouraged stowaways.

Chamonix and I worked on organizing the field packs so that they were both light and complete. We would darken the troop compartment and the group would rehearse assembling the folding kayaks and breaking down the weapons. We fitted the green Chinese uniforms and made what few alterations were required of the white camouflage overblouses and overtrousers.

I hoped to get fairly close to the Siberian coast in order to lock the raiding party out of the submarine. A lockout was a procedure in which divers exited a submerged submarine. It was a ticklish maneuver that required a rehearsal of both the frogmen and the submarine's crew. Underwater, the submarine's propellers generated a furious suction. Any error could suck a drifting frogman into the whirling propeller and certain death. The sub's captain had agreed to a rehearsal and scheduled it for the next day.

The rehearsal centered around the submarine's forward escape trunk, a compartment about the size of two telephone booths. At the top of the trunk lay a hatch that led to the outer deck of the submarine. At the bottom of the compartment was another hatch, which opened into the sub's working spaces. When the trunk was completely flooded, a small lip around the outer edge of the top hatch trapped a donut of air several inches in depth. In an emergency, a diver could just barely thrust his head into the donut-shaped bubble for breathable air.

The lockout procedure was hazardous, yet simple in principle. By operating the controls within the trunk or the dual controls in the lower passageway, we could gradually flood the trunk with water from the sub's reserve tanks. Once the pressure inside the trunk was slightly greater than the pressure outside the sub's hull, the top hatch, which was already undogged and only held shut by the outside pressure, would pop open and the divers in the trunk could swim out. From there they would glide along a safety line, which stretched from the top hatch to the periscope. The line kept the divers from drifting back into the sub's screws.

I would have preferred to use oxygen rebreathers—Draegers—which left no telltale bubbles. However, a diver breathing pure oxygen under pressure stood a good chance of blacking out at depths exceeding thirty feet. The distance between this submarine's hatch and the surface, running at periscope depth, came uncomfortably close to that depth. Draegers were therefore out, open-circuit scuba was the rig of the week.

The lockout was one way of deploying raiders in enemy waters undetected. It placed great demands on divers, especially in waters as cold as the Okhotsk, but it allowed the submarine to stay below the surface. Submariners dreaded the detectability and vulnerability of surface running.

The next evening we assembled the men for the drill. Every man wore a bulky bubble dry suit. These suits were warmer, but more cumbersome than the old-fashioned dry suits we had worn for Kunashiri.

The first diver pair, Puckins and Lutjens, climbed up into the trunk and secured the lower hatch. As the assigned safety divers, they wore single-hose regulators with octopus extensions. Puckins operated the controls inside the trunk. Dravit, his ankle cast propped on the lower knife edge of the hatchway, stood by the series of valves and pipes that duplicated Puckins's controls within the trunk. Puckins announced over the waterproof intercom each adjustment as he made it.

"Flooding."

I could hear the pumps forcing water into the trunk. Dravit repeated each message back to Puckins.

I could imagine the rising water level, first knee high, then waist high, then chest high . . .

"Tell him to have Lutjens put his mouthpiece in and test it below water level." It was a routine command. The divers had, of course, made a cursory regulator check when they had strapped on their tanks.

"Lutjens . . . is having . . . trouble."

The resonance of Puckins's words had changed as water poured into the trunk. I could hear coughing in the background over the hum of the pumps. Puckins vented the trunk.

"Try yours . . . he may have to buddy-breathe off your octopus rig."
More coughing and gagging.

"Something wrong"—cough—"getting water through the"—cough—"regulator. . . . Water's real high . . . nearly to the hatch lip."

"Get up into the bubble. Don't touch any of the controls."

"Captain Dravit, take over, using your controls. Abort the lock-out. Flood down the trunk. Whatever we do, we can't lose the bubble. Chief, we are aborting the drill."

The bubble was now their only source of air. If Dravit manipulated the controls in the wrong order, the bubble would slip out the wrong pipe and the divers would drown, trapped in a dark round coffin of steel.

"Flooding down."

The pumps reversed flow. I realized I was in a cold sweat.

When the trunk had finally emptied, Lutjens opened the lower hatch, and the two shaken divers climbed out. Wickersham grabbed their regulators and pried them open with a screwdriver.

"Mr. Frazer, take a look at these." Wickersham held out the two regulators.

"No mushroom valves."

A mushroom valve was a soft, flexible rubber disk that, during the breathing cycle, kept water from entering the mouthpiece as exhaust air escaped. These disks were missing. We examined the other regulators. Their valves were missing, too. This was no manufacturer's error. It meant deliberate sabotage—the kind a diver wouldn't normally detect until it was too late—sabotage that killed with choking horror.

"Gurung, let the control room know we've called off the lockout drill."

"Thought it might have been a Jonah back in Korea, but we've got a Judas with us. Don't we?" Wickersham thought aloud.

"Yes, it appears we do. But he hasn't stopped us . . . yet."

"Break out the kayaks. It looks like this boat's going to have to surface, after all."

CHAPTER 19

Keiko and I shared the same stateroom but barely spoke to one another. She had become distant, or perhaps I had become distant. It didn't matter since I was busy checking and rechecking, inspecting and reinspecting, planning and replanning. A chill had fallen on our relationship and I just could not spare the time to lift it. If that were possible.

A howling storm hit us three-quarters of the way across the Sea of Japan. Forty-foot waves tossed the surface-running sub around like a beer can in a washing machine. The heads became awash with vomit and we were forced to strap ourselves into our racks. Several crew members sustained broken ribs or collarbones as they caromed down passageways or attempted to climb to the sub's conning tower. The waves picked the boat up with perverse relish, hesitated, and then abruptly dropped it into the raging sea.

On one occasion, several hundred gallons of seawater cascaded down an open hatch. A lookout had opened the hatch for his watch relief. The relieving crewman was knocked senseless and the seawater short-circuited a number of powerlines. Fortunately, the seawater did not get into the sub's batteries. Seawater and batteries combine to generate deadly chlorine gas.

The storm had lasted for twenty-four hours and left everyone hungry and exhausted.

I was alone in the submarine's wardroom when Dravit and Chamonix filed in.

"Skipper, I think we'd better take a second look at this operation," Dravit opened.

His color was up. Chamonix wore a similar look of intensity. A confrontation.

I was seated. They stood over me. Dravit's cast clunked against the bench seat. I had been expecting something like this. Now the two of them had me cornered.

"We're out on a limb already and I can hear some bugger making little chopping noises behind us," he said through clenched teeth.

I searched their faces for a hint of indecision or inconsistency, and found none.

"Mister Frazer," Chamonix added in even tones, "there has been a serious pattern of acts, of, how do you say—it is the same word in English—sabotage. We cannot disregard these acts. To endure difficulties, this is admirable. To ignore clear signs of treachery, that is foolhardy."

Dravit drummed his fingers on the table softly, unconsciously.

"You mean you want me to pull the plug?" Not quite the right expression to use aboard a submarine, I thought as I said it.

They hesitated. They had come this far and now they stood before me awkward and flat-footed. None of us had wanted to be the first to say it.

"We're compromised," Dravit pleaded.

"Maybe. I don't think so."

The Frenchman looked down at his shower shoes. Dravit slumped into the bench seat across from me. Then he pulled himself up to a more adversarial posture.

It was disquieting being at odds with your second and third in command. Both Dravit and Chamonix were seasoned combatants with a wide range of field experience between them.

Dravit countered, "Well, then, who do you ken is responsible and what are you going to do about it?"

"Anyone. Everyone. Nothing for now."

They gave each other confirming looks.

"The pattern seems pretty subtle," I continued. "The camera, the Japanese police, your accident, the regulators . . . Why do they keep trying to spring the trap before they can get all of us? Why not wait and stop us once and for all?"

Chamonix cocked an eyebrow. "The *right* charge in Henry's ski booby trap could have taken us all out?"

"Yes, including the turncoat," Dravit interrupted.

"What can he do in Siberia that won't take him 'out,' along with us?"

"Maybe he wants to be in Siberia. Maybe the people he's working with are there," Dravit persisted.

That was a possibility I most dreaded.

"Why, then, take the trouble to tamper with the regulators?"

Chamonix had withdrawn enigmatically from the conversation. Evidence of his fine mind burned through occasionally, but too often his thoughts lay concealed behind a dark cloud.

"We're talking about nine men."

"I know."

"All we need is one bloke who can make contact with the wrong people at the right time and you're bloody well through."

"I've considered that."

"You run the chance of jeopardizing the sub's crew, too. That's another eighty men to figure into the balance."

"Yes, they're at risk."

His face was reddening. "We are open to retribution."

"We would be anyway."

Knockout punches were for the movies. Real fights, Dravit knew, were won by steadily pounding your opponent into rubber-legged submission.

"If they capture a single mucking one of you, they won't be gentle like my maiden aunt. Once they get out of you what they want to know, Vyshinsky will be as good as dead."

"He's nearly as good as dead already."

"Righto, so bloody well don't go!" He brought both fists down onto the table.

"Enough of this feels right. We're going. You are right, *something's* wrong, but the odds are as good as they'll ever get." I had unconsciously laid emphasis on "we're going." He wasn't and that took some weight from his arguments. "Who's ever going to expect an operation as audacious as this?"

Chamonix looked at Dravit and shrugged. The Englishman opened his mouth, then shut it. Each of them had enough military time to have run into situations like this before. Instances where the commanding officer and his senior people did not agree. There was no point in arguing further.

"The matter is closed," I pronounced. I, too, had experience, and more in positions of ultimate responsibility. Consensus was always desirable, but I had learned to trust my instincts. Kurganov had hired one man to make the final decisions. Finality was the nature of the work I did, and of the inescapable responsibility I had assumed.

Frazer, were you right this time? At what point would they stop following you?

"Remember one thing: only you, Henry, and I know the complete plan. Our turncoat isn't sure how hard he has to be trying. I'm going to settle that little question. We'll brief tonight on the entire mission. Lay out the warning order and everything. We'll begin phase planning later tomorrow."

The klaxon sounded and there was a rush of feet in the passageway. The crew were rushing to their diving stations.

That night the troop compartment was cramped and humid.

"*Bitte*, will this be an aerobic session for us, you know, as *schuss*-ing moving targets? Or is it to be a learning opportunity, say, for us to discover how many pieces of equipment can be cleverly rigged to malfunction, or perhaps blow up," Lutjens kicked off with a sweet smile, "sir?" He turned to the others with a hand gesture that invited similar challenges.

The high-living German was apparently a master of the military fine art of the border-line insubordinate question. Always end it with "sir."

I saw Chief Puckins bridle. If I was any judge, Puckins as the senior enlisted SEAL would soon be giving Lutjens a verbal blowtorching in private.

Dravit and I gave the preliminary briefing. Assignments would be made shortly and each man would be preparing a briefing to be given to the group of his portion of the mission prior to execution. Using a dozen maps, diagrams, and photographs taped to the top of an upturned Ping-Pong table, we took two and a half hours to outline the key points. More would follow, this was just the beginning. Only one or two showed any surprise. By now they had a general sense of the risks, even without knowing the countries involved.

"We *will* be putting our kayaks ashore, that's the program. I believe we can pull this off. Anyone who wants to back out now, can. Just remember that if you back out, you don't get a dime, and you won't be going anywhere beyond this submarine.

"One more thing. If we fail ashore, this submarine will be next on the list for counterattack. It won't be hard for Ivan to trace back the thread. If it turns out failure was for the lack of a man's participation, I don't really expect that man will outlive us much by staying on this boat. So you see, if any of us goes, we'd all better go.

"Stay-behinds, do I have any takers?"

No one moved. We had advanced so deeply into the maw that movement in any direction was as perilous as movement in any other direction.

"*Ja*, well, that about does it. I'm giving three-to-one odds we don't make it," Lutjens added with forced good humor.

"Just how do you expect to collect on that one?" Alvarez said as everyone cleared the compartment. The Cuban's mental discipline never waivered.

"W-w-wire his estate," Kruger replied, flipping a coin high into the air. "His posh grand-duchess aunt, or whatever she is, ought to be able to cover it."

"B-b-better idea," he added thoughtfully, "have *your estate* wire his estate."

As we drew closer to our destination they showed great care in tending to their personal equipment and developed the habit of daydreaming. Time was drawing short.

I followed the briefing with an extended calisthenics session in the troop compartment. Though the Koreans had added a snorkel, on occasion the sub ran on the surface at night with its vents open and at these times we could get enough fresh air for exercise. There wasn't room for an orthodox PT session, so each man did his push-ups, sit-ups, and flutter kicks in his rack. Nine men running in place felt as insane as it looked to the crew of the Korean sub.

Then we practiced putting the five disassembled kayaks through the after hatch and assembling them on deck. Each kayak was designed for two paddlers, though it could be paddled by one alone. Each could hold three men comfortably, and in a pinch, four. But after tying on *ahkios*, skis, and other equipment, we found barely enough room to squeeze in two paddlers.

First we assembled the simple interlocking skeleton halves of Finnish ash. Then the skeleton halves were fitted into the rubberized-fabric skin. Dual inflatable sponsons running the length of the craft provided the locking tension that kept the skin in place. Under some circumstances, the skeleton could be pre-assembled in halves below decks. However, the beams of these kayaks were too broad for the hatches of this submarine.

It was dangerous work in this climate. Everyone above decks was required to wear a safety harness. A man lost overboard at night in waters like these stood little chance of recovery. Yet the harness and the tether lines were awkward, and despite my warnings more than once, I saw men detach their harnesses to get at a particularly obstinate piece of gear.

My stopwatch read ten minutes. Too long. The low-lying fog that enshrouded the decks could only serve as a partial excuse.

Time permitted only one kayak drill. The sub's captain had said that we would be entering the Soviet radar umbrella very soon. This was one of the last times prior to launch that the sub would run fully surfaced. Since the sub had been modified with post-World War II snorkel equipment, it could run on diesel in moderate seas at periscope depth.

I favored this kayak technique over a lockout. One advantage to wet-deck launches was they could begin farther offshore and allow the sub to stay in deeper, safer water. Another advantage was that kayakers were less susceptible to currents and cold-water immersion. On the other hand, submariners like wet-deck launches as much as a poke in the eye with a sharp stick.

Later that evening I drifted up to the conning tower for some fresh air. A freak front of warm air gave the waters approaching the La Pérouse Straits a singular appearance. The sky was clear and the stars bright, but a thin two- or three-foot blanket of fog covered the sea and concealed the deck of the submarine. The conning tower floated above it like a disembodied bandstand. Here and there the underlying ocean boiled through and then disappeared as quickly as it appeared.

Occasionally a small cake of ice appeared in these glimpses of ocean. I wondered idly if in time these cakes would grow or melt.

For no reason I could think of, the expression "a snowball's chance in hell" came to mind. The expression was all wrong. A snowball had a very good chance—in a frigid hell like this. Whoever first portrayed hell as full of fire and brimstone must have taken the quick tour run by the Chamber of Commerce. Surely he had not been shown some of the more esoteric variations and did not know the true agony of severe cold . . . the way a frogman did.

Someone had once described the frogman's place in hell to me. The description involved that wizened old man, Charon, whose ferry plied the waters of the Styx carrying new arrivals to hell, or more properly, Hades. The surviving mythology has been vague as to the propulsion of Charon's craft, and understandably so. Few would grasp its poetic justice. Charon's ferry wasn't poled, rowed, sailed, motored, or drawn by some clever pulley arrangement across the inky Styx. Such efficient methods—by above-ground standards—were worthless squanderings of resources in this strange underground world with a surfeit of labor . . . and time.

No, Charon's ferry did not trifle with the conventional methods of its above-ground brothers who labored in the light of the sun. Instead, before it, harnessed in buddy pairs that stretched off into the low-lying fog where hot air met cold water, swam combat swimmers doomed to course the ice-water currents of the Styx for eternity.

In the lead traces stroked the swimmers used by Alexander to attack Tyre. Next came Beowulf and Breca, who had each fought bloody swimming battles of epic proportions. They were followed by an assortment of frogmen—French Nageurs de Combat, Italian Incusori, German Kampfschwimmers, British Royal Marines and Clearance Divers, Norwegian Marinejaegers, Japanese Fukuryu, and the older Ninja—all these warriors strained in their harnesses as clouds of vapor steamed from their mouths and nostrils. No pining, graceful Leanders here, but bruising, powerful hulks with the glazed look of the near drowned. Their common sin had been to turn a harmless pastime into a lethal occupation. And so, the punishment was made to fit the crime.

A fiendish joke caused a strange reverse evolution to work on them. They now shared a single physical trait; each had webbed feet. Among the living they had left the land to fight in or below the sea. Now their degeneration was complete and they could never again live normally on land. Their reverse evolution had stopped at this point, however. They could not develop thicker skins, and so the icy water kept them in neck-tensing discomfort just short of numbness. Their swimming would continue as long as there were doomed souls to transport from the world above. Simply, in Charon's traces there can be no rest or peace.

PART V

CHAPTER 20

The La Pérouse Straits, like the Nemuro Straits, were shared by Japan and Russia. Commander Cho had told me that he suspected that Russian sonar modules dotted the straits. These devices served to detect ships and submarines entering the Sea of Okhotsk.

As we approached the straits, he submerged the sub and shadowed an old merchant steamer closely. The resulting irregular sonar signature, he hoped, would confuse the Soviet sonar men. He banked on the fact that the shallow water of the straits, where such devices were notoriously unreliable, would cause watch standers to ignore confusing signals. Where confusion set in, any explanation, such as shallow water distortion, would be readily accepted. Anyway, the steamer was easily visible and obviously harmless.

Twice after we passed through the straits, the sub's klaxon sounded, sending the boat's crew once more to emergency diving stations. We were now snorkeling only at night and chugging along submerged at a feeble six knots. Sometimes during the long submerged periods, the air grew so foul, members of the crew couldn't keep their cigarettes lit. Condensation within the hull left everything soggy and lifeless.

One evening, Chamonix whisked by me in a passageway. "We're in Ivan's backyard now," the legionnaire pronounced somberly. "No turning back from here on out. God have mercy."

The night of the launch arrived at last. Mid-March in Siberia—it could have been worse. I had trouble visualizing how.

I kissed Keiko good-bye in the stateroom. Those big liquid black eyes held me immobile for a moment. The distance between us remained. In view of my slim chances of returning, perhaps this was the best way. I closed the stateroom door carefully. Dravit would watch out for her. "Come back," had been all she said.

I moved down the darkened passageway and took my place below the after hatch with my eight dry-suited men and a detail of Korean sailors. We crouched on our watertight bundles and waited for the signal that would send us topside for the launch. The meager red lights played lightly across pale faces with the faint sheen of tension.

The ship's head was getting a good deal of traffic. No matter how you tried to tough it out, your body always betrayed you.

Gurung came back from a trip down the ladder glistening with sweat. He collapsed on one bundle and I caught the odor of vomit. The boat was caught in a series of slow, hesitating rolls. The wave action and the mental strain had combined to make him seasick.

The Gurkha was hard and steadfast. He never groused, and grousing was to be expected. I often sensed he did not always understand all that was going on around him, and yet that did not seem to bother him. From time to time I'd pull him aside and quiz him. His responses indicated he fully comprehended all of the military aspects of our project. In essence, he functioned on an intuitive level. He sensed where to focus his attention during each evolution and in whom to place his trust. You couldn't help but admire our steady Nepalese hill man. He was like one of those epic warriors who were always wandering into mythical lands where the earthly rules did not apply. They invariably prevailed by courage and determination alone. Submarines were as far as you could get from the peaks of the Himalayas, and you could tell he was proud of his stoic ability to trudge into the fantastic and unknown.

Chief Puckins gagged. Then the freckled Texan hiccuped. He hiccuped again. And again. And again. Everyone's eyes were on Puckins.

He hiccuped loudly and something white and round popped from his mouth. As he wiped the front of his face with a towel, the object bounced to the floor. He closed his mouth and with a hiccup another white object became visible. He wiped his mouth again.

"Wass going on?" Alvarez said with a befuddled look. The husky Cuban picked up the white object and examined it hesitantly. You had to be very careful these days. Alvarez was the group's skeptic.

Soon the passageway was awash with bouncing white objects.

"I told you not to eat those Ping-Pong balls so close to a launch," Wickersham said reprovingly as he flexed his neck from side to side. "You know this always happens when you mix paddles and Ping-Pong balls at supper. The paddles get frisky and start serving the balls out. I wish you'd stick to pachinko. At least the balls stay in the machine."

"Aw, perdition (hic). Cut me some slack, Wick." He made a moue. *Don't start with me. You know how I get.* Ain't some of these fellas got enough to think about?"

Gurung, with as much dignity as he could muster, rushed down the ladder to the head again.

I was in a deep depression. It was always the same dark, irritable depression that accompanied me into action. This black mood was upholstered in equal parts of self-doubt and dark recrimination. Was all this the result of my personal madness or was it simply vanity?

This was the deep, very private gloom reserved for leaders. It was the special reserve of those madmen who went out looking for trouble, those idiots who designed nearly attainable missions and executed them themselves. Only a few military leaders experienced this special torment. Others were passively drawn into battle, responding to directives and reacting to threats. Not you. In special operations, the initiative, the organizing, and the execution were often all rolled into one. You sought out trouble spots, generated your own proposals for authorization, and bore the heavy burden of the power of life and death alone.

The mood came before every evolution where I might lose a man. It was like this before every night parachute jump, before every night ship attack, before open boat passages, before assaults up a sheer rock cliff, before every hazardous engagement.

I kneaded my right shoulder. It was throbbing again.

What made me so foolhardy? Who was I to think I could pull this off? Very likely we would all be dead by this time next week.

It was always eerie to be able to see the future in such stark alternatives and be able to set your watch by them. In a week we would all be alive or we would all be dead. Would my name be the last name cursed on one of my own men's lips? With black humor I wondered if perhaps I had been selected to rid the world of its dangerous, violent, overeager people. People who loved rough sports, danger, and a bizarre camaraderie.

As always, I would persevere and see it through. I was driven to make sense out of nonsense. I was haunted by the need to see that good men were not wasted on mediocre causes and enterprises. I burned with the desire to forcibly turn past experiences in personal pain, discomfort, and courage into something worthy of the price. I would take every ordeal, humiliation, and hardship that we had suffered collectively to end up where we now crouched, and make it worth something. Let something else take that away from us. I would not turn back. They wouldn't.

Nearly all of us were veterans. Each of us had been badly battered and in the end had become associated with a failed undertaking. We would not accept that assessment as a final score. We would take these failures, but only as setbacks on the way to some larger justifying victory. Someday, perhaps.

I understood all this, as I always had, but I still invariably plunged into black depression. For I had forced the issue, and brought everyone to the test, and after tonight not one of our lives would ever be the same.

Then Dravit beaned me with a Ping-Pong ball.

*   *   *

Once we surfaced, the hatch was tossed open, and men and equipment spewed onto the exposed deck. Whitecaps smashed across the sub's flatback bow, leaving the deck wet and icy slick. The quarter moon shed just enough light to give the quick-frozen icicles on the cigarette-deck railing a crystalline sparkle. The breeze did not feel unusually cold at first, but you soon knew where you had exposed skin.

We assembled the kayaks just aft and in the lee of the conning tower. Rapidly, the kayaks took form and absorbed our watertight bundles of equipment. We clicked through assembly and loading like a well crafted breechblock with finely fitted tolerances. The mechanism showed a single flaw. Lutjens—in Chamonix's boat—seemed to be an uncontrolled swarm of thumbs. The weight of the risks of a mission seemed to fall all at once during the last twenty-four hours before a launch. You became so intent on trying to visualize the future that you forgot the present. It was not unusual for even crack troops to become punchy with anticipation.

The sub's deck left little freeboard, and its guardrails had been removed. One moment the elegant German was standing next to his kayak, the next moment a comber running the length of the deck swept him off his feet and the deck.

Chamonix lunged for him, but had no play left in his safety harness. Someone tossed a line, but by then Lutjens had disappeared under the submarine. Moments later, bits of stained neoprene bobbed in the submarine's wake.

"Why wasn't his harness fastened?" Alvarez demanded. The big Cuban sighed as if his worst suspicions had been confirmed. "How could it happen? Not another accident."

"That Judas-Jonah is still with us," said Wickersham glumly. He worked his bicep. "I don't like it, not a bit."

Chief Puckins interrupted, "I can't figure it out, either, but one thing's for sure. If we don't launch pretty damn quick, the Russki radar is going to draw a bead on this boat." He drew his hand across his throat.

Matsuma and I eased into our kayak. The old Japanese fisherman took the bow seat, and I the stern seat with the rudder pedals. I waved "all clear" to Dravit and in seconds the submarine began to submerge. The rush of white water tossed the kayaks around mercilessly, but our spray skirts kept us dry. The submarine slipped like a shadow beneath the waves, carrying Henry Dravit, former Royal Marine, and Keiko Shirahama, onetime Ama diver, away—perhaps forever.

"One man dead for sure in exchange for one man's possible rescue. At best, there can be no net gain," Chamonix called over the darkness.

I steered a course based on the sub's last fix. Matsuma suggested course modifications to guide us through the large chunks of free-floating ice.

"I don't fight to balance any books," I returned. "Those are the values of someone else's vocation.

"I fight to bring hope," I added, addressing no one in particular.

CHAPTER 21

We had severed the logistic umbilical. For the next ten to twelve days, we could forget any outside support. As a small covert force we would be hard to detect, but if detected . . .

Our kayaks dodged floes as needles of wind-driven spray tormented the paddlers. My use of an azimuth was of secondary value, the real navigation rested in Matsuma's hands until we reached shore. In March, much of the pack ice began to break up, he had assured me, and the great tidal range and strong currents along this stretch of coast left it navigable to within one or two miles of land.

March weather varied as unpredictably in Siberia as it did elsewhere. Though Siberia averaged only twenty inches of snow a year, a great part of this figure fell in March. March temperatures were generally milder than deep-winter temperatures, but they could plunge to sixty below without warning.

Matsuma and I held the lead position. The synchronized flutter of our double-bladed paddles moved us briskly up and over the rolling black waves. The seawater, which dripped from these paddles, or which splashed over the decks, froze in sheets down the length of our seventeen-foot craft. As we approached land, free ice became more plentiful. Clear passages through the ice fields became narrower and narrower, fanning into small, wandering channels, which forked like branches of a tree. Matsuma showed an unerring instinct for picking the fork that meandered toward pack ice. Then, for a quarter of a mile, we manhandled floes with our paddles to clear a path. Finally, we reached pack ice. There we climbed out and hauled the kayaks onto the ice. We portaged a mile, then hit a belt of open water. Once again we slid the kayaks into the sea. The belt was only a few hundred yards across and then we were back on pack ice. Before us lay disjointed piles of ice in pressure ridges. Here, a false step on seemingly secure ice could flip a man into water far colder than his dry suit provided for.

One by one we dragged the kayaks across the unstable ice. Then we portaged them a quarter mile before dismantling them. Once during the portage, Gurung stepped into a crevice. A sharp crystal ripped a small hole in the leg of his suit as his foot plunged to the knee into the water beneath. We weren't able to unpack one of the portable stoves until ten minutes later. By then his foot was encased in rime. As we thawed his foot with the stove, it looked to me as if he'd have to be scratched from the remainder of the raid. Reading my mind, he shrugged off further attention and limped on ahead.

We hiked another mile across ragged ice before we reached a tree line, the first positive indication of solid land. We had reached the edge of the taiga, the vast, virtually unbroken expanse of larch, spruce, fir, and cedar that covered most of Siberia. There, at a distinctive stand of stunted birch, we buried the four kayaks in the snow and covered them with a white tarp, which we froze in place with melted snow. As an added measure we pushed a rotten tree over the tarp to keep the wind from blowing it over. I pointed out several terrain features that would help identify this spot to the returning raiders in the event that I was not with them. Then I went over each leg of the journey on the map once again to be sure that if we became separated, each man would have a chance, however remote, of rejoining the party. We then changed into our quilted Chinese uniforms and donned the white overtrousers. With the dark taiga background, we didn't need overblouses.

We melted snow to quench what was now an overwhelming thirst.

"Why the Chicom uniforms?" Wickersham asked, putting on his fur hat. "If we're going to wear someone else's uniform, why not a Russian uniform? It's a Russian camp."

"Where were you at the briefings, Wick?" Chief Puckins scolded. "Cinders of hell, from here on out we're Chinese to the rest of the world, *remember that*. The sub's Chinese, the kayaks are Chinese, the weapons are Chinese, the skis are Chinese, and the sledge is Chinese. Folks around you? They're a crack advance force of China's People's Liberation Army."

The Texan had a point to make and he was not going to let up. "What did I ever teach you? Didn't you catch the Chinese markings those Korean submarine fellows had painted on their boat when we boarded in Chinhae? Russkis are gonna think it's made of grade-A fine porcelain.

"Now mind me, if I hear you thinkin', there'd better be Chinese subtitles on your thoughts or you're on report. Why, if you break out any rations, you'd better finish up the meal with an almond cookie and a wise saying."

"Just throwing a little confusion in the game," I added. "If we're detected or pursued, I want the Russians to be worried about some larger movement by the Chinese and not devote all their energy to us and some insignificant corrective labor camp. We're a little over four hundred miles from the Chinese border in a sparsely populated corner of the USSR. I want them to wonder if half a dozen Chinese divisions haven't infiltrated through their back door. Also, it'll confuse them as to our ultimate destination on the way out."

"If we get out," added Chamonix.

"We are not having radios," Gurung interposed. "Is that being for the same reason?"

I turned to the steadfast Gurkha.

"No, too high a risk of RDF intercept. Russian radio direction-finding equipment is quite good, and in any event, for most of the mission there won't be anyone to call for help."

I didn't add the second reason. I didn't want our turncoat to be able to communicate with his sponsors, or to be able to trigger RDF triangulation.

Puckins hummed "White Christmas" and whirled like a Fifth Avenue model showing his new uniform with the jacket open, then closed, with and without gloves. This was the Puckins I remembered. In Japan and Korea, he had appeared distracted and lifeless, but since leaving the submarine he had reverted to form.

"What about our chances of detection?" Alvarez questioned, watching Puckins's fashion show. He was forever filing information for future use.

"With luck, we should make it to the camp. There are fewer people per square mile here than at the same latitude in British Columbia. Siberia's lack of settlers was the reason for establishing the camps here in the first place. It's not the sort of climate that encourages people to be outdoors noticing strangers or following unexplained tracks very far without good reason. Survival out here is enough of a struggle to discourage idle curiosity. We'll just have to keep a lookout for trappers and herdsmen.

"As a small unit, camouflaged, and making the best of available cover, we should do all right. The wind will drift over our tracks in the open areas and the trees will hide them in the thickly foliated areas. Ivan may have a dogsled patrol like Greenland had during the Second World War, but I doubt it. He isn't on a wartime basis, not way out here. I'd say our chances are respectable, but don't hold me to it."

The North Star was too high in the sky to use for bearings, so I had to rely on Ursa Major, or Cassiopeia, or Deneb, and selected times to find North. Taking out my barometer/altimeter, I checked the reading. The Dzhugdzhur Range paralleled the coast. As long as we were gradually gaining altitude, we could not be too far off. About eighty miles from the coast, before we reached the crust of the range, we should stumble on a railroad spur. The spur worked northward from the main trunk of the Trans Siberian Railway and terminated at the camp; If we reached the summit of the range first, we were too far north.

We shouldered our packs and donned our skis. Movement was slower than I had anticipated. The kayak voyage and ice portage had worn us down. Alvarez and Kruger broke trail while Puckins and Chamonix strained in the *ahkio* harnesses. We had fastened the two sleds together like a giant oyster. Though the fused container held the recoilless rifle, much of our ammunition, and the tents, it was relatively light. These remaining four skiers traded positions with these men at regular intervals.

About an hour before sunrise we stopped and pitched the Norwegian tents. Within each two-man tent, each pair fashioned a cold well and sleeping benches above it so that they would not be sleeping in the lowest, and therefore coldest, portion of the tent. Stripping down to his Norwegian-made polypropylene underwear, each skier brushed down his boots and outer clothing, then stuffed them into the foot of his sleeping bag in a waterproof bag. Then from his sleeping bag, one member of the pair boiled water for the freeze-dried food under the tent's outer fly. A single slow-burning candle combined with the pair's body warmth to keep the inside of the tent relatively warm, but hardly comfortable. It was an unwieldy, time-consuming way to camp on a long-range patrol, but in cold-weather operations, eighty percent of your energy went to survival, fifteen percent to military activities, and five percent to fighting.

My thermometer read fifteen below zero. When I awoke, a fine coating of frozen condensation covered the inner ridge of the tent.

The next night we moved with better speed through the rolling, rising taiga. Our file looked like a long green-and-white caterpillar with piston legs as it threaded its parallel tracks through the widely spaced trees. Kick, slide, kick, slide. Packs clung to backs and pounded at kidneys. Our weapons, never designed for ski troops, were heavy and awkward. Periodically we stopped to check the stars and melt snow.

"What is that white concoction?" Gurung asked, watching Wickersham wiping a lotion into his face and hands.

"Cold cream," Wickersham quipped.

Kruger shifted his weight from foot to foot and clapped his hands against his sides. The cold was worse when we stopped. "I don't s-s-see where it makes *you* look any better."

"Oh yeah? Well, you saw what happened to the movie lady in Shangri-la, didn't you? Well, it just so happens I have a limited supply available. . . ."

"You have any vanishing cream?" Alvarez chimed in sardonically. The big Cuban was not about to let any of Wickersham's pranks get past him. "That would sure make this jaunt a lot easier. Invisible raiders, yeah . . . 'Stealth' ski troopers."

"Nope. Chief Puckins handles vanishin' and materializin'. Different department altogether."

The cold, dry air stung bitterly. Occasionally the wind swept down the valleys with such intensity that we had to wear suede face masks for protection. Once, when we were caught in a full-blown williwaw, we had to turn our faces away from the wind and seek whatever windbreaks we could find. Kick, slide, kick, slide.

As the second dawn approached, I estimated we had covered nearly thirty miles as the crow flies—ten in the first night, twenty during the second. Unfortunately, we could not ski as the crow flew because the increasing gradient often forced us to traverse slopes.

Even if the gradient had permitted, it was unwise to travel too long in a straight line. Since you couldn't cover your tracks you had to hope they'd drift over, but often they didn't. Each night before bivouacking, we left tracks in an ever-diminishing coil—resembling a watch spring—with the campsite at the center. In this way, we could hear pursuing trackers as they traipsed around us. At this point in our journey it was too demanding a drain on our manpower to post sentries. Half the group would be dead on their feet the next morning. Instead, we relied on our mobility and camouflage to protect us. As a further safeguard, Gurung strung alarm trip wires around the camp—high enough so animals wouldn't trip them, low enough so humans would.

I realized we would soon have to change from night to day travel. The terrain was growing more rugged and we were hitting stretches of black taiga—thick expanses of fir and spruce, which made hauling the *ahkio* a nightmare. Secondly, cloud cover was creeping in from the west and would soon obscure the stars. Soon I would be forced to navigate by terrain features and my sun compass alone. Clouds did not hamper its value, but it required daylight.

Fatigue began to show in the men's faces. No matter how well you prepared your tent and sleeping gear, you were never quite warm. Every time you shifted position in your sleeping bag, it took five minutes to get warm enough to sleep again. No one slept soundly and a heightened sense of survival stirred you awake at the snap of a frozen twig. Cooking was a miserable cycle of fumblings. First taking your mittens off to adjust something, then hurriedly jamming the same mittens on to numbed fingers in the futile hope of getting them warm again. Yet though cooking was torture, not cooking—and thereby forfeiting the fuel that kept you warm and moving—meant disaster.

The psychological strain was telling, too. Bundled in innumerable layers of hooded clothing, you found it easy to withdraw into yourself. It was called going "into the cocoon." Though the hood brought warmth, it restricted your hearing and field of vision. Your thinking became sluggish and you were soon oblivious to all. When an entire group entered their individual cocoons, lethargy gained the upper hand and carelessness set in.

I decided to stop though we had only covered fifteen miles. Over the past hours, as each pair had taken the *ahkio*, their irritations erupted into hushed arguments, and those arguments generated wasted heat. It was time for a rest. I noted the temperature was thirty degrees below zero and the barometer steady.

I awoke at midday, bundled up, and left the tent to relieve myself. This routine function was always one of the most traumatic chores of cold-weather travel. When my urine sizzled as it hit the snow I knew something was wrong. I checked my thermometer again. It read fifty degrees below zero.

"Pass the word to the others," I called to Wickersham and Gurung's tent. "We're not traveling until the temperature goes up. It's fifty below. Not safe to move." Chamonix rolled over in his sleeping bag and muttered some elegant French profanity. The sun played lightly on the side of the tent—very lightly.

Chamonix boiled water for the rations over the small stove. In the next tent Puckins was doing sleight-of-hand tricks for Gurung. Gurung gave amused yelps.

The ascetic old legionnaire whistled tunelessly. For the first time since I had known him, the muscles at the ends of his mouth had unconsciously bunched upward. My curiosity was aroused.

"Why all the radiant good cheer? Fifty below doesn't usually hit people that way."

Torn from his thoughts, he looked up at me puzzled. "I don't know. Perhaps it's we're out here—free of them. Free of noncombatants who retain us, and more often than not, betray us. No one's really free of them, I guess, but at least out here I can cultivate the illusion. Yes, for the moment I'm free of their fickle hypocrisy, and among warriors whose codes are simple, often constant."

Chamonix poured the hot water into the ration wrapper and stirred it into the freeze-dried contents. The aroma of pork and rice filled the tent. He remained quiet for a time but I sensed he wasn't through.

"It's more than that. Funny, no? How some things can set you thinking. This useless little burner reminds me of my wife and Algeria."

"Wife? I didn't know you had a wife." I knew very little about his private life. He'd revealed only the barest minimum of personal background to apply for the assignment.

"A wife and child, both dead."

He became silent again. I knew not to prod him.

"She used to cook over a small burner for me, not a gas one, though. She was Moslem, you know. Very pretty . . . big, liquid brown eyes. The French army discouraged such marriages, especially when officers were involved. Our marriage was totally against regulations, but my colonel understood. Unlike many, he knew you can't fight for long in a country without becoming involved with it. 'You can do far worse in La Légion,' he used to say."

He handed me the steaming ration.

"It had all started after I had graduated from St. Cyr and requested posting to the First Foreign Parachute Regiment in Algeria. Rumor had it they were fighters and knew something about this new phenomenon, guerrilla warfare.

"The rumor was right on both counts. Many of the legion's paratroop officers were Indochina veterans who, as prisoners of war, had been indoctrinated in Viet Minh ways. They had abandoned the quantitative approach of the rear-echelon generals to warfare. That view was that any insurrection could be stopped by pouring immense numbers of men and munitions over a problem. These Indochina vets had formulated a new doctrine, *la guerre révolutionnaire*. That doctrine worked by offering a revolution of its own.

"You must see the stage on which this drama was played. Sector Q of Algeria—where I was stationed—contained several small towns, numerous vineyards, and many cork plantations. Beneath the lazy Mediterranean sun, Moslems cut settlers' throats, and settlers cut Moslems' throats. Yet in reality, each group needed the other. Corruption riddled many local governments, more perhaps than usual for metropolitan France, less than usual for North Africa. Algeria was something worth saving. It had grown productive through the settlers' efforts since the nineteenth century. The Moslems had demonstrated a belief in common ideals with France and proven their courage and loyalty alongside French troops in World War One and World War Two.

"The fellaghas, the communist-backed insurgents of the FLN, promised a new order—one perfect and glorious order. This new order would redistribute wealth, integrate the society, and put incorruptible men in power. The points that the fellaghas made were valid, their promises knowing lies. But it was a wonderful banner to fight under, this dream.

"Enough of politics," said the legionnaire, dismissing the concepts with a flick of his mitten.

"You can't fight a dream with the tarnished status quo. *La guerre révolutionnaire* offered a revolution of its own, which aimed to set straight the wrongs of old Algeria. We recruited from the captured fellaghas. *They* were the fighters and idealists. Many fellaghas weren't interested in communism, just a new Algeria with political rights equal to Frenchmen. I recruited a Moslem commando company. It wasn't easy to win them over but I did. We did.

"'Put your faith in me, lads,' I promised them wholeheartedly. 'I won't leave you in the lurch. I'll shed my blood right along with yours. Together we will fight for one country from Dunkirk to Tamanrasset. I give you my word.'

"The Moslem commando company worked far more effectively than our troops did. After all, it was their home ground. Hassim, their elected commanding officer, grew from a comrade in arms to a brother. Lean, with the chiseled features of a born leader, he had studied to be a doctor before the FLN had sent him to Prague for training. We spent months in the field setting ambushes in the wadis for FLN *kattibas*—companies—and fending FLN bullyboy tax collectors from the small settlements. Through Hassim I met and eventually married, with his blessing, Fatima, his sister.

"My colonel managed to clean up the governmental corruption in the sector. Settlers and wealthy Arabs alike had been lining their pockets at Algeria's expense. Hassim and I attended to the fellaghas. Within three months, FLN activity had become a mere trickle where it had been a torrent.

"My daughter, Odette Aicha, was born at the end of my first year in Sector Q."

He looked up at the top of the tent. I knew the light well-being had gone from Chamonix as quickly as it had come.

"The FLN, which had always spiced its dream with terrorism, turned to it full scale. The carnage sickened my most hardened NCOs. It was a sort of tantrum, I guess. They couldn't win by vote or military action so they showed they'd be grisly spoilers of anyone else's dream. A tantrum can wear some people into submission, too.

"They'd go into cafés with machine guns and mow down everyone—Europeans, Arabs, anyone, it didn't matter. Fatima and baby Odette were in an outdoor café one day. Cafés were an Algerian institution, everyone patronized them. Fatima was sipping mint tea one moment, she and the baby were bloody lumps of meat the next."

He gave a short sob, then regained control.

"I could have understood, though not justified, it being some perverse form of revenge against me. But it wasn't revenge. They were just people in a café. Hassim and I hunted down these particular FLN terrorists ourselves. After capture, they laughed at our revulsion at their act. 'That is the way to win, Frenchmen, in these times,' one had said. Hassim had them executed fellagha fashion. They died very painfully, very slowly. I felt no remorse; the punishment fit the crime.

"The terrorists were right. *La guerre révolutionnaire* required the courage and insight of those in Algeria, and the resigned conviction of those at home. My country betrayed me and the Moslems that believed in me. All I could ever promise the Moslem company was that the French army would fight until a conclusive victory . . . or defeat. But self-indulgent France did not have the resolve of its soldiers. France, I learned, talked high principles and sought the luxury of world adulation. It was willing to conduct crusades as long as they didn't prove too inconvenient. Terrorism put the soldier's burden of courage on all civilians—and worse, it threatened to spread to France. In other words, France could be high minded as long as the going didn't get too distasteful. Sordid situations required emotional commitments. The average Frenchman didn't want the front page of his evening paper upsetting his digestion. Crusades were fine at a distance, but all-consuming conflicts were a bother.

"Eventually the French government caved in and virtually offered to hand Algeria over to the FLN—not the loyal Moslems who had stood by us—the FLN whose mindless terrorism had been decried throughout the world.

"The Moslem commando company deserted to a man. That day I found Hassim staked to a cork tree with bayonets. He cursed me with his dying breath. Painted in blood across his chest was the message: 'This is what happens to fools who trust the two-faced Europeans.'

"I couldn't begrudge the company. 'Trust me,' I had told them. 'Trust me.' But the country behind me had said, 'Well, so long, have to be going now. Take care.'

"My regiment, the Premier Regiment Etranger Parachutiste did the honorable thing. It mutinied. Now it is no more—sort of institutional suicide on the grand scale. Matsuma would understand. As for me, I resigned my commission.

"In subsequent years, I have served as *un mercenaire* with the Sixth Commando of Katanga and for many other causes, but never as an officer. I lost any right to be an officer when as a stupid patriotic junior officer I asked to be trusted and couldn't be trusted. I am now Sergeant d'Epinuriaux. As *un mercenaire* I put my faith in no one but my comrades and gauge the sincerity of a cause by the money they'll pay. And when they betray me it will be with a bullet, not sweet-tasting poison in my mint tea."

His face flushed.

"I have had my fill of clever-tongued types who can find grand reasons to begin fighting for a cause and as quickly gather splendid reasons to abandon it.

"All we have here are ourselves, and I'm glad of it."

The steam rose from his ration and curled defiantly around him.

The temperature climbed slowly through the day and next night until by the following morning it was safe to travel. Clouds seized more and more of the available sky. We glided on. Kick, slide.

The gradient, too, was increasing and we were compelled to traverse more often. Finally I had each man affix mohair climbers to the bottom of his skis. Surprisingly, we were covering ground quickly now.

About midday I spotted a musk deer trotting along parallel to us. Perhaps curiosity had overcome its fear of these clumsy green-and-white walking bundles. As my eye followed him, it caught an irregularity. I pulled my binoculars from my jacket.

"Matsuma, have a look. What do you make of that?"

He focused them on a frozen river and then scanned left and right. "Dogsled tracks, a day or two old. Probably Evenki. But maybe we should keep away from them, just the same."

As if this new development weren't enough, a disturbing new thought plagued me. Since we'd left the submarine, there hadn't been a single act of treachery. We'd lost Lutjens and left Dravit. Could Dravit have been the turncoat? The thought stuck in my mind and put a hollow feeling in my chest. There was no man on earth I trusted more than Dravit. We'd been through much together. But hadn't every man his price? He wasn't getting any younger and it was time to think of retirement. It would be easy. Dravit was our representative on the submarine. On his say-so they could abandon us with a clear conscience. A large part of our fate rested in his hands.

No, it was all wrong. Men like Dravit never thought of retirement. They slipped into it unconsciously or went out in a blaze of glory. I mulled the situation over and over in my mind. If the little Englishman left us to die, was there any point in fighting it? No, that was wrong, too; the cold must be warping my mind. I wanted to live, to survive. Yet if we did live, and Dravit had betrayed us, life would be marred by one very large void.

We made good progress during the next day, too. All indications were that we were very close to the camp. We seemed beyond exhaustion now, but had to keep moving. The *ahkio* drained away our strength, but we could not afford to abandon it or its contents. With the closing proximity of the camp, I reminded the point men and rear security people to stay alert.

During one water stop, Puckins deftly pulled a rubber ball from Alvarez's ear, causing Gurung to laugh uproariously. Puckins had been working on the trick since we'd left the kayaks. Gurung had seen it many times before. Still it was a tough stunt to do with shooting mittens on. Chamonix was clapping his hands together to maintain the circulation when Puckins snatched a sponge cube from the Frenchman's hawklike nose.

"Enough," Chamonix barked with mock severity as he motioned everyone up off their packs.

"March or die," he growled in parody of the well-known legion order. He skied off whistling "*Je Ne Regrette Rien*" in wavering notes, which mimicked Piaf's mournful rendition. A significantly haunting tune to hear from one of the Premier Regiment Etranger Parachutiste, it generally foreshadowed bloodletting with a vengeance.

By now fatigue and stress had made everyone giddy. It was our fifth day of sub-zero weather.

CHAPTER 22

The railroad line cut through the tree-covered contours like a child's finger through cake icing. The absence of drifts over the individual rails meant a train had been by recently. I dead-reckoned we were somewhere southwest of the camp. We paralleled the tracks, staying behind the tree line until twilight, then pitched camp. I didn't want to stumble onto the camp in the dark.

At about noon of the sixth day, we found the camp in a broad open valley ringed by spruce-covered ridges. Caution required that we study the camp's routine for at least a full day. The size of the garrison necessitated a night attack. Since it was already noon, that meant we should reconnoiter the camp for the rest of the day and attack during the evening of the following day. We burrowed well back into the tree line and in pairs took turns watching the camp through binoculars.

The camp had been erected in the shape of a large isosceles triangle, with its base parallel to the railroad line. On the opposite side of the line lay large pyramids of logs. Between the camp and the logs, the line split into two spurs. A string of half-loaded flatcars, together with a wood-burning locomotive, rested on the outer spur. The sides of the triangle stretched roughly 250 yards on each side and 150 yards at the base. The triangle had been truncated with internal fences into three bandlike sections. An empty parade ground, scarred by half-track treadmarks formed the base section. Four prison barracks, a mess hall, and some other buildings composed the waist section. We had no trouble identifying each of the commandant's, officers', and guards' quarters in the apex section. A magazine; the radio shack; its electrical generator; and a tall, well-maintained antenna were also located in the apex section.

Near dusk, four gangs of prisoners marched out of the taiga toward the camp. "March" was the charitable term; they stumbled in unison before four half-track trucks. As we watched, a woman near the rear of one formation faltered and collapsed. The half-track behind her didn't swerve an inch. It continued on, leaving a red stamp at even intervals, from the spot where it had crushed her under its treads.

As the gangs approached the railroad gate, they began to stumble for lead position. Intuitively I knew that the first gang through the gate ate first, and the last gang through ate last . . . what was left. Like scarecrows trying to fly, they seemed to gain speed by flapping the black rags that covered them. Many dropped out of formation, lacking the energy to continue the race. One man from one gang was the first to reach the gate, barely cutting off a second gang. Two gray-coated VOKhk guards beat back the second gang, swinging their rifles like clubs. At the inner gate, one at a time, the prisoners were searched by two more VOKhk guards. Then they were allowed to enter the section that contained the prison barracks and mess hall. My breath kept fogging up the binoculars. After dark, I switched to the Starlight sniper scope. The scope didn't work at first so I had to rush back to our bivouac to warm up the batteries while Alvarez covered for me with the binoculars. Using the scope, I studied the three sentry towers at the corners of the camp and recorded significant movement within the camp. Each relieving pair did the same. I noted there were lights on the perimeter but the towers stayed dark.

Reveille for the camp came about two hours before dawn. Men lined up at the mess hall and at another building, which must have been the sick bay. Apparently if a *zek* claimed to be sick, he lost his chance to eat. Then the men lined up at the inner gate and were frisked as they entered the parade ground. Any extra clothing was confiscated and the *zek* had to strip it off right there in the fifteen-below open air. When concealed food was discovered, it was ground beneath a guard's boot.

"Look at that." Wickersham, who shared my watch, pointed to the gate. Something shiny glittered in the snow near a prisoner held by two guards. A sergeant with three yellow stripes across his sky blue shoulder boards was lashing the *zek* across the face with a quirt.

"Must have tried to smuggle a knife out with him," Wickersham offered as he watched the scene intently.

The VOKhk sergeant was built like a beer barrel. He had to look up at the prisoner—until after the savage, methodical working-over, the prisoner sagged to the ground. Another guard, a major, walked over to the squat sergeant. At first I thought he was going to put a stop to it, but he just put his hands on his hips and watched. When the prisoner passed out, the major had two other prisoners carry the unconscious *zek* to a building within the triangular apex section of the camp. It was probably the punishment block or "cooler."

Wickersham watched the beer-barrel sergeant strut away. "Fellow sure likes his work. I think he's got it in for that work gang now."

Then, as if to prove his words, six of the guards hustled back to the guardroom and came out with crowbars. They walked to one barracks and pried out the window frames. The effect on the gang was visible. They slumped dejectedly. No windows on a barracks in sub-zero weather was a virtual death sentence.

Wickersham shook his head. He pointed to the punishment block. "That may be the cooler"—he swung his quivering mitten toward the windowless barracks—"but it'll be no cooler than that one."

It was a play on words, but no joke.

I sketched the camp with a ski pole in the snow. "That's the camp generator. That, we think, is the camp magazine. That building is the guardroom and guards' quarters. Does everyone understand what he has to do?"

Each man nodded as I caught his eye. Matsuma had a distant look. I guessed he was meditating his way through some samurai purification ritual on his feet.

"Matsuma, let's keep a clear head through this. Your responsibilities to the living of this group take precedence over revenge for the dead."

"I will do duty to all." He bowed his head slightly.

I studied the camp through the Starlight scope, carefully avoiding the perimeter lights, whose brightness could burn out the scope's delicate sensors. The whole valley seemed agonizingly still. Occasionally the moon poked through the clouds, but its effect was fleeting. Once or twice a door slammed in the officers' quarters or the guardroom. The valley was so quiet that each door slam seemed only yards away.

Puckins and Gurung crawled down to the barbed-wire fence. They advanced, sliding their skis under them, with their hands in the toe straps and their rifles around their necks. Puckins cut the lower five strands between two posts on the apex section's perimeter. He left the top electrified strands alone. Puckins's cut breached an opening about four feet wide and three and one half feet high. He then cut through the second perimeter fence. He bowed with a flourish, gestured Gurung through, and then handed him the wire cutters.

As with most penal institutions, this one had been designed with the primary aim of keeping certain people in, rather than keeping others out. The camp's officers had mimicked the camp's design in setting their priorities. As ordered, the three sentries sat inert in their towers wearing heavy sheepskin coats. With their rope ladders drawn up into their tower crow's nest, they focused their attention on the prisoners' barracks, occasionally standing to stretch their legs, clap their hands, or adjust the tiny wood stove, which seemed to add little to their comfort. Most of the time they sat so still it was difficult to tell if they weren't dozing.

Gurung had to cut through two additional fences, but he was the first to reach his designated tower. I saw his *kukri* flash from its scabbard as he left his skis behind and began to feel his way up the tower struts. Puckins reached his tower seconds later. He ascended quickly, pulling himself up hand over hand, letting his legs hang slack. When he reached the sentry's platform, he drew a length of wire, with toggles at either end, from his coat. A quick flick of the looped garrot and the sentry was clawing at his neck. In a minute the struggle was over. Puckins pushed the body aside and, unslinging the Dragunov, covered the third sentry on the far side of the camp carefully gauging windage and elevation.

Gurung was having a difficult time. He had barely had time to swing under his sentry's platform when that sentry had stood up to load more wood into his stove. When the sentry sat down again, Gurung waited. Then in a rapid succession of movements he was at the railing, then slashing his *kukri* toward the back of the sentry's neck. At this moment the sentry chose to stand up again. The razor-sharp *kukri* slashed through several layers of clothing into the sentry's back. The sentry screamed and fumbled for his rifle. The scream echoed through the valley—then stopped abruptly with Gurung's second stroke.

The third sentry on the far side of the camp stood up and took aim. A cracking report shattered the valley's peace for a second time. In the far corner, the sentry dropped his rifle, pitched forward, and toppled to the snow beneath his tower like a broken gray doll.

Puckins raised the barrel of the Dragunov, satisfied with his shot.

CHAPTER 23

"Stand by."

From their position on top of the ridge, Chamonix and Alvarez fired an armor-piercing round from the recoilless rifle into the mobile generator. The generator supplied power for the radio shack and most of the camp. The distant whine of the generator stopped with a resounding thump and a shower of sparks. Chunks of metal clattered against the side of the radio shack.

"Let's hit it . . . now!"

The rest of us pulled our suede face masks into place, patted our body-armor vests, and placed our ski tips parallel. I could hear shouting from the guards' barracks. The wind whistled under my fur ear flaps, knocking back my white hood as I made a few clumsy turns to keep my velocity under control until I shot through the gap in the fence. Moments later I was barreling through the breach. I could hear the hiss of six sets of skis behind me. I could hear snow being kicked aside as they, too, plunged through the two fences and across the camp yard. Someone fell behind me—in time with a rifle shot from the barracks—but was up before I dared to look back.

Several half-clothed guards—I thought I recognized the beer-barrel sergeant—were already out of their barracks' side door. I fired a fan of tracers from a crouch, never bothering to reduce speed. Chamonix and Alvarez, with the recoilless, took cover near the radio shack and took aim at the door of the snowdrift blister that was the magazine. The magazine erupted in a terrifying geyser of iridescent flame. That signaled the end of the garrison's hope for automatic weapons or additional ammo. I turned to watch the recoilless crew, only to see Alvarez stagger as blood gushed from his upper thighs below his body armor. Three more hits made him do a macabre soft-shoe before he collapsed, leaving a trail of bright red snow. His feet still moved, pushed, drove the body another yard, leaving a slushy, scarlet skid mark.

Shifting his position a few degrees, Chamonix waited for Alvarez to load the next round. He hadn't seen him go down. The next target was the guards' barracks.

The SKS fire from their barracks was withering. Wickersham, Matsuma, and I had to take shelter behind an ell of the cooler. Kruger, at another corner of the cooler, was covering the officers' quarters and had eliminated the watch-standers in the radio shack. I felt a round rip through the side of my quilted jacket, deflect off my body armor, and scrape hotly up the inside of my left arm. Wickersham was laying down automatic-weapons fire with the Type 67. Matsuma had disappeared.

Then he reappeared amid a cat's cradle of tracer streaks. He sprinted recklessly across the open area between the cooler and the guards' barracks. Halfway across, he took a hit, which knocked him over as if he'd been hit with an invisible I-beam. He'd been hit in his armor vest. Then he crawled to the corner of the barracks and began cutting down anyone who tried to leave the barracks. Seconds after, Wickersham and I rushed across, smashing the Type 67 through an already-shattered window. Wickersham began raking the inside of the barracks. Out of the corner of my eye I saw Chamonix dragging the recoilless and its ammo across to the far door of their long barracks. The building was propped up on blocks. I crawled under the gauntlet of windows to help him. I knew we were also taking ragged fire from the officers' quarters, and I could see gray uniforms working around back of the cooler toward the half-tracks.

I jammed a canister round into the recoilless. Canister was the descendant of grapeshot and had the same devastating effect. Chamonix fired through a window. The back blast created a great cloud of snow. I loaded a canister again. Chamonix fired. He was talking but I could no longer hear anything. The roar of the blasts had been too loud. I loaded again and he fired. He turned and said something but it sounded as if he were talking through a calliope. I began to load again but he tapped my arm and shook his head no.

I kicked open the door. The inside glowed brightly. A stove had fallen over and several bunks had caught fire. The place was a slaughterhouse. Grisly chunks of body and bone were smeared everywhere. I tripped over an ownerless boot. In one corner of the barracks I thought I saw something move and aimed to fire. A body tumbled to one side and a woman who had been beneath it rose calmly. She was naked and unmarked. Hard, dark circles had been etched beneath her eyes. I could tell she had been pretty a long time ago—a ballerina, perhaps. She kicked aside the body violently and reached for her prison clothes, which lay in a mound nearby. She looked Chamonix and me up and down with bitter defiance. Who were these grisly specters; masked, cloaked in deathly white, and splattered with blood? New jailers? Probably.

Chamonix found two other women weeping in a concrete-walled shower room. They'd all learned how to survive in this camp long before we arrived.

Outside, small-arms fire peppered from the cooler. Several officers in a rush for the half-tracks had been unable to make it past the cooler. So they had dug in. A few bodies sprawled in the snow outside the officers' quarters. Puckins and Gurung had picked them off from their eyries. No more than four or five officers could have made it as far as the cooler.

A guard using two *zeks* as human shields moved out of the shelter of the cooler in the direction of the half-tracks. It was the beer-barrel sergeant. With his free hand he wrenched the prisoners between him and the guards' barracks. Seconds later he flopped forward, leaving the two *zeks* bewildered. Puckins had, from on high, plinked the beer-barrel sergeant off with a single round. The *zeks* hesitated, then scurried out the gate into one of their barracks.

Wickersham, Kruger, and Matsuma had the Type 67 inside the guards' barracks now and were considering whether to place it out a window or on the roof.

"Can't return fire on the cooler. Might hit a prisoner," someone said.

Kruger fell forward with a dark blue hole in his forehead. We ducked instinctively.

"Don't bother. Just keep the fire aimed up over the cooler until Gurung and Puckins can work up behind the bastards." Puckins and Gurung had already left the towers and were making a wide circle behind the barracks.

"They've stopped firing," said Wickersham warily.

Three VOKhk officers in *gymnasterka* tunics hung out the cooler windows by their heels. Each had a prison spoon handle thrust deep below the corner of his jaw. All were decidedly dead. The *zeks* had settled old scores.

Two shadows raced out the inner fence gate toward the half-tracks.

"The recoilless," I yelled. Matsuma and Chamonix grabbed the weapon and its ammo. Putting on our skis, we flashed through the gate. One VOKhk guard worked frantically to bring an RPK machine gun mounted in the half-track to bear, as the other started the engine. Chamonix kneeled and Matsuma loaded. The half-track blossomed into flame and the two guards—what was left of them—slumped forward, burning like candles.

Other than the ringing in my ears it was very quiet.

"Shall we," Chamonix bellowed into my deafened ear, "attend to the liberation."

"Look what we found."

Gurung and Chief Puckins herded five Russian guards in front of them—the only survivors. I didn't like the look in Matsuma's eye. *Giri* again.

"Matsuma, gather up the four gang bosses and invite them to the commandant's quarters. It's time for that briefing you've prepared. Tell the other prisoners not to start running off on their own—we're going to help them with an organized escape."

It was better to keep Matsuma busy. The Japanese say that with some debts of honor one can only begin to pay one one-thousandth of the debt. I didn't want him reducing the fraction's denominator.

Matsuma turned to a group of prisoners standing uneasily on a barracks' stoop. Their features were a map of the Soviet Union—Yakut, Kazakh, Uzbek, Belorussian, Armenian, Ukrainian, Russian. One Mongolian girl reminded me of Keiko. Ivan bestowed his favors with equanimity. The USSR is an equal-opportunity oppressor.

"We come as friends . . . ," he began.

I turned to Puckins. "Lock them up in the cooler. Some of their friends should be by to release them shortly. Then take some of the C-4 and blow out the insides of the radio shack after you pull those items we need. That way Ivan won't realize what's missing.

"One other thing, Chief. Have someone smash the radios in the half-tracks. Then have Gurung and Wickersham gather up any ammo they can find. We may need it."

"Right, sir."

He returned in half an hour.

"Here they are, the crypto assembly and the code books." He held out several looseleaf binders and a mass of electronic circuitry about the size of a typewriter. "The charges are set."

"Good. Very good."

The radio shack erupted in fiery splinters, shattering the false dawn. Tiny bits of knobs, wires, and metal plate hummed down around us. What was left of it burned in indifferent competition with the guards' barracks/pyre. Prisoners, in a festive mood, milled about the two bonfires. In Siberia, holidays were where you found them.

CHAPTER 24

"Who are you?"

The four gang bosses sat in the center of the commandant's office. We stood along its sides. Light flickered from a kerosene lantern onto the commandant's well-appointed oak desk. Matsuma and Gurung stood in front of them without their exposure masks.

Matsuma pealed off his white overblouse to reveal a green quilted jacket with red collar flashes but devoid of insignia. He moved stiffly. I guessed the hit to the body armor had broken a rib or two. "We are soldiers of the People's Republic of China. We are liberating all the concentration camps of the Russian imperialists in this area and seizing the Trans Siberian Railway."

"Are we your captives?" asked an Armenian gang boss with a heavy beard.

"By no means. We have admired the courage of you who have challenged the Kremlin adventurists. You are free to go. In fact, that is why we have asked you here. One gang will divide up the camp's food and supplies into four equal parts. Then, by lot, the other gangs will be allowed to choose which quarter they want. It will be up to each gang boss to parcel up the supplies among his individual gang members.

You should take the three remaining half-tracks and the train. That'll give you a head start. Head in different directions for about half a day, then abandon them and split up. We figure a VOKhk relief detachment will get here by rail within twenty-four hours."

A straw-haired old boss with deep-sunken eyes stood up. "Can you help us get into China?"

"No," Matsuma stated firmly. "We have liberated you, that is all we can do. Escape for us, in the event our army does not succeed, will be difficult enough."

"How can we possibly survive?"

"I don't know. All I can say is winter is nearly over and this is a large, sparsely settled region. With the guards' portion added in, you're going to have more food than you would have had otherwise. Anyone who wishes can of course stay in the camp until the raid has been discovered and the new guards arrive."

"Not bloody likely," another gang boss said, then spit for emphasis. It left a dark spot on the commandant's Persian rug.

"They don't look very Chinese to me. Some of these men are too big, even for northern Chinese," a short gang boss with Mongolian features and no teeth said, pointing to Chamonix and Wickersham, "and why are they still wearing masks?"

Matsuma looked to me.

"Tell them we freedom fighters of the People's Republic do not observe class or race distinctions. Ours is an international struggle." I said to Matsuma in Japanese. He translated.

They guffawed.

"And it is in your self-interest for us to be Chinese. If we are Chinese, the Kremlin must order a border-long mobilization. If any *zek* reveals to anyone we are not, then the Kremlin can concentrate all its resources into catching us and recapturing you. Convince your *zek* gangs that we are all dog-eating Chinamen and be content. There is an ancient Chinese proverb: 'Don't look a gift horse in the mouth.'"

They nodded understanding.

"One more thing," I said. "Where is Special Prisoner Seven Thirty-four? . . . Vyshinsky?"

"That goner? He's in sick bay."

*   *   *

The old man raised himself up on his elbows. There was no color in his drawn features and his eyes were rheumy. *Those pallbearer's eyes.*

"You're from Kurganov, aren't you?" he started timidly. "I've been expecting you."

Only a few *zeks* remained in the sick bay. Most of the ailing had been carried to the half-tracks by their friends. Outside I could hear the bustling of prisoners dividing up the supplies.

"Yes . . . how did you know?"

"Myshka. Myshka told me."

It was clear he felt uncomfortable with direct communication. His life had been built around double meanings and oblique references.

"Myshka told you? Here?"

"A queer twist of fate brought him here—just a few weeks ago. We were in the same work gang. He died here . . . just a few weeks ago."

Vyshinsky fell back onto his cot. His breathing was heavy and erratic. He couldn't have lasted much longer here.

"He told me Kurganov had considered rescuing me. The young man said it was a useless hope. He hadn't had time to obtain some special information there in Moscow for you people outside."

Vyshinsky's voice had a mournful, wheezing quality to it. "He wasn't made to survive in these camps—too dreamy, too proud. He was a poet, you know. Funny how those literary ones are—either they're like Kurganov and survive forever, or they're like Myshka and get their brains kicked out in a matter of weeks."

He coughed and his pipe-cleaner body shook uncontrollably.

"All right, let's get you bundled up for transport. You're going on a sleigh ride."

"*Troika*?" he said with a frail smirk.

"*Ahkio.* Not as enjoyable by half."

Wickersham lifted Vyshinsky from the cot effortlessly.

By midmorning we were ready to evacuate the camp. There was enough talent among the *zeks* to drive the train and the half-tracks. Probably enough to drive a space shuttle.

The riders of one half-track had broken into the commandant's liquor supply and were passing a bottle around. They sang bittersweet Russian folksongs in a haunting harmony.

A wizened old Ukrainian whirled through one of those Slavic dances, where the dancer alternately squats and kicks with his arms crossed, on the bed of the vehicle. He whirled and kicked, and kicked and whirled like some sad and marvelous mechanical toy. The old *zek* drew from some invisible source of energy.

As a group they were no worse off than before. There was little else I could do. The decision to flee had been theirs. My inexpert opinion was that the majority would be dead within a month. In any event they would die free . . . with hope. Who really knew what their chances were? After all, it was their country.

Chamonix stepped forward and saluted. "All secured and ready for departure."

The gang bosses assumed Matsuma was in command of our party. Each walked up and gave him a hug. That was Lutjen's, Alvarez's, and Kruger's memorial. For three good unfaltering men there would be no other.

We skied east, avoiding our old trail. Clouds were building in the west at an alarming rate. The barometer had dropped, indicating an impending weather change. The temperature hovered at five degrees below. Kick, slide.

In the early afternoon, I heard the drone of a plane overhead. It was a troop transport with four propellers. Paratroops.

The plane flew to the camp a couple ridges behind us and circled twice. Then it spilled out a chain of parachutes. It took less than a minute to deploy one hundred Soviet paratroops. The paratroopers wore white camouflage uniforms similar to ours. Suspended from their harnesses were skis and equipment bags. Their 'chutes drifted lazily behind the last ridge.

I had assumed we would have more time to make our escape. I had also assumed that we would be pursued by prison guards rather then elite shock troops. Over the years Ivan had claimed to have invented many things. He truly did invent airborne military operations. Ivan has seven airborne divisions—Uncle Sam, one.

I called to Gurung in the point position, "Veer southeast, we'll try to intersect our old trail. Let's pick up the pace, under the circumstances a little sweat might be permissible. " It was a bad tactic to go out the same way you came in, but a broken trail would let us maintain our position relative to our pursuers. At present they had the advantage of following a trail we had broken. Well, we had a few tricks that would change that. I hoped that I was reading the sky right. We were in a race for time. Kick, slide.

Within an hour my binoculars picked up paratroopers on a distant ridge. They were fresh, and moving quickly. Within ninety minutes they'd be on us. In two hours it'd be dark.

I focused the lenses on one paratrooper. From the deference given him by the others it appeared he was an officer or NCO. His face showed clean-shaven and athletic features under his dome-shaped helmet. His features betrayed smoothness and arrogance, molded by the easy successes of garrison service, unweathered by the ravages of genuine conflict. He stopped and drew his field glasses from within his white jacket. Their lenses reflected light and suddenly I realized this smooth-faced officer was studying me as I had studied him. I slipped back into the trees.

We covered ground rapidly as we moved downward and seaward, but we still hadn't intersected our old trail. As they drew closer I counted about thirty men. So they had rated us a full third of their complement. The half-track trails they could understand, the ski and *ahkio* tracks must have mystified them. Once we reached a new ridge and began to climb, I gave the order to prepare to ambush. I sent Matsuma and Puckins on ahead. I had them ditch one *ahkio* and cram Vyshinsky and the recoilless into the other. We fanned out behind the ridge, took off our skis, and waited.

"Fire one magazine only, then rally at the *ahkio*. Wickersham, no more than fifty rounds with your 67."

"Couldn't fire much more than that if I wanted to. I'm nearly out of ammo." The firefight at the camp had consumed more ammo than expected.

"Make the rounds count."

We waited a long twenty minutes. Finally I could hear puffing and at a distance, the hushed talk of wary troops. Their point man skied right through us. He didn't stop until he noticed our tracks had divided. By that time Chamonix had drawn a bead on him with the sniper rifle. We placed our elbows on our skis and pushed the skis to the top of the ridge. Chamonix dropped their point man with a shot to the head, just below the helmet.

The paratroops were caught in the open, going uphill. Most immediately dropped into the soft snow and had difficulty bringing their weapons to bear from the prone position as their elbows sank in the white stuff. Others turned and skied back down the ridge. Their movement was slow, encumbered by the overequipage of conventional combat troops—shovels, gas masks, steel helmets, chemical-contamination musette bags. One-third to one-half of them went down in our volley. Of those, I hoped all were wounded. A wounded man in the cold needed someone to get him back to a medical station.

We pulled back and raced to catch the *ahkio*. These paratroops were elite but green. Their fire continued for a full ten minutes after we had stopped firing. It was a colossal waste of ammunition and time on their part. It gave us more space and left the Russians smarting. They would move more cautiously now and their next point man would be more alert.

We caught up with Matsuma, Puckins, and the *ahkio* just as they came upon our original trail. It was nearly dark.

"We're going to ditch all but one pack. Get rid of the tents, sleeping bags, armor vests. Save your candles, ammo, cooking gear, and half the food. Save only the clothing you can stash on you. We're going to be traveling for speed from here on out."

It was ten below zero and the barometer had plunged five millimeters. We crashed along at breakneck speed through the darkness, more than once losing the trail. After an hour or two I could hear the Russian paratroopers behind us again. They were getting their confidence back.

"Wickersham, break out the four ski booby traps. Gurung, cover him."

He set the first one in a ski rut where the trail entered a thicket of spruce. I was right; they were close on our tails. The booby trap detonated behind us not five minutes later.

"Again."

This time he placed one just outside a rut near a bend. Several skiers could pass it unnoticed but one man skiing randomly at the bend would trip it off. He placed a second not far from the first. It was where a Russian paratrooper, in moving the first casualty clear of the trail, would stand.

Once more a detonation shook the snow from the trees. A minute later another detonation followed the first.

"Wait awhile on this next one, it's going to have to get maximum mileage."

My throat was brick dry. We were sweating despite the ten-below-zero reading. At each stop my sweat cooled, making me shiver uncontrollably.

It was well past midnight before I could hear the Russians again. This time they were more difficult to hear. Our people were cursing under their breaths with every spill, and fatigue was making them clumsy.

"Put out the last one."

He laid it in a rut on a steep incline and covered it with snow. We schussed on. Five, ten, fifteen minutes passed . . . but no detonation.

"They must be breaking their own trail now," Wicker-sham whispered. "Why don't they call in air support?"

"Probably aren't sure where we are. They're probably waiting for daylight."

"What'll we do now?"

"Did you ditch that nylon utility line?"

"No."

"Good. I think I have a use for it soon." We felt worn and brittle from the cold. Every moment became an effort. Extremities began to numb with cold, ski poles banged stupidly against branches, skis clattered as tips came close to crossing.

"Leave me behind," Vyshinsky gasped to Chamonix. His sad eyes flared with intensity. "I'm only holding you up. Your men are spent. They can't keep this up in this cold."

"No," said Chamonix, not wishing to draw any further on his limited Russian vocabulary.

"I'm telling you leave me behind. I'm not worth all your lives." This was as direct a challenge as he'd made in his life.

"No, we need someone to keep the recoilless rifle warm."

Vyshinsky became quiet.

The trail ran close along a ledge. On the left the ridge ran straight up. On the right, seven feet over, it dropped off rapidly. The trail itself inclined downward at about thirty degrees.

"I knew this ledge was along here somewhere. Where's that nylon line? Here I'll take it."

I stretched the line from a tree at the base of the rise on the left, about five inches above the trail, to a tree that hung over the precipice. The line itself did not cross the trail perpendicularly, but at a forty-five-degree angle. The lowest end of the line was at the precipice. With momentum a skier would catch the line at ankle height and then slide sideways out of control—over the cliff. Not fatally, the drop wasn't that far, but enough to break that skier's leg . . . and put him out of action.

A full half hour later we heard an agonized scream that ended suddenly. At last we were putting distance between them and us. But it was only a few hours until dawn. I checked my thermometer. It read ten degrees above, the first above-zero reading in eight days.

"Snow, dammit, snow." Wickersham grumbled. "It's going to snow, I know it. Why can't it snow now?"

We were all waiting for the snow. The weather was giving all the right signs. If we could only run into a sheltering snowstorm. It would cover our tracks and hide us from aircraft.

"Okay, okay. All ahead flank, let's redline for the next half hour. It'll be dawn in another hour. If we can get a lead, and if it snows, we can shake those bastards."

Kick, slide. My polypropylene underwear was soaked with sweat. If we ever stopped for long it would freeze solid. SNOW DAMMIT. We were low on ammunition and that dwelled on my mind. We had traveled light from the very beginning and had now been in two firefights. Furthermore, we showed signs of the punchiness that meant extreme fatigue, and which adrenaline might not override. The *ahkio* was difficult to control down the steeper slopes, but we couldn't risk letting

Vyshinsky slide free. Everyone prayed for snow—track-concealing, aircraft-downing snow.

We had to get off our old trail. If it didn't snow, other paratroopers dropped ahead of us in the daylight would find it and work back. Going downhill at this pace we had covered four days ground in a day and a night. I fretted a half hour away without knowing it.

"All right, veer northeast. Break a new trail," I said to Matsuma ahead of me. He sent the word up.

"Which way is northeast?" was the reply back.

I skied up to Puckins. "That way, I think."

Not a star was visible through the cloud cover and it was too early for the sun compass. We began breaking a new trail as the sky lightened in the east.

The Russian squad slalomed down a slope to our left. They tumbled into firing positions mere yards from us. I sensed they were as surprised as we were. Apparently our pursuers had divided into two uneven squads, and this squad had been told to flank us from the north. They had expected us to be farther south—where we would have been, had we kept to our old trail.

Under the circumstances a retreat would have cost about the same as an assault. We assaulted. I cut down a tall Russian with a three-round burst and my weapon went silent, out of ammo. There were too many trees and we were too close for grenades. Still moving forward, I flicked the AK's bayonet up and drove it into another Russian paratrooper, all the way up to the muzzle. Everyone had kicked off his skis by now.

Out of the corner of my eye, I saw Puckins fall, red splashes covering his white overblouse. I felt light-headed.

A terrifying, ungodly screaming filled my ears.

The Russians must have been short of ammo, too, because within seconds all firing had stopped.

The screaming wouldn't stop. I thrust below another paratrooper's bayonet, I impaled and lifted his body off its feet, and flung it at another charging Russian. The charging Russian's bayonet stuck fast in his comrade as I pulled free. I smashed into his temple with a driving horizontal butt stroke.

Die, Frazer, die. You let them down. Two more Russians came at me from behind. I parried one's bayonet—not before it tore into my triceps. The other thrust at my face, knocking off my fur cap and searing my scalp with his blade as I ducked low. From a squat I swept away his knees with another butt stroke. Brittle from the cold, the rifle stock splintered apart in my hands.

Still the ghastly screaming continued. As I searched for another weapon, powerful arms began to choke me from behind. The hands tried to twist my neck enough to snap it. I crouched and dived at a tree. The tree hit the Russian with sufficient impact to loosen his grip. I turned and, grabbing the insides of his collar, started choking him. I hammered his head against the tree. Then he went limp. I looked at the big red stain around a small hole in his chest. It was the smooth-faced officer. He'd been dead before he'd throttled me, he just hadn't known it.

I looked around. Wickersham stood erect with his legs braced in the center of a pile of bodies. Chamonix swayed with a bloody shoulder. Matsuma was down on one knee wrapping some cloth around his thigh. I could not see Gurung. Then a Russian body rolled aside. Gurung lay flat on his back, soaked in his victim's blood. He rose stiffly, unsure of his balance.

The screaming had stopped. It had been mine.

CHAPTER 25

"Take a look at this." Chamonix held forward a brace of Russian ammo pouches with his good arm. "Only a quarter full. They must have lightened their equipment, too, but they jettisoned ammo. They must have been pretty confident, those heroes of the Soviet Union."

Puckins, barely conscious, sat propped against a tree. Several bullet holes had perforated his midsection. A stomach wound developed irreversible peritonitis if not attended by a surgeon promptly. We had no surgeon nor would we be able to get one in time. Moreover, we could not stop his bleeding. He only had hours to live. We knew it. Puckins knew it.

"Mister Frazer," he said. "I owe you, sir."

"Owe me? I owe you—if anyone owes anything to anybody."

"No, sir, you don't understand. I was partially responsible for those . . . those things. You know . . . the camera . . . the police bust . . . Captain Dravit's leg . . . the regulators."

"You? Why?"

I felt myself wobble with despair and squatted down to have my eyes even with his. He looked old for once. His eyes were glazed with pain, but there were lines of sadness around them, too.

"It was Lutjens and me. Lutjens only at first, but then I got pulled into it. From the very beginning I suspected he . . . Lutjens . . . was up to something, from back when we made our little excursion to Kunashiri. He just wasn't behavin' quite right. Couldn't put my finger on it for a long time, until later I remembered Lutjens braggin' . . . during the arm-wrestling match . . . about the big debts he'd run up in Germany before he had been forced to skip the country. I guess he was among the high-rollin' damned from the very first, and he owed some shadowy characters no mean stack of silver. Must have noticed me watchin' him because just before the police raid in Hokkaido, he bore down on me with a heavy lean."

What color he'd had seemed to have drained from his face. A snowflake on his cheek refused to melt.

"You know the wife's a Viet. Somehow . . . I can't figure how. . . . Lutjens had connections in Washington. He had her records checked and of course her application for entry was irregular, awful irregular—enough to win her a quick deportation if someone wanted to press it. When we got married, she thought someone might stop her papers 'cause of her old man being a Saigon deputy police chief. . . ."

The Saigon deputy police chief, the one in the photograph executing a VC terrorist with his police pistol. What the U.S. newspapers hadn't said in their captions was this incident had occurred in the midst of one of the most cold-blooded, vicious attacks on noncombatants of the war. Special VC assassination squads had been sent into the homes of pro-American Viets and began—as planned—to execute family members one by one, youngest first, while the rest had been made to watch. The deputy police chief had managed to apprehend one of these terrorists.

"So she gun-decked it. Her old man was a hard old Viet. How was she to know they couldn't deport her for her old man's righteous anger—but they sure as hell's fire could deport her for a falsified application. Lutjens kept saying he had a friend named Denehy who'd have her back in Ho Chi Minh City faster than you could say '*di-di mau.*' Then he'd laugh."

I'm sure Puckins hadn't laughed. His eyes now reflected the haunting faces of nine laughterless children.

"I played along for a while to get a little thinking space. There was something wrong with Lutjens, more than just a pile of bad debts. He didn't seem to have been issued a full emotional register. I've seen people like him before. They see other people as just objects to be used. Anyway, he was a nasty customer but not really very sharp, if you know what I mean. So I managed to steer him into relatively harmless dead ends—except for Captain Dravit's booby trap—he did all that on his own. Trouble was, Lutjens was getting thinking space, too, and next thing I know, he plunked a threat to get me yanked out of the Nav' on top of it all. Mentions Commander Ackert, too. *What was I going to do?* First no wife, then no job, and nine kids under fourteen? Sulfur and salvation, there just wasn't any way out I could see in the short run."

His head sagged. Wisps of steamy vapor seeped from his torn stomach.

"God forgive me, I helped them, I *did*. Why, I even thought of the psych . . . psychological angle. It was my idea to help your girlfriend stow away on the sub. A woman can really *work* on your mind, I know. Really get you dizzy when you're about to set in motion something really wild, like this project, even if they never say a word. She didn't, did she? She was something, Mister Frazer. The regulator screw-up would have given you an excuse to back out.

"Aw, damnation, I'm nearly a deacon and it's just beyond me to do things the wrong way for long. Lord's truth. Dep, my old woman, she'll understand and forgive me, I hope. I just bided my time and trusted in Grandpaw and Uncle Ho."

He read the question in my expression.

"Sounds crazy, doesn't it? What I mean is, I pulled back in the face of a superior force—guerrilla style and waited for an opportunity. You know, playing it the way Uncle Ho—or really General Giap, I guess—told his troops to play it against our conventional ground-pounders. It was a strange feeling having to fight those fellows, Mr. Ackert and the others, that way. I waited and then on the submarine I saw my chance.

"You know my grandpaw was an old gimlet-eyed circuit preacher. Well, he used to say as a good Christian he couldn't pass judgment on a fellow mortal, but that didn't mean he couldn't put that mortal in a position where the scales of right couldn't make their own decision. I unhooked Lutjens's safety line—but no mortal's hand swept him overboard."

It was an unusual way to justify a killing in self-defense and in the defense of others. Puckins was an unusual man, a man of hard courage and convictions.

"Well I'm glad Lutjens and his friends failed. Bullheaded officers like you, Mister Frazier, are *just* a nuisance to try to stop. I was glad when we landed on the ice, that meant there was nothing else they or I could do."

So there it was, all laid out neatly.

"The whole thing's kind of funny." He laughed, and then choked weakly.

"How's about wrapping me with a little belt of that leftover C-4, and unscrewing the detonator from one of these grenades? I might as well take a Russki or two with me.

Wickersham brought over the plastic explosive. With his massive hands he worked it around Puckins as tenderly as a mother would with an ailing child. He handed Puckins the grenade works. When it was over, the chief threw back his head and sighed.

"I'm sorry. . . ."

"Cut it out. If you wanted to screw us over you would have! You didn't."

He grinned halfheartedly.

"Chief, here take this," Wickersham said. It was an old coin with a square hole in the center. "It's for luck."

Then Wickersham walked away. He began picking up paratroopers' rifles mechanically. One by one he smashed them into useless chunks of wood and steel against a large tree. His eyes were moist.

As were mine.

An hour or so later we heard an explosion behind us, up the valley. Whether he had taken a Russki or two, or whether he had just passed out and taken pressure off the grenade spoon, I would never know.

Chamonix placed his hand on my shoulder. "In a way, our betrayals have something in common. We men of causes and violence exist in their eyes to be used, expended, or betrayed. Oh, their glorious manipulations through things or people! The only ones we can trust are one another. Now they want to use and destroy that small bit of solace, too."

Puckins didn't owe me a thing. Ackert was another matter.

The fresh snow drove down in large, awkward flakes, as if churned in some giant glass paperweight. The visibility was fifteen feet, which, given the speed of our withdrawal, meant we were skiing blind. With the snow and direction of the wind, it was understandable why Gurung didn't notice the dark forms ahead of us. The forms congealed into a herd of reindeer, the cattle of Siberia. Nearby an Evenki drover and his son loomed out of the swirling snow. Unfortunately they saw us at the same moment we saw them.

Instantly they stood at the convergence of five gunsights. Chamonix looked back at me. He had already sized up the situation. The Evenki drover could give pursuing Russian patrols details of our strength and direction of movement. Additionally, none of us was wearing an exposure mask, so the detected presence of Caucasians might upset our China ruse.

Chamonix ran his finger across his throat quizzically. The cold, rational, old-school decision would be to dispatch any witnesses. Chamonix had been through a rough school in the Congo and knew the price of leaving talking trail markers. Shaking my head, I beckoned to Matsuma. After a few false starts, it was soon clear these Evenki did not speak Russian. Fortunately Matsuma knew their language from his early fishing days and his stay with the Evenki after his escape.

The drover and his son had at first assumed we were a Soviet patrol, since the Chinese and Russian winter camouflage uniforms were very similar. Our wounded, and our worn-out condition, aroused their suspicions. They questioned Matsuma, and at the same time he questioned them. The drover and his son huddled together. The father's face was round with flattened cheekbones. The son, about ten, looked like an Eskimo cherub. Though his father was transmitting caution signals, the boy was overwhelmed by the curiosity these white-suited strangers aroused.

I pulled Matsuma aside. "What do you think?"

"Poor, hardworking Evenki drovers. They get nothing from *Roshiajins* but a visit from the agriculture commissioner once a year and many publications—which they can't read but burn well—on reindeer husbandry. They need all this kind of help like they need a ten-kilo block of ice. Kremlin, to them, is as remote as Argentina."

I studied their faces for any sign of duplicity.

"Frazer Commander, I will tell him we are deserters and corrective labor camp escapees, all right? They are not to mention anything to any soldiers unless asked. I will request they give us food. We need food, rest, shelter, many things. Without them escape can still be very difficult. Vyshinsky is very weak, *ne*?"

I nodded. Chamonix nodded in agreement. He had fulfilled his duty as devil's advocate.

Matsuma talked with the drover for a long time. Finally the father indicated that we should all follow him. His son trudged alongside us, his eyes wide and inquiring. We moved into an open area in the taiga and soon I lost all sense of direction. It was reassuring to know that if the snow didn't cover our tracks the reindeer herd would. In less than an hour, we reached a deserted cabin ornately trimmed with Siberian gingerbread.

Matsuma searched in his jacket for his survival kit. When he found it, he pulled out several ruble notes. As he did this he winked at me. The drover deftly palmed the notes, pulled off his cap, and said something with a little hop.

"We are welcome to share this humble dwelling with him. He plans to graze his reindeer here for a week or so. By then his brother will have returned with his dogsled. You can trust him, I think. He has no use for *Roshiajin*, either."

We brushed the snow from our boots, clothing, and equipment and entered the cabin. It had no windowpanes—either they had been taken out or never installed originally. Slat shutters, closed against the wind, helped to keep some heat within the cabin—but not much. The drover and his boy had a pile of reindeer hides in one corner, which they used for bedding. A small-hearthed fireplace that did not draw correctly provided the only heat. The fireplace was constructed in the massive Russian style. Its flue did not rise straight up but wound upward in the ancient labyrinthine manner of tradition. In this efficient way each brick managed to capture some heat and radiate it into the cabin. As time had destroyed portions of the cabin's wall and roof, and its windows were nonexistent, it was a wonder this fireplace could keep the cabin habitable at all. The drover lent us a few hides but we found the best protection against the cold was huddling together like beach seagulls on a rainy night.

In contrast to our trek toward the camp, when we hadn't posted sentries, this time I decided to use them. I had three reasons for doing this. First, we were closely pursued. Second, this wasn't a camouflaged encampment. Third, the watch-spring technique only helped in situations where fresh snow hadn't concealed your tracks. I divided the party into two watches. One watch would maintain a lookout while the other watch tried to steal some sleep. Since the visibility outside had dropped to less than five feet, I saw no reason to post sentries outside the cabin. They could see just as much peering between the shutter sluts.

As the first group prepared to sleep, Vyshinsky spoke up, still bundled in *ahkio* blankets.

"Who are you men?"

Chamonix, closest, responded tiredly, "Friends."

"You are not Chinese . . . or Russian, that is clear. . . ." He raised his head, feebly looking us over with his pallbearer's eyes. "In whose country's service do you fight?"

The morose Frenchman fingered his bandaged shoulder. "No country's."

"No country's? You are bandits . . . no, wrong word. There is a discipline here. You are mercenaries?" he asked tentatively.

"Yes, I suppose you could say that," he replied with growing irritation. Wickersham turned away from his window.

"You do this thing for money?"

"Sure, you know us mercenaries—anything for a price. A well-known type, just a ragtag mob of misfits who couldn't make it doing anything else. Unloved losers, martial orphans."

"Yeah, no momma, no poppa, no Uncle Sammy," Wickersham recited acidly, "the scum of the earth in uniforms cammy."

"'What God abandoned, these defended/And saved the sum of things for pay,'" I added.

Vyshinsky realized he had made a mistake.

"Well, as one misfit to five others," he said gently, "I'm grateful to you all."

The ninth day wore by slowly. In the faint glow of the fireplace I saw Wickersham wave the Evenki boy over to him. He pointed to the bone amulet the boy wore around his neck on a hide thong. Then he pulled an object from under the bottom of his trouser leg. It was a boot knife with a double-edged, stainless-steel blade and a micarta handle. The boy shied back and then realized the knife was being offered in trade.

The boy picked up the knife with the same calculated indifference he had probably seen his father use bartering with other drovers. He cut a thin strip of hide using the knife and then inspected the edge. He hefted it in his hand. He tapped the handle against a joist. He measured it with his palm, horse-trader style. He shook his head. The knife was too small.

"Hell's bells," Wickersham grumbled, and then pulled a flier's survival mirror from his breast pocket. It was made from some unbreakable material and it had a clear glass peep sight in the center of a Morse code decal on the back. The boy inspected it without returning the knife. He studied his reflection in it. Wickersham showed how to aim it for signaling by using the peep sight. The boy handed him the amulet, keeping both the knife and the mirror.

"Gave away my good-luck piece awhile ago," he said to himself. "Kid trades harder than a Singapore Chinaman, but I just had to have that neckpiece. Can't afford to be without a charm now. No, don't want to run out of luck this far from home."

I could feel everyone tense. This talk of luck put everyone on edge.

CHAPTER 26

It snowed until late the tenth day, the day of our first scheduled submarine pickup. We set out that night for the coast. We were still about a day and a half's travel from where we'd buried the kayaks. We would have to travel as far as we could by night and then burrow into the snow during the day. I dreaded this impending day bivouac in the snow. We would be without tents or sleeping bags.

Another matter made me anxious. The submarine was scheduled to be on station to pick us up at midnight of the tenth day and if we didn't show, to try again at a different location on the eleventh day. We weren't going to make that first pickup. Making the second pickup would call for fine timing. We *must* make the second pickup. I didn't expect the Korean sub to wait around for us if we didn't.

We skied through the night as rapidly as we could, and when day came we fashioned snow caves. We crawled into three separate caves and waited for dark. One slow-burning candle and two bodies per cave brought the interior temperature of each up into the high thirties. No one slept much. It was too cold, anyway the constant drone of SU-19 jets overhead dispelled any thought of rest. The jets flew search patterns in and out of the surrounding ridges. Twice, pairs of jets cracked by right overhead.

"Flamin' jets are up and down more often than a hooker's skivvies," Wickersham observed with typical hostility. For the most part we shivered in silence.

That night we covered the last miles to the coast. By some freak of nature the temperature rose above freezing. We hit the coast north of our original landing point and had to ski south until we found the stand of stunted birch that marked the kayaks. We departed quickly, abandoning a kayak and not bothering to pull on our dry suits.

After a brief portage, we found a freshly formed channel and slipped our three remaining kayaks between the masses of ice. The rise in temperature had brought fog with it. It seemed we were never very far from fog. This stuff rolled by in uneven patches, which at no time permitted visibility of more than one hundred yards. The mist that glided over the ice fields was like smoke passing over some burned, broken, forgotten place.

With Vyshinsky tucked into Chamonix's kayak, we brought the kayaks into single file. We began to paddle up the narrow channel, which opened into a larger channel, and then, we hoped, open water. Unfortunately we were not moving as fast as I had hoped, though it appeared we would just make the rendezvous.

Matsuma heard it first—the slow gurgling noise of marine engines at near idle. Carefully laying our paddles across the kayak thwarts, we drifted and waited. If we kept still perhaps the danger would pass. Matsuma opened his end of the spray skirt, reached down to the recoilless, and hefted it to his shoulder. I searched the fog hoping that the noise was coming from a not-too-watchful fishing boat. The chances, however, of meeting a civilian powerboat in these waters were slim.

Then, abruptly, I could trace the outline of a Russian P-class torpedo boat. And then a second P-class. For a second their silhouettes were clear, then they faded back into the fog. I armed several high-explosive projectiles. Armor-piercing rounds would just go in one side of their thin-skinned hulls and out the other. Riding as low in the water as we did, with the mist and icy backdrop concealing us, we still had a chance. I agonized over whether we should initiate fire.

There was only one possible answer once they began their turn into our channel. Now they lay between us and the open sea.

Matsuma and I rotated the bow of the kayak forty-five degrees so that the back blast of the recoilless wouldn't hit the kayaks behind us.

"Get the rear boat's pilothouse," I whispered. Matsuma studied the sights. With the rear torpedo boat out of control, neither could turn or back out of the narrow channel. Then, if I could load and Matsuma could resight fast enough with 25-millimeter and .51-caliber fire raining down on us, we might have a chance.

"Ready?" Matsuma said without turning his head.

"Fire in the hole," I yelled, and tapped him on the shoulder.

Bawhummp.

I looked up to see the pilothouse on the second torpedo boat had flattened over to one side like a folded top hat.

Fifty-one-caliber fire began to rake the ice floes around us. The 25-millimeter mounts fixed without aiming. They weren't sure where we were. The lead boat fired a torpedo blind and it boiled under all three boats, exploding a hundred yards behind us into ice.

The wet cold made my fingers clumsy as I loaded the second round. We had to keep the lead torpedo boat from transmitting a call for assistance.

"Fire in the hole."

Bawhummp.

The pilothouse of the lead boat burst open at its seams. The helmsman on the O.O.D. were tossed high into the air.

The deck gunner on the rear boat had the right direction but the wrong elevation now. Rounds whined overhead. The twin 25-millimeter mounts were making wild slashes at the ice fields. All their guns winked fire without stop. My ears were ringing again. I jammed another round in. The lead boat was beginning to turn, using only its engines for steering.

Bawhummp.

The lead boat exploded into a burning hulk, its fuel tanks ablaze. It lit the area and melted away the fog. The deck gunner on the remaining boat could now see us clearly, though the crews of the 25-millimeter mounts were still firing blind from their shielded positions. I loaded.

The deck gunner had us now and stitched a burst into Wickersham and Gurung's kayak. He placed rounds below their waterline.

Bawhummp.

Matsuma had rushed the shot. It blew away a section of deck and the deck gunner fell away from his machine gun. I loaded. Another figure darted out of the hull for it and swiveled the muzzle toward us once again.

Bawhummp.

The second torpedo boat broke into two flaming halves and burned intensely. All that remained of the first boat was a smoking hole in the latticework of free ice. The stench of burning diesel fuel was overpowering.

We had no way of knowing if either boat had transmitted. Gurung had lost a chunk of upper thigh to a .51-caliber bullet. It was all he could do to muster the strength to stuff bits of his torn jacket into the bullet holes below the waterline. I could tell he was close to spiraling into shock. He couldn't paddle. Wickersham taped over the other holes and tied together the splintered thwart braces, then bailed the kayak dry.

The men were at the end of their ropes. We felt weak and rickety from the unrelenting strain. Each kayak crew had to watch the other to make sure no one fell asleep or collapsed unnoticed.

Our second pickup point was near a stone reef. We paddled to where I figured it ought to be. It wasn't. I wondered if it mattered, we were already two hours late for the rendezvous.

We paddled in an ever-growing circle until we found the reef. Everything seemed vague and hazy. It took me ten minutes to make thirty-second decisions. Was it exhaustion or hypothermia, and did it really matter anymore? The submarine was nowhere in sight. We were overdue. By rights we would never see the submarine again. I decided not to decide what to do next. We secured a grappling hook between two icy bits of rock on the reef, rafted together, and slept beneath the blanket of fog. If we were going to be discovered we were too exposed and weary now to resist.

It had turned cold again by the time I awoke.

*   *   *

We bobbed in the low chop off the reef in the predawn light. We had missed our primary and secondary rendezvous. Earlier, during the briefing aboard the sub, I had noticed Commander Cho had only half-heartedly acknowledged my mention of a secondary rendezvous. People who missed their primary did so for a reason and seldom made their secondary. I wouldn't be surprised if the submarine was cruising the Sea of Japan now.

"There! There! It's over there. I am seeing it very clear, there." Gurung pointed north. There was nothing there.

The effect of strain and fatigue on the minds of men adrift in small boats was well known. Sometimes only one man was affected, often there were group delusions. That would be the final humiliation, to go out in a series of phantom ship chases across the Sea of Okhotsk.

"Take it easy, you sure you saw something over there?"

"Yes, being right over at the edge of the fog bank. Right. . . ." He pointed again and began to feel foolish. He looked down at his wound. "Well, I guess . . ."

"No, he was wrong. It was over that way!"

Now Wickersham. Was this how it was going to end? I tried to follow his outstretched arm. I had trouble concentrating.

Then, like some plumber's sea monster, the dull black periscope cut the sea, leaving a feather of white foam. It headed straight for us, then surfaced. It lay dead in the water not more than a few hundred yards away. Though it remained stationary, it seemed to move in and out of the fog, sometimes disappearing altogether.

In the distance I could hear a high-pitched hum. At first I thought it came from the submarine. It grew louder. Then as it drew nearer I gasped in recognition and dug deeply with my paddle.

"We have to make it to the sub—now! Fast as we can make it. Dig in. Chamonix, you're first aboard with Vyshinsky. Just get him aboard, forget the gear. . . ."

The hum changed pitch as two fox-bat jets broke through the fog bank forty feet above us. One had to veer radically to avoid the conning tower of the sub. I could make out people on its deck moving agitatedly. Its deck gun began to pivot.

She's not going to dive—she's going to slug it out on the surface with jets! It was a brave but foolhardy stance.

Matsuma and I were paddling as fast as we could—the bayonet wound in my left arm made it nearly useless. Chamonix's kayak had almost reached the sub.

I could imagine the radio exchanges between the pilots. They had a *Chinese* submarine in their sights. Our deception was complete, if that mattered anymore.

The jets cracked overhead on a reverse bearing. The sub's gun popped away ineffectually. They bracketed the sub with bombs. No use wasting rockets on a surfaced, dead-in-the-water, putative Chinese sub. Geysers of water spouted all around us.

I could make out Dravit with his leg still in a cast on deck. Incredibly, Keiko was standing right next to him and they were tearing a pipe out of a crate. Except it wasn't a pipe, it was a U.S.-made Stinger ground-to-air missile. Two Korean crewman handled another pipe.

The jets made another pass. A rocket split off from the vapor trail of one jet. The other released a stick of bombs. The single rocket thrust up a geyser just beyond the sub. The fog had somehow upset its tracking system. The bombs detonated near the bow of the sub and tore away a portion of decking. They knocked everyone on the sub's deck flat. Dravit, just aft of the conning tower, righted himself. He kneeled with his missile and a Korean sailor sighted the other. I couldn't see Keiko. Where was she? Why wasn't she standing?

The jets started another pass, again coming from behind the sub. The Englishman and the Korean pivoted—and fired. Matsuma and I were twenty yards from the sub, all the rest were scrambling aboard. One side of the lead jet burst into flame and its engine began stopping and starting like a hiccuping Waring blender. The other jet made a hard turn and evaded the second missile. The lead jet still hung in the air, headed toward the sub—and in the last seconds I realized it was going to hit us.

A great wall of ice water capsized the kayak. Inverted, I tore away the spray skirt and felt my body numb. Survival in ice water was a function of energy, and I was totally spent. I looked around for Matsuma. He was gone . . . smashed by the dying plane. I tried to swim but my numbed arms barely moved. I could see the sub clearly, as clearly as I had ever seen anything in my life—even make out faces of people as they vaulted down the hatches, preparing to dive the sub. I was sinking, waves washed over my head. In the corner of my eye I saw a splash. Where was Keiko?

So this was what it was like to die.

It was a peculiar dream. Keiko was swimming with me, crying. She kept tugging at my hair. I tried to make her stop but she wouldn't; Dravit was on a dark black riverbank with the muzzle of a grease gun pointed into a hole with a hinged lid like a garbage can. He kept looking over at us anxiously and talking into the hole. It took forever for us to get to the riverbank, but when we did men came out of the hole and dragged us into it. I didn't want to go.

Dravit had played dirty. It had occurred to me when we had loaded the sub that we had an inordinate amount of ordnance. Dravit had arranged to load several extra crates of C-4 and the Stinger missiles in Chinhae. He had concealed charges throughout the sub as a precaution. When the sub's skipper had been reluctant to wait extra hours for us, Dravit had played his wild card. Only he knew how to disarm the already-armed charges—which he promised to do once the sub had recovered the raiding party. An insane, and altogether genuine gleam in Dravit's eye was all it took to convince the sub's captain that Dravit would willingly blow up himself, the sub, and its crew. The sub's captain had decided then, Dravit later related, that "the proper thing to do" was wait for us.

The sub and its skipper redeemed themselves on the way back. With the entire Soviet navy looking for us, they eluded Russian antisubmarine-warfare forces, using shallow water, coastal ice, thermoclines, and other tricks I did not quite understand.

CHAPTER 27

After we negotiated the La Pérouse Straits, it was just a matter of tying up loose ends. I was told Vyshinsky, in improving health, demanded to shake the hand of every sailor on the boat as we left the straits.

Matsuma was dead. The Sea of Okhotsk had finally made its claim, and I did not look forward to returning to that Ainu fishing village with news of a dead patriarch. I knew how they would take it, though—with the same samurai-like stoicism Matsuma had shown.

As for Puckins, I intended to have Kurganov set up a generous trust fund for his family.

Gurung's thigh, it appeared, would take about six months to fully recover. The hollow scar would never fully disappear, a prospect he relished. Chamonix's shoulder would heal in three months but remain stiff for life. My arm would take the same amount of time to heal. Wickersham, untouched, thought better of his horse trade for the Evenki amulet.

I turned over the crypto assembly and code books to the sub's classified-materials officer. The procedure for securing them was so complicated I knew he wished they'd deep-sixed with one of the kayaks. Well, that was done and Mr. Kim hadn't even had to sell his mother.

Keiko, who hummed Japanese songs to herself when she thought I wasn't looking, gave me such a scolding I knew all was well again. She was a woman to come home to.

We transferred to picket boats outside Chinhae. Vyshinsky had recovered enough strength while on the sub to walk by himself. Only Gurung would have to be carried off by stretcher.

Kurganov stood at the end of the pier in a heavy coat with a fur collar. Several men surrounded him, including reporters with cameras. Sato stood inconspicuously off to one side.

"Who invited him?" Wickersham growled, pointing down the pier. Far behind Kurganov stood Ackert in a knee-length fur coat. He had several men with him, including a U.S. Navy captain in a reefer jacket.

Vyshinsky, still very weak, moved to the rail and braced himself against a stanchion. Kurganov's face metamorphosed into a melancholy smile. Throughout his life, smiling had been a pleasant but infrequently enjoyed exercise. He called out something to Vyshinsky that I didn't catch. Almost before the lines were over, Vyshinsky and Kurganov were embracing in moist-eyed joy.

We dodged the reporters as professional hazards. They would have a good enough story, venturing how Vyshinsky escaped from Mother Russia. After the four of us had jostled our way through the clicking cameras, we . . . I began the long walk down the pier. Ackert took a few steps to meet me, with his hand outstretched.

"Fine job, simply fine job. Thought I should try an' stop you, you were going against current policy, ol' buddy. If my superiors had ever . . . Well, no harm done and the Koreans have agreed to share the crypto gizmo with my Company buddies. Why, they're real pleased. Hell, no hard feelings, Fraze."

The punch started somewhere down near my knees. It caught him in the side of the jaw and jarred him, but that was all. He took a couple little half-steps and swiveled his head as if to shake the punch off. His face flushed. For once he lost his honey-tongued composure.

"You take this sleazy band of no-count trash on a little ski trip and now you're a bunch of heroes. So what? For me, it all counts the same toward twenty. In your case it don't count toward nothin'. Well, boy, stand by, cause ol' Ackert's gonna mess you up so bad, your Nip honey ain't gonna want what's left."

He swung flat-footed into the bandaged part of my left arm. My knees sagged and nearly buckled. The pain made my eyes water. His football instincts made him dive for my legs but I sidestepped and brought my knee up into his face. When he came up I slammed him hard below his left ear and he stumbled by.

He straightened up with a surprised look on his face; one eye was puffy and the side of his face was discolored.

Some of the men with him tried to intercede but Chamonix and Wickersham checked two of them off the pier. Dravit swept the legs out from under a third with his crutch. The Navy captain stood by impassively.

Ackert came again, this time wailing in with a flurry of punches—then dived for my legs before I could dodge. I hit the concrete with a wrenching thud. I could tell he meant to get me down, hold me down, and rain the punches from on high. But as soon as I hit the pier I rolled into him so he could not make full use of his massive arms. I could not afford to fight him rolling on the deck—he had too many pounds on me.

My tanto dagger had clattered to the concrete during my fall. Ackert grabbed for it, but Wickersham kicked it skidding down the pier.

I faked an attempt at a choke, then scrambled to my feet. He followed me up. Without missing a beat, he aimed a volley of punches at my head. It felt as if my head was going to be snapped clean off and I could feel one eye closing. I tasted blood in my mouth.

Ducking under one of his punches, I crouched into *ippon seoi nage*, a judo single shoulder throw. My execution wasn't clean and for a second Ackert hovered head to earth before he came down, with his full weight, against a bollard. He brought himself up on all fours, holding his right shoulder lower than his left. His collarbone was broken.

He climbed to his feet and then registered a punch that seemed to snap my head clean back to my shoulder blades. He followed with a kick at my kneecap. I had barely time to raise my leg. He hit my shin instead. His kick stung unbearably and my leg wouldn't bear weight. He tried again. I counters wept with my left leg. Caught off balance, he hit the pier with the back of his head.

He put up his hand to signal enough. I would have none of it. All I could see was Chief Puckins bleeding his guts into the snow with a guilty look on his face. I raised Ackert to his feet by his collar. He put my bandaged arm in his bear-trap grip and brought his knee up into my groin before I could turn my hip. I slumped but adrenaline was pumping into my system out of fifty-five-gallon drums and the pain was filed for future appreciation. A hard right cross had effect this time, and Ackert's knees buckled. He sank to his knees. Arm weary, I managed to drum a boxer's speed-bag tattoo into his wobbling head. Right, right, left, left. It must have taken two dozen punches before he toppled face first into the pier.

I stumbled a bit, at last feeling the full impact of the knee to the groin. My left arm was bleeding again and I couldn't see out of my right eye. My shin was swollen but unbroken.

The captain remained where he had been. Then he did something strange. He winked. He winked as if in slow motion—a restful wink, a peaceful wink.

But—simply—in Charon's traces there was no rest or peace.

CPSIA information can be obtained
at www.ICGtesting.com
Printed in the USA
BVHW080823050721
611157BV00008B/384